Forces of Love by Susan Downs
While stationed in the European theater, Captain Jack Johnson, a fighter pilot, begins correspondence with pen pal Caroline Harrington of Boston. Yet a tangle of miscommunication threatens to destroy their deepening relationship. Will things get straightened out in time for Jack to meet Caroline face-to-face when he passes through Boston on holiday leave?

The Missing Peace by Rebecca Germany
Viewing the world from the perspective of an army nurse serving in Europe during 1944 has changed Joyce. She is ready to cut ties with her sheltered upbringing and her childhood sweetheart. What path will her letter home take? And will a chance encounter in an evacuation hospital remind her of the source of true peace?

Christmas Always Comes by Darlene Mindrup
Kenshin receives a letter that his brother is breaking his engagement with Mitsu and plans to marry a girl he met in France. When word comes that his brother was killed in action, Kenshin goes to Mitsu at the Japanese-American relocation center to comfort her and see if she was aware of the broken engagement. What will Kenshin find?

Engagement of the Heart by Kathleen Paul
Betsy Anderson has received a letter from a soldier in an army hospital informing her that her fiancé has died. Betsy is confused. She wrote many patriotic letters to soldiers in service, but she has never been engaged. She goes to the hospital and meets Sargaent Kevin Coombs. Will she be taken as a flirt or a soldier's Christmas Angel?

Christmas Letters

Letters and Romance Tangle Across
WWII Battle Lines in Four Novellas

Susan Downs
Rebecca Germany
Darlene Mindrup
Kathleen Paul

BARBOUR
PUBLISHING, INC.
Uhrichsville, Ohio

Forces of Love ©2001 by Susan Downs.
The Missing Peace ©2001 by Rebecca Germany.
Christmas Always Comes ©2001 by Darlene Mindrup.
Engagement of the Heart ©2001 by Kathleen Paul.

Illustrations by Mari Goering.

ISBN 1-58660-243-8

All Scripture quotations, unless otherwise noted, are taken from the King James Version of the Bible.

Published by Barbour Publishing, Inc., P.O. Box 719, Uhrichsville, Ohio 44683 http://www.barbourbooks.com

Member of the
Evangelical Christian
Publishers Association

Printed in the United States of America.

Christmas Letters

Forces of Love

by Susan Downs

Dedication

To David. . .my beloved husband and hero.

Prologue

September 12, 1944

*D*ear Miss Harrington,
  You don't know me, but Capt. Johnson slept in the bunk next to mine and we flew in the same squadron. I'm writing to fulfill a promise I made to him. I've started this letter a couple dozen times, but I can't ever seem to get the words right. I don't know of any easy way to break this news to you, so I guess I ought to just tell you straight out.

Jack said that if anything ever happened to him, since you weren't kin and wouldn't receive any official notice, that I should make sure you got the word. He also asked me to return your letters to you, rather than let them go to his parents with his other things. Since this box includes your letters, you can probably guess that means he met with disaster.

On the 25th of August, Jack's P–47, the Sweet Caroline, was shot down over enemy territory while we were conducting a strafing mission. I was flying in formation just ahead of him, and when I circled back around, I saw his plane

9

engulfed in flames on the ground. Neither I nor any of the other pilots in our squadron saw an open chute or any signs of life around the plane. So it is with great sadness that I have to tell you that Jack has officially been listed as killed in action.

We all knew Jack as not only a good fighter pilot but a great guy as well. Although we've seen plenty of our buddies go down, Jack's death has hit us really hard. We'll all miss him.

Jack never was one to go drinking or into town on a skirt patrol. He used his cigarette rations to barter for sweets to give to the local kids. Whenever we'd head out for a little R&R, he'd stay behind to write letters or to read the latest mail from a certain Boston address. But even though he was quiet and kept mostly to himself, we all knew he thought the world of you. You were the only gal he ever talked about, and we caught him staring at your picture constantly.

Every night, no matter how tired he was, he'd read his Bible and say his prayers, but even though he had religion, he wasn't the kind of guy who preached at us or crammed his beliefs down our throats. We all respected him for that. Knowing Jack, I'm certain that he's in heaven, flying higher than any of us now.

Well, I guess I'd better be going. If the weather holds, we're flying tomorrow so I've gotta get some shut-eye. Sorry to be the bearer of bad news.

Sincerely,
Second Lieutenant Mike Yeats
56th Fighter Group, 63rd Fighter Squadron
Eighth USAAF

Chapter 1

WESTERN UNION

DECEMBER 11 1944 PM 1:00

CAROLINE HARRINGTON
26 SPRING BRANCH ST.
BOSTON MASSACHUSETTS

SAFE AND COMING STATESIDE. . .
ARRIVING BOSTON HARBOR. . .
WOULD LOVE TO MEET YOU.
NOON SATURDAY DECEMBER 23.
FISH PIER #1 RESTAURANT. . .
WILL EXPLAIN ALL THEN. . .
                    YOUR FRIEND JACK

#1 Fish Pier

Capt. John "Jack" Wesley Johnson rubbed his watering eyes and looked again. A yellowed life preserver hung askew on the weathered oak door and served as a makeshift sign. The hand-scrawled lettering confirmed the address he had cabled Caroline. He breathed a deep sigh of resignation, filling his nose and throat with a metallic taste of rancid fish, and hurried into the dilapidated warehouse-turned-restaurant. Pushing the door shut against the icy nor'easter wind, he removed his hat, then brushed the melting sleet from the shoulders of his bomber jacket.

"Set yourself down anywhere, Soldier Boy." A frumpy, platinum blond waitress nodded at him and gave her gum a good crack. "I'll be with you in a jiff." Her pink uniform twirled around her knees as she turned away to quarrel with a crusty old salt about his steep price for haddock.

Judging from their attire, all of the other restaurant patrons appeared to be dockworkers and fishmongers. Over the din of clattering pots and pans resounding from the kitchen, "White Christmas" wafted from a static-plagued radio. Jack winced as some unseen and off-key Bing Crosby wannabe crooned along. No doubt the food would be great, but this wasn't exactly what he'd meant when he'd asked Richard, the native Bostonian on his P-47's maintenance crew, for the name of a good restaurant where he could meet Caroline. He considered the dumb grease monkey pretty lucky that the Atlantic Ocean now separated them.

Jack glanced at his watch—11:25—early for lunch hour—yet only a couple of tables near the door remained unoccupied. He'd obviously failed in his attempt to beat the lunch crowd and get a table with a view of the harbor—a cozy, quiet, out-of-the-way table for two where he and Caroline could really talk. At least with an unobstructed view of the door, he'd be able to spot her the moment she walked in.

He tossed a small, gift-wrapped package onto the table and covered it with his hat. Favoring his tender left shoulder, he shrugged off his jacket and draped it across the back of a rickety chair. Jack sank into the seat and rested both elbows on the table before burying his face in his hands.

In light of his recent behavior, he couldn't bring himself to pray. He didn't dare ask for any special favors from God. Yet he hoped against hope that Caroline would come. If she did, then today would signify a fresh start—a whole new life for him. She was the only person on earth with whom he felt comfortable enough to share the details of his recent horrors. She represented his only hope in overcoming the haunting memories that shadowed his every thought.

But what if she doesn't show. . . .

His temples throbbed, and he rubbed them with his cold fingertips. The idea that she might stand him up left Jack longing for a stiff drink. Then, again, he didn't need a new excuse to imbibe. Lately, the desire to drown his warring thoughts and tortured memories in booze seldom left him. Escape from his raging battle with guilt came only after the warming numbness of a third or fourth shot.

"You look like you could really use a cup o' jamoke, Hon." Coffee sloshed over the side of the rattling cup and into the saucer as the waitress shoved the steaming brew across the table toward him. She slapped a plastic-encased menu down on the table beside the cup, then pulled an order pad from her apron pocket and a stubby pencil from behind her right ear and poised to take his order. "By the looks of how your uniform hangs on your shoulders like a pup tent, you could use some fattening up as well. Why don't you let me bring you a big bowl of our famous clam chowder? There's none better in Beantown."

The brassy gal appeared ready to head for the kitchen and retrieve the soup, whether he wanted a bowl or not, so Jack waved to get her attention.

"Yeah?" She popped her gum between her molars and hiked her hands over her hips, causing her uniform to strain at the buttons.

"Just the coffee is fine for now. I'm waiting for a lady friend to join me for lunch."

The waitress nodded and the hint of a smirk lifted one corner of her mouth. "Yeah. I bet a handsome officer like you has a string of sweethearts from here to Führerland."

"No, Ma'am. I couldn't say that." Jack focused on the crocheted Christmas tree that adorned the waitress's lapel. "I keep pretty much to myself."

"I can take a hint, Dearie." She poked her pencil behind one ear and slipped her order pad back into her pocket. "But I'll still bring you a few slices of sourdough to tide you over 'til your gal arrives. If you change your mind, just holler. Name's Fern." Before he could protest that he hadn't been hinting at anything, the waitress shuffled on to the next table.

He peered at his watch again—11:30. Jack ran a finger around the neck of his borrowed Class A uniform and wiggled his necktie back into place. Even though, according to Waitress Fern, his shirt resembled a pup tent, the collar pinched his neck like a noose. Because some overzealous company clerk had shipped all of his personal effects back home in September, he'd found it necessary to beg a uniform off another captain before he set sail from England. He'd suffered much greater discomforts over the course of the past four months, and he could endure the torture of the pencil-necked Capt. Peavey's too-tight collar for a few hours more. He wanted Caroline's first impression to be a good one, and women seemed to flock around an officer in full dress.

A cold blast of air swept in through the opening door, and Jack looked to see if, by chance, Caroline might have arrived early. A mouse-faced woman rushed inside, her bare hands clutching at the lapels of a shapeless brown coat. For the briefest of moments, Jack wondered if she might be Caroline, but a kid wearing a U.S. Navy uniform followed close behind her and encircled her waist with one arm while he led her to the only open table. The woman in no way resembled Jack's mental image of Caroline, but her arrival made him question whether or not he would be able to recognize his friend. For although they had shared their deepest secrets and most private thoughts with one another, they had yet to meet face-to-face.

What if she looked nothing like the Caroline in his picture? He pulled a tattered and soiled photograph from his breast pocket and propped it against the bill of his hat. He could describe the grainy, black-and-white image of Caroline with his eyes closed, yet he never tired of looking at her just the same. According to the photo's accompanying letter—her very first one—the snapshot had been taken after her graduation from college a year and a half ago.

"No, I'm not a Ha-Ha-Harvard girl," she'd written with little flourishes and curlicues punctuating her perfect penmanship, "but a proud alumna of New England Christian College, a small liberal arts school on the South Shore."

She had gone on to explain in her introductory letter that she'd found his name on a list of military pen pal prospects posted at the Salvation Army center where she volunteered. For some reason or another, until seeing Caroline's picture, he'd always imagined members of the Salvation Army as dole-faced matrons. That certainly didn't describe the woman in the photo he studied now. Although she was average in many regards—average height, average weight—just to look at her broad smile brought a smile to his own lips.

For all he could tell from the monochrome print, Caroline might just as easily be a redhead as a brunette or a blond. He could only guess at the color of her eyes. Brown? Gray? But they sparkled with sweetness. Tenderness. Compassion.

In the early days of their long-distance friendship, her V-mail letters had offered a generic accounting of her day-to-day activities at her new job and an update on her volunteer work with the Salvation Army. He'd answered each letter with a tamed version of his perils and adventures as a fighter pilot. Fear of the censor's scissors kept him from sharing many specifics about his assignment or location, and she never pressed him for details.

Within a month or so, their weekly correspondence had turned into a daily ritual. Formal pleasantries swiftly gave way to heartfelt sharing. Even during the famine stages of the military's feast-or-famine postal delivery, when mail took days or weeks to catch up to him, he knew to expect a fresh batch of letters from Caroline at the moment he needed them most. Just the anticipation made his spirits soar.

Jack's gaze darted to his watch—11:53. He wished he could pass the time by reading a few of Caroline's letters right now, especially the mail he never got to see that arrived after August 25. But the whole batch should have been safely back in Caroline's possession long ago—at about the same time his parents were to receive the remaining contents of his footlocker.

Guilt assaulted him, and he shook his head, struggling to stem the unwelcome thoughts. Even though he'd sent his folks a telegram to let them know he was alive and safe, perhaps he should have gone home to Indiana for Christmas. His mother's heart would be broken if she ever learned that he had arrived in the States in time for the holidays and had chosen not to spend the week with them.

Jack hated the idea of hurting his mom, but he wasn't ready to face his dad. Not yet. He wasn't sure he would ever be.

He startled at the touch of someone leaning over his shoulder. "Here's that bread I promised and this morning's *Herald* to help you bide the time." The waitress set her serving tray on his table and leaned in so close Jack could smell the peppermint flavoring from her gum.

"May I?" Without waiting for a response, she snatched the picture of Caroline from the table and began to scrutinize it through squinted eyes.

"You met this girl before?" The waitress's eyebrow hiked, and Jack fought the urge to tell her that it was really none of her business.

"Only through letters."

"Ah." She rocked her head up and down. "Yes."

The falling of her tone, her hesitation, spoke volumes. Jack had the strong impression she'd seen this scenario before. Suddenly, his situation didn't look all that unique. Perhaps dozens, hundreds of soldiers had returned from the war, hearts empty, clutching a picture, desperately longing to meet the girl of their dreams. Words of defense for Caroline rose in his throat, but for some reason he couldn't utter them.

"Well. Don't you worry none." The waitress returned the photo to Jack and reached for her tray. "Your pen pal don't look like the type that would leave you in a lurch. I just was wondering if she'd seen you up close and personal is all. I don't figure any woman would miss a date with a fella whose eyes are blue as yours." She offered him an exaggerated wink. "Tell ya what. If she's not here by fifteen-after, ol' Fern here'll be your date—and lunch'll be on me." Her pink skirt jiggled up and down as she laughed at her own merrymaking. Jack offered a silent plea to Caroline, asking her to hurry and save him from such a fate.

"Uh. . ." His mouth opened and closed as he struggled for an appropriate response to Waitress Fern. Finally, his shoulders heaved in a sigh, and he stared up at her in silence.

Her expression sobered, and she gave his hand a gentle pat. "Ah, I see how it is. I can always tell the boys that's coming home from the boys that's just heading off to war. You vets are such a somber bunch." Waitress Fern tucked her tray under one arm and began backing away from his table as she spoke. "I'll pray you learn to laugh again soon, Soldier. Maybe that pretty gal of yours can give you a quick refresher course when she gets here."

Jack could only manage a weak smile and a nod.

He held his watch to his ear and listened for the soft tick of the second hand before confirming the time again. Two minutes before twelve. Caroline would be coming through the door at any moment now. He slipped her photograph back into his pocket. He moved his hat away from the center of the table. He flounced the red bow on top of her gift. He shifted in his seat, first to the left, then right; pulled his shoulders back and sat erect. Finally, fearing that he would appear too stiff and formal, he decided to put on a more casual air, and he opened the newspaper with a snap.

The bold headlines announced the latest war news— U.S. TROOPS SUFFER HEAVY LOSSES IN ARDENNES—but Jack wanted to forget all about war, if only for the next couple of hours. So he let his gaze wander over the advertisements for liver pills and secretarial schools. He skimmed the police report and learned about the seedy side of Boston. His gaze darted over the social calendar, and he thoroughly perused the sports reports. Before every page turn, and at every minute in between, he stole a glance at his watch.

Each of the countless times the door opened, he expected to see Caroline sweeping in. Each time, his heart sank in disappointment. By twelve minutes after noon, he no longer noticed the words on the printed page. His attention focused on a growing list of excuses as to why Caroline might be late. The telegram should have arrived in plenty of time. He'd had time to cross the Atlantic by boat since sending his message, and unlike military mail, Western Union always got through. Maybe she was one of those free spirits who always showed up fashionably late. Perhaps she couldn't leave work to meet him for lunch. Possibly her grandmother was ill and needed her help and Caroline couldn't find anyone to deliver a message to him. Conceivably, one of those crooks he'd read about in the police report could have robbed her and left her unconscious in a dark alley. Or...

He squeezed his eyes shut and his stomach sank. Maybe the waitress's unspoken suspicions were right and he had read too much into their relationship all along. Maybe Caroline had no interest in meeting him.

At 12:25, Waitress Fern slapped at Jack's paper and placed a steaming bowl of chowder in front of him. "I'm not saying that your gal won't show. But you aren't looking too perky, and I figure you need to eat. When your date comes, I'll bring you another bowl. Go ahead and chow down now. This one's on me."

"Ma'am, this really isn't necessary. You don't need to buy my lunch."

The look she gave him reeked with pity, and he clenched his jaw against a responding flash of anger.

"Just consider it an early Christmas present, Darlin'." She whisked away before he could protest any further.

When 12:35 rolled past, Jack reconciled himself to the fact that, for whatever reason, Caroline wouldn't be coming. To wait any longer would simply be a waste of time. He pushed away his empty soup bowl, folded the newspaper, and slipped her gift back into the inner pocket of his bomber jacket. However, before he rose to leave, he determined to write one last letter to Caroline. Then if she chose not to contact him during his ten-day leave, he would take her lack of response as an unwritten "Dear John" letter and he'd forget all his troubles at the nearest bar.

He fished his date book out of his coat and ripped a page from the back to use as stationery. Since receiving her first letter on that summer day a year and a half ago, he had, one page at a time, exposed his very soul to her. He wouldn't make that mistake again. In brusque strokes, he dashed off a brief, no-frills note. He waved the page back and forth to dry the ink and tucked it into his shirt pocket for safekeeping until he could find an envelope.

As soon as Waitress Fern disappeared into the kitchen, he pulled enough cash from his wallet to cover the cost of his soup plus a hefty tip, and hurried out the door, waiting until he was outside to slip into his coat. Over three months spent eluding Nazi capture had perfected his disappearing act.

Jack jogged down the wharf's boardwalk toward the street. He buried his nose in his jacket's lambs-wool collar as he ran to block the biting chill of the December sea winds and to muffle the overpowering harbor smells. When he reached the street, he searched left and right for an open cab until a disturbing realization hit him. He had no reason to hurry anywhere. He had no place where he had to go. He had no missions to fly. No daring escapes to make. No appointments to keep. No one to meet.

Today's long-fantasized rendezvous with Caroline had been the driving force that kept him going when he felt like giving up. The keen disappointment of her truancy left him as deflated as a ruptured weather balloon. Still, he couldn't quite bring himself to concede to a cruel and premeditated rejection by the Christ-like Caroline. He needed to know for certain that she had deliberately chosen not to come.

He felt compelled to hand deliver his last letter to Caroline, and he resolved to slip the note into her mailbox at the address on Spring Branch Street.

Jack scanned the city skyline, seized with a renewed sense of mission. If he could make his way across occupied-Holland, he felt confident that he could find Caroline's residence. He'd committed her address to memory long ago, and from her letters he knew she lived with her grandmother in a brownstone close to the famed Boston Commons. Since it was Saturday and the Christmas break, he didn't hold much hope of finding her at the Buckingham Private School for Girls, where Caroline taught English Literature. But should all else fail and he mustered enough courage, he might go so far as to seek her out at the Salvation Army mission where she spent all her free time.

In the absence of any cabs, Jack set off on foot in the direction of downtown, sloshing through the sludge of trampled, days-old snow. Trying to skirt along the quay's edge, he wandered through the city streets until he began to feel hopelessly lost. Finally, he stopped at a roadside stand and bought a tourist map of downtown

Boston. The vendor who sold him the map took the time to trace his finger along the quickest route to the Commons from where they stood. Jack thanked him, and following the merchant's advice, he headed into an enormous indoor farmer's market referred to as Quincy Market. He was beginning to think all of Boston smelled of bad fish. But the indoor market would keep him out of the sleet and cold for a long city block, and he considered the unpleasant odor the lesser of two evils. According to his map, he should emerge from the market just opposite the historic landmark Faneuil Hall.

The moment Jack stepped outside, he startled to hear the tune "Onward Christian Soldiers." He followed the music to where a five-member Salvation Army band played their horns and tambourines at the base of the steps leading up to the famous site.

Pausing to listen to the familiar hymn, his thoughts carried him back to that distant summer day when he set sail for Europe on the *Queen Elizabeth*. He, along with thousand of other recruits, had waved good-bye to America, as a band on the dock played this same tune. With tears of pride and patriotism coursing down his cheeks, he'd hummed along and softly sung what lyrics he could remember. "Onward Christian Soldier, marching as to war, with the cross of Jesus going on before. . . ."

Today that old Sunday school hymn held new meaning for him. War embodied more than lofty ideals and righteous principles put to song. War also meant blood and death and misery.

"No son of mine has any business getting into the business of war." His father's oft-spoken words rang in his ears and Jack suspected that his father might have been right all along.

Determined to purge his thoughts of war and other unpleasantries, Jack studied the members of the Salvation Army band. Immediately upon conclusion of the old hymn, the quintet launched into a hurdy-gurdy rendition of "Hark, the Herald Angels Sing." None of the three women in the band came close to resembling Caroline. And once when he'd asked Caroline if she played a musical instrument, she'd replied that, unlike her parents, the only thing musical she knew how to play was the radio. Even so, he wondered if any of them might know her.

A few yards away, stationed at a red kettle, another woman wearing the traditional navy blue garb of the Salvation Army stood with her back to him. In one hand, she jangled a brass bell. Since the band showed no signs of slowing, Jack decided to approach the woman at the kettle and ask if, by chance, she might know a Miss Caroline Harrington.

"Excuse me, Ma'am." I'm wondering if you might know an acquaintance of mine who's a member of the Salvation Army here in town. Her name's—"

Jack dropped a dollar bill into her kettle, then raised his eyes to look at her. His heart leaped to his throat, and his voice squeaked like a prepubescent choirboy.

"Caroline."

Chapter 2

October 16, 1944

Dearest Miss Harrington,

Thank you for your kind note of sympathy over the loss of our son. From the day he went off to flight school, I began praying that the Lord would send a good Christian girl just like you across John Wesley's path. I'm so glad to learn that God answered my prayer. I'm sure your letters were a real blessing to him.

John Wesley's father always had such high hopes that our son would follow in his footsteps and enter the ministry. He was against him going into the service from the very beginning. Perhaps way back then he sensed this tragedy would come. (His own father had died in battle when he was just a teen.) I can't say as I understand why God took our only boy from us at such a young age. Some things we just have to trust to Him and figure the Good Lord knows best.

I wish you every future happiness.

Cordially,
Mrs. Naomi Johnson

Caroline Harrington. Do you know her?"

"Know her?" The man's question caught Caroline completely off guard. She cast a quick glance at the stranger to make certain that he wasn't blind. Any personal acquaintances ought to recognize her at first glance. *Except maybe Jack.* The wild idea sent a shiver down her spine. She looked again at this blue-eyed stranger wearing an Army Air Corps uniform replete with the two silver bars of a captain's rank. His resemblance to Jack's photographs left her woozy and weak in the knees. The loud ringing in her ears drowned out the gentle peal of her habitually swaying brass bell. She tried to formulate a response, but she couldn't think over the melancholy chant that echoed through her brain. *Dear Jack, how I miss you! I miss you so!*

Since receiving word of Jack's death, her grief-stricken mind often played tricks on her, and these frequent instances of mistaken identity were its cruelest trick of all. Every uniformed soldier, regardless of his rank or branch of service, sent her imagination on the rampage and reopened fresh wounds of sorrow.

She thought the worst of her mourning should be over by now. She kept reminding herself that she'd never met Jack in person or even spoken to him on the telephone. Yet her disconsolate sense of loss only increased with time. This man couldn't possibly be Jack. Jack was four-months dead.

She tried to study the man's face without being too obvious. He did look so very familiar. There had to be a logical explanation as to why he reminded her of her dear deceased friend, a sensible reason behind their strikingly similar features—the same square-set jaw,

Roman nose, laugh-lined eyes—she had memorized from Jack's pictures.

This man who knew her name, and whom her heart wanted so desperately to believe to be a living and breathing Captain Jack, was probably just some guy she'd spoken to at the mission center when he'd stumbled in after a drinking binge. Her name must have stuck in his inebriated head even though he'd forgotten her face.

She masked her maelstrom of emotions behind a syrupy smile and replied in her most professional sounding voice. "I'm sorry, Sir, but for safety's sake, we aren't allowed to divulge any personal information about our corps soldiers to strangers on the street. However, if you would like to give me your name and an address or phone number where you might be contacted, I'd be happy to pass the information along."

The man's sky-blue eyes clouded in bewilderment, and Caroline squirmed beneath his gaze.

"I see. That makes sense, I suppose." He looked past her to the band and back over his shoulder in the direction of State Street, then turned around to look her squarely in the eye again. "I've written everything down already." He reached into his pocket and pulled out a slip of paper. "But if I give this to you, you will make certain that Miss Harrington receives it, won't you? It pertains to a matter of some importance to me."

Caroline's curiosity spiked even higher at his words, but she maintained her cool demeanor. "Of course. I'll personally see to it that she reads the note. You can count on me." She tucked her bell under her arm and pulled off a mitten so that she could properly receive the note extended by this supposed acquaintance of hers. Feigning an air of nonchalance, she slipped it into the pocket of her overcoat, donned her mittens, then raised her bell to resume her kettle-drive duties.

"You have a Merry Christmas, Sir. Remember, God loves you."

She intended to give him a quick nod and turn away, but he hesitated and their gazes locked. The momentary visual standoff provided Caroline with a flashing glimpse into a tortured soul. He seemed to be pleading with her—for what, she had no clue.

"Ma'am." Their interchange broken, he took his leave by ticking the bill of his hat in an informal salute. His form melted into the crowd of holiday shoppers, but he stood head and shoulders above the rest, and Caroline could easily mark his progress down the street. His note burned in her pocket like a live coal, and she could hardly wait until he was out of sight so that she could read the message. However, he stopped some fifty yards away and sat on a public bench, facing her. During a lull in the pedestrian traffic, their gazes met again. Caroline jerked her head away. Yet again and again, her attentions wandered back to the bus stop, and she found herself snatching a quick peek toward the mystery military man at every opportunity. Always when she did, she caught him looking back at her. Even when she turned away from him, she could feel his watchful stare. At each glance, he looked increasingly forlorn.

She forced herself to focus on the donors who were dropping their contributions in her kettle, but her repetitive thank-yous, God-bless-yous, and Merry Christmases took on a hollow tone of insincerity. She yearned for a private moment to calm her emotions and collect her thoughts. She wanted to find a secluded place to read the note and discover what business this pecurliarly familiar stranger had with her. The remaining half-hour of her volunteer shift seemed to stretch on for an eternity.

At last, an unmarked truck pulled to the curb. At its arrival, the members of the band ceased their carol playing and began to pack up their instruments. A middle-aged Salvation Army soldier jumped out of the passenger side of the cab. He opened the cargo doors and walked toward Caroline, slapping dirt from his trousers as he approached.

"God bless you, Sister. You've done a noble job of collecting. I can hardly lift the kettle off its frame." His shoulders slumped with the weight of the pot while he waddled back to the truck to trade the full kettle for an empty one.

"I'm ready to relieve you now. Lucky for me, there's a break in the weather." He reached for Caroline's bell, and her arm felt lighter than air the moment she released it from her grasp. His experienced hand picked up Caroline's steady cadence on the bell.

"Brother Fred will drive you and the others back to the mission. He's got a thermos of hot coffee in the cab."

"I appreciate that, Brother William, but Grams is returning from the Cape today, and I need to get home to see her. I've also got one last Christmas present yet to buy, so I may head to Filene's too. You don't think anyone would mind, do you?"

"Not at all. Not at all. You run along." He tipped his head in the general direction of the large department store as though urging her on. Before she could slip away, one of the trumpet players from the band leaned in between Caroline and her replacement bell-ringer.

"Say, Sister Caroline, are your parents still on tour in the Pacific with the USO? You know, when they get tired of globe-hopping, they can always join our merry band."

Caroline's ears tingled with embarrassment at her fellow soldier's innocent remarks. For the greater portion of her life, she'd felt like the parent rather than the child in her relationship with Harry and Lill, as they preferred to be called. The vagabond couple traveled year-round with a jazz band. They didn't even own a home. Whenever they breezed through town on their way to another gig, they'd take over the third floor of Grams's place. A few months back, they'd signed on with the USO and were currently accompanying a gaggle of Hollywood celebrities on a Christmas goodwill tour.

As much as she loved the eccentric old soul, Caroline didn't view Grams as much more mature than her son. She was forever gallivanting off on some bizarre mission. Just today she was returning from Cape Cod, where she'd been for over a week with a trio of her kooky friends. For an early Christmas present, she'd requested a spyglass so she could serve her country as a spotter and search the shoreline for Nazi submarines.

All of Caroline's family had ridiculed and mocked her when she announced that she had accepted Christ as her Savior and joined forces with the Salvation

Army to help the city's poor.

"Now that you've got religion, you'll never have fun anymore," Harry had warned.

Then Lill had chimed in. "Those holy-rollers don't wear any makeup or jewelry. Are you ready for that?"

"You'll turn sour and crotchety before your time," Grams added. "Mark my words."

But Caroline had found her new life in Christ to be just the opposite. She'd never felt happier or more fulfilled.

Looking back up at Brother William, Caroline hid her embarrassment behind a flashing smile. "I'll be sure and pass your invitation along next time I see the folks," she said. "But I don't think they could keep up with your snappy beat. You might need them to audition first." Her playful remarks met with a round of laughter from the musicians.

"You're still planning on joining us for all the Christmas festivities at the mission tomorrow and Christmas Day, aren't you?" Sister Grace wagged her tambourine at Caroline to get her attention. "We're expecting to feed a record crowd at the Christmas dinner."

"Grams will insist on making her biannual pilgrimage to church tomorrow, so I won't be there in the morning. But I'm supposed to see to the preparation of the elements for tomorrow evening's candlelight communion service, and Major Stanton put me in charge of the potatoes on Christmas Day as well." Caroline slapped her forehead with a mittened hand. "Oh, speaking of Christmas dinner reminds me. I promised Grams that I'd pick up a couple of Cornish hens from Haymarket

Square for our own little holiday celebration. Aren't we all glad they've eased up on meat rationing?"

She didn't wait for a response but began sidling away from the circle of co-workers. "Listen, I must run. I'll see you all at the Christmas Eve service, if not before." She waved a quick good-bye and plunged into the tide of people. While she made her way toward the subway station, she bobbed her head up and down, back and forth, trying to spot the uniformed stranger. In his place on the bench now sat a mother with a baby cradled on her lap. A thorough scan of the area convinced Caroline that Jack's look-alike had gone. The realization brought an uncanny sorrow mixed with expectancy at the chance to read the note unobserved.

She ducked into Waltham's Pharmacy and took a seat at the soda fountain counter. While the soda jerk filled her order for hot cocoa, Caroline removed her mittens and pulled the piece of paper from her pocket with a certain measure of ceremony. Her hands started to quiver as she unfolded the jagged-edged page. She recognized the handwriting instantly, and her hand flew to her mouth to smother the squeal of joy that threatened to escape. Blinding tears kept her from reading past the first line, and she hurried to whisk them away. She skimmed the note once, twice, three times to make certain her eyes weren't deceiving her, then she jumped off her stool and grabbed her mittens. On her way out the door, she called over her shoulder, "Forget the cocoa. I've got to go."

Caroline prodded her way through the crowd until she came to the place where she'd last seen him. Setting aside all thoughts of propriety, she climbed up to stand on the bench and began to frantically scan the sea of shoppers in hopes of catching sight of a man in a USAAF uniform.

"Excuse me, Miss. Are you all right?" The young mother still sat on the bench, but she had pulled her baby close to her chest. She looked up at Caroline. Dismay etched her face.

Reconciled to the fact that he was really gone, Caroline stopped her search and climbed down to take a seat. "I'm sorry to have frightened you. I'm fine. I was just trying to locate a friend." The woman's eyebrows knitted in consternation, and she rose from her place on the bench to hurry off down the street. Caroline took a deep breath and pondered what she should do next. She reread the note, this time slowly and deliberately, making sure she hadn't misread the message.

Dear Caroline,

In the event that wires got crossed and you didn't receive my cable, I want you to know that I am alive and well and in Boston as of yesterday. If you want to contact me, I'm billeted at the Bay View Inn until 2 January, at which time I will travel to Westover Air Base for processing to my new assignment. Perhaps we'll get a chance to meet. If not, I wish you a very Merry Christmas.

Your former pen pal and friend,
Jack Johnson

Alive and well. Jack is alive and well. And just minutes before, he had been standing right in front of her. She envisioned his dark wavy hair, ruddy complexion, brilliant blue eyes. At last she could add color and depth to the one-dimensional, sepia-toned image of him she'd held for so long. Her heart had recognized the living and breathing Jack even when all logic said, "Impossible."

Fresh tears spilled unchecked down her cheeks, and she prayed without shame in a voice loud enough for all those around her to hear. "Thank You, Lord, for this modern-day Christmas miracle. Whatever the explanation, You've given Jack back to me—back from the dead—and I give You praise."

Alive and well. The words were too fantastic, too miraculous to be believed, but she embraced them as truth and praised the Lord. She couldn't wait to hear the resurrection story from Jack's own lips.

She held the note to her nose and inhaled the faint essence of leather and engine oil it had absorbed from his jacket. With a feathery touch, she rubbed an index finger over the ink. On her fifth or sixth read-through of Jack's letter, a flash of curiosity seized Caroline as to why she'd never received the cable he mentioned. She also found Jack's wording a bit odd and formal compared to his friendly letters of old. What had he meant by the words, *"former* pen pal and friend"? She shrugged off her concern as a symptom of her overactive imagination and tucked the precious missive away for safekeeping.

She would go to this Bay View Inn and wait for him to come. She'd camp out in their lobby if necessary. She'd throw her arms around Jack's neck and smother him with kisses when he walked in the door. Her heart refused to stop thumping in double-time, and her tangent thoughts would not be tamed. She had to think this through.

Caroline checked the time. She wanted more than anything to rush right over to the Bay View Inn, but she had no idea how to find the place. Besides, Grams would be expecting her any time now. She longed to change out of her uniform and shed the scratchy wool bonnet for more comfortable attire. She shouldn't wonder that Jack hadn't recognized her from the picture she'd sent. She must look a fright.

In light of all this, she decided to run by the house to welcome Grams back from her trip and share with her the happy news of Jack. She could call for directions, change clothes, and be riding the MTA to meet Jack in less than an hour's time.

"Anybody home?" Caroline stepped into the foyer. "Grams, you here?"

Darkness engulfed her when she closed the door, and she realized she'd forgotten to raise the blackout shades that morning before she raced out the door.

"I'll be down in two shakes of a lamb's tail, Toots." The familiar voice, laced with the unmistakable accent of a native Bostonian, resonated from the second floor. "Brought you a surprise."

Caroline shucked off her coat, then groped for an empty place on the coat rack behind the door. She let her uniform's bonnet dangle by the ribbon ties on the same peg that held her overcoat. Grams refused to allow the use of electric lights until six o'clock, and Caroline didn't want to be greeted with a lecture. She stretched her arms out in front of her in order to feel her way to the parlor windows and let in some light. However, her shins collided with an inanimate object in the middle of the entryway, and she nearly went sprawling. Through the murky black, she managed to grab the banister and right herself.

"Welcome home, Grams," she muttered and rubbed her smarting legs. The dear woman would never win any awards for good housekeeping. Caroline's eyes finally adjusted to the faint light filtering from Grams's bedroom at the top of the stairs, and she was able to pick her way around the clutter to the parlor. No one would have ever guessed that Caroline had come straight home yesterday after her classes dismissed for the holidays and stayed up past midnight to clean.

Icabod, the stray calico kitten Grams had welcomed as a permanent resident at the first frost, leaped from his favorite napping place on the ottoman and tangled himself around Caroline's legs. Rather than risk another shin-bruising spill, Caroline crouched down to rub and scratch the cat behind his ears. Icabod bolted up the stairs, having evidently received sufficient attention.

Caroline walked back through the entryway and skirted an apple crate filled with a wide assortment of seashells—no doubt the very item she'd tripped over moments before. She followed a woolen trail of a scarf, gloves, and a stocking cap that led through the hallway and ended at her grams's overcoat draped across a kitchen chair. On the dinette table lay a foot-long jagged strip of iron lacquered with a thick coat of gunmetal-gray paint. Caroline lifted the heavy metal piece and turned it over and back and over again. She shrugged her shoulders and returned the curiosity to the table.

"I see you found your surprise." Grams came up behind her, and Caroline startled at her voice. "Can you guess what it is?"

"I don't have the vaguest idea. You'll have to fill me in on the origins of this treasure."

"Well, the rest of the girls expressed some reservation and I'm not one hundred percent sure, but I have a strong hunch that this is a piece off a German U-boat that our boys sunk. If you look close, you'll see a bit of black paint that looks all the world to me like a corner of a swastika. I stubbed my toe on this chunk while I patrolled the shoreline yesterday." To add a bit of dramatic flair, she glanced down and wiggled her feet, bedecked in a pair of pink chenille house slippers. "I'm most certain that stretch of beach was pristine the day before."

When Grams lifted her head again to look at Caroline, a silver pin curl fell over her left eye and she sent it back into place with a puff of breath. Instead of a housedress, she wore a doctor's lab coat that her husband used to wear on his hospital rounds. Caroline didn't remember her grandfather at all. He died when she was two. However, from all indications, she had inherited her level-headedness from him.

"Grams, I never heard any reports of our navy sinking an enemy sub off the Cape." Caroline lifted the scrap metal again and examined it with suspicion. "Where did you get your information?"

"You don't expect our boys to release that type of scuttlebutt to the general public, do you?" Grams's voice lowered to a whisper. "Why, can you imagine the mass panic that would ensue if word got out as to just how close to our own shores the enemy lurks and the battle rages? But just between you and me, let me tell you that the waters off the Cape were alive with covert activity, and not even the military can keep such things secret from a sleuth the likes of your ol' Grams."

The elderly woman's runaway imagination filled the room with an infectious sparkle of suspense. However, Caroline knew from experience that Grams' assumptions and hunches seldom found basis in fact. She had to force herself not to roll her eyes.

"Regardless of where this comes from, Grams, I'll cherish it forever. I can always use another paperweight or doorstop. Thanks for thinking of me." Caroline pulled Jack's note from her pocket and dangled it high in the air above her grandmother's head. "Now I have an even bigger surprise to share with you—and I'm on my way to verify this one as soon as I can change clothes and make a telephone call. I hold in my hand a letter from my dear pen pal, Jack Johnson, the pilot everyone presumed to be dead—"

"Oh, my sweet Toots." Grams slipped a comforting arm around Caroline. "I know how hard you took the news of your little friend's death. Grief can do such awful things to one's mind, especially around the holidays. You simply mustn't lose your grip on reality."

Caroline attempted to escape her grandmother's embrace and turn to face her so that she could explain, but Grams's bony fingers tightened their grip on her shoulder.

"I imagine those radical Christians you mingle with are filling your head with silly ideas, what with all their preaching about life after death. But nothing will bring that pilot back from a fiery grave—no matter how much you might wish otherwise. I'll bet you that an old letter he wrote before his crash is just now catching up to you. I've heard such things happen often to family members of the deceased. What's the date on the letter? Let me see what it says."

Caroline sputtered a protest, but her grandmother pried the piece of paper from her hand.

"Aye! Caramba!" Grams only used the foreign interjection upon a sudden remembrance. "Your letter reminds me. . ." Holding the note in one hand, she reached with the other into the deep pocket of her lab coat and withdrew an envelope. "This came for you as I was leaving the house on my way to the Cape. I'd already locked things up, and the girls were waiting in Mabel's car with the engine running. I couldn't waste gasoline, you understand. . .and, well, I didn't figure it was anything too urgent as I'd just received a telegram from your folks saying they'd arrived in Hawaii just fine."

Caroline took the official-looking envelope from her grandmother and pushed her finger under the flap to break the seal. With Grams chittering around her like a magpie, she found it difficult to concentrate on the telegraph message the envelope contained.

"Maybe you inherited some money from your mother's nutty third cousin, Ida Belle, who passed on last month. Wouldn't that be nice? You could use a bit of good news to lift your spirits and help you forget about your little pen pal friend. . . ." Her grandmother fell silent when Caroline closed her eyes and laid an open palm on top of her head.

"Oh, Grams. How could you? I've got to find Jack right away and explain."

Chapter 3

Dear Guest,

We want to thank you for choosing to stay with us here at Bay View Inn. As an expression of our appreciation, please present this certificate for a complimentary cocktail at The Pirate's Cove, our hotel nightclub.

We appreciate your patronage and hope you enjoy your stay.

The Management

Jack waited at the Park Street Station for the next subway, struggling to stand his ground against the marathon of holiday shoppers who pressed and pushed him on every side. With only a few hours left until the stores closed on this final shopping day before Christmas, the crowd raced past him with a mounting sense of urgency. He, on the other hand, felt no need to hurry anywhere.

He pinched Caroline's photograph between his thumb and index finger and inched his way over to a wastebasket. Intent on ripping her image into confetti, he paused with his fingers poised. Knowing now that her eyes were a rich, maple syrup brown and her hair a soft shade of doeskin blond only increased his suffering. He could no longer bear to look at her contagious smile after seeing with his own eyes the kissable pink of her full lips. All hopes of pursuing a deeper relationship with Caroline had been dashed when she first looked at him. Even so, he couldn't bring himself to destroy the photo of the woman he loved. He breathed a deep sigh and tucked her picture back into his pocket.

The moment his gaze met hers, he had recognized her, and he knew by her stunned expression that she had recognized him as well. She looked miserably uncomfortable at having been caught so soon after their scheduled meeting. For the longest time, he had contemplated whether or not to address her outright about the missed date. But he'd given her ample opportunity to reveal her true identity, and she'd refused to come clean and admit to being the woman he sought. She obviously didn't want anything to do with him, and he wasn't about to grant her the satisfaction of knowing how much she'd hurt him. He had decided to pretend not to recognize her in hopes of saving a shred of dignity.

She must have fallen in love with another man. Maybe she'd even married in the course of the past four months. He'd watched and waited in hopes of catching a peek at a ring, but she'd never removed the mitten from her left hand.

Despite the endless list of possibilities, he still clung with desperate optimism to the thinnest thread of a chance that she hadn't really recognized him. . .that she hadn't gotten his telegram. . .that she still thought he was dead. . .and that, once she read his note, she'd rush to meet him before the day's end. However, the frayed strand of hope could snap in the slightest breeze of more bad news.

A pervasive weariness washed over him, and he felt as though he could sleep without stirring straight through Christmas. Unless a brighter prospect came along, he planned to succumb to the temptation of a good, long nap—right after he redeemed his coupon for a free cocktail, courtesy of the Bay View Inn.

Jack looked over his shoulder to see if anyone noticed him passing from the hotel lobby into the Pirate's Cove lounge. Each time he entered a bar he suffered from a paranoid suspicion that his father was watching him. The thought of his father's disapproval heaped coals of fire on a conscience already sizzling with guilt.

Up until his final combat mission, Jack could have counted on a duck's toenails the number of times he'd entered this type of place or tasted their wares. However, the lure of the liquid painkiller overpowered all his moral rectitude.

He dipped into a secluded booth and inspected his surroundings. The room's nautical theme seemed an ill-suited backdrop for the sounds of Cole Porter's hit, "Don't Fence Me In," that blared from the corner jukebox. A lone sprig of mistletoe over the doorway constituted the only holiday decor.

His cheeks puffed with a sigh of relief to discover that he shared the room with only one other patron. A man about his age sat at the bar, cradling his chin in his left hand. A safety pin tacked an empty shirt cuff to the shoulder of his other sleeve. Half a dozen empty beer mugs cluttered the counter in front of him, and another frothy glass of fresh-poured brew waited to be nursed. Rather than going to the trouble of leaving his post, the bartender hollered across the room.

"What'll it be?"

Jack screwed his face into a puzzled frown. "Excuse me?"

"What can I get you to drink? Or are you just claimin' squatter's rights to my valuable real estate?" He tacked a humorless chuckle onto his retort. Jack figured that the guy must serve double-duty as a bouncer, his forearms looked like mortar shell casings.

"I have this coupon for a free cocktail. Why don't you just bring me your specialty." In the past, due to his lack of experience along these lines, he'd always deferred such decisions to his drinking buddies. He wondered if his ignorance appeared obvious now.

"Hey, Pal." The one-armed man swivelled on his barstool to face Jack. "No need for the both of us to drink alone when we could share our Christmas cheer. Mind if I join you?" Jack waved him over, and the man carried his drink with him when he came.

"Forgive me for not shaking your hand," he said, clipping his head in Jack's direction instead. "But when I promised to give Uncle Sam my right arm, he took me literally. I'm Bob Landry, recently discharged from my duties as a corporal in the army infantry. You a military man?"

"Captain John Wesley Johnson, U.S. Army Air Corps. But please, just call me Jack. I packed my title away with my uniform this afternoon, and I'm planning to spend the rest of my R&R incognito."

The man paused in mid-crouch as he prepared to slide into the booth opposite Jack. "You sure you don't mind fraternizing with an enlisted man?"

Jack swiped at the air. "Have a seat. I insist. We're just fellow battle-scarred soldiers. Although my wounds can't compare to yours." He tried to not stare at the dangling sleeve.

"This thing wouldn't qualify as a scratch compared to the injuries I've suffered in here." Bob poked at his chest with his thumb. "A warrior's deepest injuries never show, and something tells me you're nursin' a few of those too." He fell silent when the bartender approached and slid an amber-colored drink across the table. The burly waiter interrupted without a hint of an apology.

"I guarantee this here will put hair on your toes. I call it the Polish Pirate, made from my own secret recipe. Just let me know if and when you're ready for another. I won't be far." Turning toward the corporal, he asked, "Another beer for you?"

Caroline maintained a discreet distance and tried not to eavesdrop as an elderly, hunch-backed, male desk clerk registered a room to a dress-uniformed sailor with a Greer Garson look-alike hanging on his arm. In light of the grains of rice that speckled their hair and the lady's fragrant gardenia corsage, she pegged the lovey-dovey pair as newlyweds.

While the attendant described for them, in painstaking detail, the way to the honeymoon suite, Caroline transposed herself into the bride's dyed-satin coral shoes and matching pillbox hat. Jack's face replaced that of the doting groom. All her long-dormant dreams of a future with Jack broke to the surface again and bloomed like a Christmas rose.

She wondered if he still sensed a call to the ministry, and at the same time, she worried that she might not have the gifts and graces necessary to be a pastor's wife. She choked back a bubble of laughter. Her runaway imagination already pronounced her married to the pilot-turned-pastor John Wesley Johnson and living happily ever after in a quaint village rectory, when she had yet to have a real conversation with him. Then again, she might find herself conversing with Jack in a matter of moments. She could think of a thousand different things she wanted to tell him first. Her face flushed with heated excitement over the possibilities.

Caroline wedged her pocketbook between her feet while she shed her heavy coat and tucked it over one arm. Then she straightened the lace collar of her sweater and smoothed her skirt. She stole a quick peek at her compact's mirror to verify that her lipstick hadn't smudged, and she patted her upswept bangs into place. If only this droning receptionist would cut short his Bay View Inn history lesson and send the inattentive lovebirds on their way, she could confirm whether or not Jack was in his room. There didn't appear to be any other employees on the premises nor a quicker avenue to get the information she needed.

She crossed her arms and tapped her foot on the wood floor. Tilting her head to one side, she stared at the prattling clerk and sighed loudly in hopes that he would sense her urgency, but he didn't even glance her way. The thought occurred to her that she might be faced with an equally tedious lecture when her turn came to approach the counter. Caroline searched the lobby, trying to cook up a quick plan to rescue both herself and the captive newlyweds. When she spied the telephone on a table beside a threadbare velour davenport, she crept stealthily toward it.

Facing away from the front desk, she lifted the heavy, black handset from its cradle. Caroline tugged the rotary dial through a series of ticking clacks. KEN-5555. She still remembered the exchange and simple number after calling the inn earlier to ask for directions. At the loud jangle of the front desk telephone, Caroline stuck a finger in her open ear to muffle some of the nearby noise.

"Excuse me just a moment while I answer this." From across the room, the clerk's nasal whine penetrated through Caroline's plugged ear.

"Bay View Inn, where George Washington really did sleep, this is Mr. Pratt speaking, how may I assist you?"

Out of the corner of her eye, Caroline noticed the newlyweds tiptoeing toward the hallway leading to the guestrooms. "Yes," she said. "Could you please connect me with the room of one of your guests—a Captain John Johnson?"

"Regrettably, no. You see, Miss, we don't have telephones in our guests rooms, for, by and large, we've found that most of our patrons prefer not to be interrupted—" Caroline tried to jump in before he could expound any further.

"I understand. Then perhaps you could—"

"And even if we did have phones in the guest rooms, you wouldn't find Captain Johnson there to answer it. He walked through here a few minutes ago on his way to our nightclub, the Pirate's Cove, speaking of which reminds me of a true tale that occurred some number of—"

From Caroline's vantage point, she could look across the lobby and see directly into the entrance of the dingy lounge. Her heart skipped a beat to learn how near to Jack she might be.

"I do wish I could listen to your story, Mr. Pratt, but I'm pressed for time. Thank you for your kind help, Sir." Caroline eased the receiver onto the telephone and the connection broke with a soft click. She hated the thought of being rude to the man, but when she copped a quick glance at the registration desk, he didn't appear to be the least bit offended, nor did he seem wise to the fact that she had been the one on the other end of the line. Before he could hold her gaze or detain her in any way, she hurried toward the entrance to the bar and paused in the doorway to survey the room.

A noxious odor of alcohol mixed with cigarette smoke permeated the air. Behind the bar, a brawny man stood drying glasses. He nodded at Caroline to acknowledge her presence, and the lecherous look he gave her made her skin crawl. In the farthest smoky corner, two men huddled in a booth, deep in conversation.

She hesitated, uncomfortable at the thought of stepping any farther into the room. The one who sat facing the entrance could not be mistaken for the man she'd met on the street earlier that afternoon. Perhaps Mr. Pratt was confused when he thought he saw Jack enter the nightclub. The Jack Johnson she knew didn't frequent bars. She started to spin on one heel to leave, but she paused mid-turn, struck by something familiar in the man with his back to her.

Caroline cried out, unable to contain her desperation or control her resuscitated dreams a moment longer. "Jack!"

The man twisted in his seat and sprang to his feet. He took one step toward her, then froze. For a split second, his slitted eyes seemed to be sizing her up, trying to decide if she came as friend or foe.

"C–Caroline?"

She couldn't keep a silly grin from spreading across her face. A shiver raced through her and she clapped her hands together over her chest, then rushed to close the distance between them.

They both dodged around tables and a few scattered chairs, finally meeting in the middle of the room. Without pause, Caroline threw her arms around Jack's neck. He encircled her waist in one strong arm and swept her off her feet.

The smell of alcohol clung to Jack's clothes and hair, but she attributed it to their surroundings and tried to ignore it. Caroline nuzzled into his warm neck, and her heart tamped furiously against her chest. Waves of euphoric joy pushed to the surface in gale-force sobs. Jack caressed and patted her back and breathed tender shushings in her ear until her weeping dwindled to silent, happy tears. He pulled her even closer, and she ran her fingers through his dark hair. Wordlessly, she savored this long-imagined, hope-forsaken moment. Her only regret was that their first real meeting had to happen in a shabby, smelly bar.

"Oh, Jack, I'm so sorry," she said with her head still tucked in the crook of his neck. "You must have thought me just awful for not meeting you or acknowledging your presence earlier. I didn't see your telegram until just minutes ago. I thought when I saw you on the street that I must be imagining things. You're supposed to be dead."

She planted a light kiss on the spot where her lips rested against his clean-shaven skin. Never would she have done such a thing upon first meeting anyone else, yet she felt wholly comfortable in his arms.

She pulled back slightly. "Now put me down and let me look at you," she insisted.

He eased her down until her feet touched the floor, and she pulled a starched white hanky from her sleeve. She proceeded to dab her remaining tears from under her eyes, replaced her handkerchief in its hiding place, then tipped her head back to look into his face. "Jack, is it truly you back from the grave or one of Dickens' Christmas visions standing here before me now?" She pressed his cheeks between her hands, and his smile pushed at her palms.

"It's me in the flesh. But for awhile this afternoon, you had me wishing I were dead," he said. He traced along the side of her face with the back of his fingers. "I'm glad to hear there was some kind of a mix-up and that you weren't intentionally avoiding me. You don't know how happy you've made me, Caroline. You're everything I thought you'd be and more."

With utmost tenderness, he lifted her chin and bent to kiss her. In that instant, Caroline thought that she, too, had died—and gone to heaven. But before his lips met hers, the sound of someone clearing his throat interrupted her fairy-tale meeting with Jack. The man she'd seen sitting in the booth now stood just inches away from them, accompanied by an overpowering stench of stale beer. She shot a glance at his dangling sleeve while he spoke.

"Looks like my company's been outranked by that of a dame. Not that I blame ya none. I figure before things get too involved here, I'd be best sayin' my good-byes."

Caroline immediately recognized the slurred speech and glazed look in the stranger's eyes. She had observed these same symptoms all too frequently while working at the mission, and she'd lost count of the number of lives she'd seen destroyed by a bottle. *Jack must have been witnessing to him,* she thought.

"Enjoyed sharing a drink with you, Captain. Maybe we'll run into each other again before you leave town. If so, next round is on me." The tipsy, disabled vet presented a sloppy, left-handed salute.

"Sure thing, Bob," Jack offered. He released his hold on Caroline long enough to return the proffered salute. The man backed away, stumbling over a chair and running into a table before he teetered under the mistletoe and lunged out the door.

Upon their interrupter's departure, Jack drew her into his arms again. "Now, where were we?" He dipped toward her again, but when his lips touched hers, Caroline thought she caught a fresh whiff of booze. Even his kisses tasted like alcohol. She decided it had to somehow be related to the lingering odor of the one-armed man. She knew for certain that Jack didn't drink. During their back-and-forth correspondence, they had often discussed the fact that neither of them imbibed in spirits of any kind. His buddy's letter, which told her of Jack's death, had confirmed this fact as well. She tried to shake off her niggling suspicions and focus her full attention on Jack.

"We have so much to talk about," she said. "Now that I've seen you with my own eyes, I'm itching to know where you've been these past four months and why it is that the army pronounced you dead. What do you say we get out of here and go someplace where we can converse privately?"

Caroline glanced toward the bar where the bartender leaned, his head in one hand, blatantly eavesdropping on them.

She brightened. "We could go back to my place. Grams had a few errands to run, so she may not be there for the first little bit we're there, but she insisted that I bring you home to meet her if I found you. When I left, she was putting a pot of venison stew on the stove to simmer so we'd have something to feed us all. In fact, she wants you to pack your bags and stay with us for the remainder of your leave. You can have the whole third floor to yourself, since we don't expect Harry and Lill back from their latest tour until the end of January. Grams says—" Caroline began to imitate the warbling falsetto of her grandmother's voice. "Listen, Toots, that distinguished pilot officer of yours shouldn't be hanging around Sculley Square in the midst of all those raucous sailor boys." Dropping her imitation, she continued. "What with my mission work, Grams long ago gave up in her attempts to keep me away from the rough parts of town, but she still makes me carry a whistle so I can call for help whenever I travel down this way." She raised her right arm and jangled her charm bracelet in the air to display the prominent silver-plated whistle.

"I apologize for bringing you down to this neighborhood," Jack said. "When I wrote that note this afternoon, I guess I didn't really expect you to respond. The stew sounds great. And I certainly don't like the idea of you traveling these streets alone. I'd be more than happy to see you home." He took her by the elbow and guided her out of the bar.

"Frankly," he continued, "I can't wait to meet your grandmother. After all you've written about her, I feel as though I already know her well. Besides, I figure I'm helpless to protest or decline her invitation. I can see her bursting into my hotel room after curfew, pulling me out of bed, and dragging me to your place in my skivvies." They shared a flutter of laughter, and Caroline's spirit brimmed with pure delight.

She heard a clanging bell and looked through the lobby's plate-glass window in time to see a streetcar pulling away from the corner stop. She glanced at her watch. "The streetcars run every fifteen minutes or so. Do you think we can catch the next one? They don't run as often as the subways, but they only cost a nickel, while the subway costs a dime."

Jack sent her a sly smile. "The army owes me four months of back pay, so I think I can afford to fork out the extra dough for the subway ride. Still, I won't need but a minute to reload my Val-Pak. I left Europe in such a hurry after getting back into Allied territory that my entire wardrobe consists of what I could beg and borrow from the guys in my old barracks."

Caroline watched while Jack's face clouded with seriousness.

"I'll share my story over a bowl of stew with you, Caroline, but I need to warn you now. After you've heard me out, you may want to withdraw the offer for me to stay around. If that's the case, no matter what your grandmother wants or says, I'll honor your wishes and hightail it back here to the Bay View Inn." Jack lowered his head and appeared to intently study his fingernails. "You see, although I wasn't actually killed on August 25, a part of me did die. I'm not the man you came to know through our letters. I've changed."

Chapter 4

Nearly midnight

Dear Diary,

Who would have thought when I woke up this morning what today would bring? My dear, supposedly deceased Jack is not only ALIVE, but as I write these words, I can hear him walking across my parents' bedroom—right over my head!

Jack Johnson is more handsome *and* sweet *than I ever dreamed he'd be!!! How heartbreaking that the awful experiences he's been through have left him such a tortured and tormented soul. He seems eaten up with guilt—even doubting his call to the ministry, which disappoints me for more reasons than one. I am desperately praying that God will show me how I can help him.*

I'll need pages and pages to explain today's miraculous chain of events, and I'm too exhausted to write more now. Even though I'm not likely to forget a single detail of this day anytime soon, I'll spell everything out sometime tomorrow. TO BE CONTINUED. . .

S ince the streetcar carried them closer to their destination than the subway, Jack and Caroline decided to take the cheaper mode of transport to her neighborhood after all. During the twenty-minute ride, amid the jarring stop-and-go traffic and jostling crowds, they shared a comfortable companionship, exchanging frequent smiles and general pleasantries. Jack appreciated the fact that Caroline didn't press him for information in this too-chaotic, too-public place.

"Beacon and Charles Street," she said. "This is our stop. We've only got a short walk from here."

Jack hitched his bag over his right shoulder and held onto Caroline's arm with his free hand, allowing her to guide him through the jam of people exiting and boarding the trolley. They left the busy sidewalk which bordered the Commons and turned down a residential side street. The bare oak trees lining the walk sent long shadows dancing among the diffused light of winter's dusk.

Thanks to the graphic word pictures Caroline had painted over the course of their correspondence, Jack didn't need to look at the post marker to know their location. He felt like he'd come home. In stark contrast to the crumbled, battle-scarred dwellings and debris-filled streets he'd grown accustomed to, everything here looked so clean. Inviting. Whole.

Jack halted abruptly in the middle of the sidewalk and spread his arms wide. "Ladies and gentlemen. . . drum roll please. . .we have arrived on Spring Branch, that renowned street where America's melting pot begins to boil and home of Boston's sterling citizen, Miss Caroline Harrington."

She responded with a dramatic curtsy and said, "Allow me to introduce you to the neighborhood—"

"Stop." He held up a hand to punctuate the command. "Don't tell me. Let me guess. I bet I can name the people who live in each place." He pointed to the house on the corner they'd just rounded. "This one's easy."

Two abandoned hockey sticks, four well-worn ice skates, and a kickball littered the tiny yard. "We now stand before the residence of the twelve-year-old Arnold twins, Phil and Steve." Through Caroline, he'd sent them two of his squadron's insignia patches and a couple pairs of pilot wings.

On prominent display in the next home's front window hung a red-bordered, white banner with a vertical row of three stars—two blue and one gold.

"That's where the Randolphs live." He stopped and removed his hat as a show of respect. "I see by the 'Sons in Service' flag that one of their three boys was killed. Which one? How'd it happen?"

"Tim," Caroline answered softly. "The youngest. Killed somewhere in France about the time you went down." She clutched his arm and let out a deep sigh. "His mother is still grieving so hard. I'm praying the other two make it home soon. We'll all breathe a little easier then." They walked on by in silence.

Paint-chipped shutters, pulled tight against the outside world, and an unswept stoop denoted the home of Ruby Dildine, the widowed recluse who seldom ventured outside her doors. Hers was the only brownstone on the street that didn't boast a V-Home sign indicating the residents had done their part in supporting the war effort.

"As I recollect, your friendly Civil Defense warden, Sam Burns, and his wife, Ida, live there, across the street from Widow Dildine. And only one house stands between the Dildine place and yours. Am I right?" He looked to Caroline, and she nodded her confirmation. "But here's where I'm stumped. The last letter I read from you said the place next door to yours was being fixed up for new tenants and you hadn't yet learned their names."

She spoke so softly he had to lean in close to hear her response.

"A professional photographer by the name of Izzie Bernstein moved in there, along with his mother. The poor folks may have been spared the brunt of Hitler's hate, but they still face plenty of discrimination right here in the good ol' USA. They moved into our neighborhood because, after years of scrimping to buy the house they were renting in the south shore suburbs, a village ordinance denied them that right because they are Jewish." She shook her head slowly from side to side. "I'll never understand such prejudice. They're really nice people. Mrs. Bernstein hosts Grams's bridge club every Tuesday morning."

Jack clinched his fists in reflex to the searing anger spreading through him. He'd watched many good men—most of his buddies—die in an effort to stamp out such evil. Instances like this made him believe they'd died for a hopeless cause.

Caroline gently touched his sleeve and tugged for

him to start walking again. "What man meant for evil, the Lord used for good. The Bernsteins are happier here than they were in their old neighborhood. For the most part, we're all one big happy family on Spring Branch Street, you know."

He swallowed his anger and forced himself to return her smile. When they reached the walk leading up to her home, they paused. Centered in the tiny plot of brown grass, a ship's mast had been converted into a flagpole. In the still air, a limp Old Glory dangled from the top. Against the pole's base leaned a rusty anchor. Caroline swept one arm in a wide arc and pointed the way to the front door with an extended palm. "I welcome you to our humble abode. I warn you, though. The place is a mess."

"I expected no less," Jack said. She responded by feigning a punch to his chest.

"Hey, I try. But Grams prefers that 'lived in' look."

"Your Grams and I are going to get along just fine." He motioned for her to go ahead. "Please. Lead the way."

Once inside, Caroline showed Jack to his room and excused herself to serve up the stew. He joined her in the kitchen as soon as he'd hung up his uniform and made use of the facilities. When she had everything on the table, she took her seat and held out her hand for him to hold. "Jack, will you say the blessing for our food?"

He enclosed her soft hand in his and cleared his throat. "Uh. I'd prefer it if you'd do it this time."

She raised an eyebrow but simply nodded in response and began to pray. She offered up to the Lord a sweet and simple prayer of thanksgiving not only for the food, but also for bringing him safely to her when she'd long since given up hope. As she prayed, Jack realized that he used to commune with God in a similar, personal way just a few short months ago. As she said, "Amen," she gave his thumb a squeeze and pulled her hand away.

Caroline picked up her soup spoon and sunk it into her stew, and he followed her lead. Raising it to her lips, she blew at the rising steam, speaking in short sentences between puffs. "Don't get me wrong. . . . I'm glad they were mistaken. . . . But it seems to me. . .like a cruel and inhumane thing. . .for the military to do. . . to a soldier's loved ones. . .declaring them 'killed in action'. . .when they aren't one hundred percent sure." She stuck the spoon into her mouth and dove it back into the bowl while she chewed.

Jack swallowed his bite and swiped over his chin with his napkin before he spoke. "The Army Air Corps isn't to blame. They told me at debriefing that this kind of thing hasn't happened but a few times over the course of the war. Maybe a couple dozen accounts at most. Three fighter pilots die for every one injury, and in my case, the odds of surviving that crash should have been nil. My squadron had every reason to believe I'd been killed." He dug his spoon into his thick soup again.

"Well, if you don't tell me the whole story soon, I'm going to die of curiosity." When Jack looked at her, she winced. "Whoops. I suppose that was a poor word choice. These past few months have taught me that death is no laughing matter. Even so. . ." She pointed her empty utensil at him like a weapon. "I've been patient long enough, Captain Johnson. Out with it."

With a loud clatter, she dropped her spoon onto her bread plate and pushed back in her chair. She crossed her arms and waited in silence for him to respond, but her sparkling eyes betrayed her mock expression of anger.

As leavened dough left untended, a rising quagmire of dread oozed over Jack's spirit. He couldn't postpone the inevitable any longer. He had to tell her everything—including the parts he had glossed over during the CO's interrogation for his official report. He'd come to Boston, in part, to bare his soul to the only person he knew who might understand and not judge. Only Caroline held the potential of helping him come to terms with his guilt.

"I'll tell you the whole sordid story, but you need to know before I begin that I don't ever plan on sharing with another soul the dark revelations I'm about to share with you now. You're the only one I trust." He looked into her eyes to find the playful expression of anger had changed to one of utmost seriousness.

"I'm honored that you feel you can confide in me." She reached across the table and rested her hand on his wrist. "I pray I won't ever do anything to lose that trust. I was only teasing, you know. If you aren't ready to talk about it yet, I can wait."

"No. There's no better time than the present. I need to ask one favor, though. Let me spell it all out without interruption, 'cause I don't think I can say it more than once."

"My lips are sealed." She twisted her fingers over her mouth as if turning a key in a lock.

"I'll start at the beginning then." He stared out the

window at a barren tree while his mind's eye carried him back across the Atlantic to a warm summer day.

"Early morning August 25, we took off from Boxted Station into a clear blue sky. Our patrol team of four left the mission briefing in high spirits after hearing reports that the French Resistance Fighters had managed to regain control of Paris. Our mission that day called for us to strafe a portion of the Rhine to prevent a Hun infantry battalion from transporting replacement troops from the Netherlands into Belgium. I remember praying as I prepared for take-off, asking God to go before me and enable me to play a part in destroying the enemy so we could all go home soon." He reached for his glass of water and took a drink.

"True to the scouting reports, we spotted enemy troops crossing the river on barges and just about anything else that would float. I flew Tail-End Charlie that day behind the other three planes, and when I made my first strafing pass, I witnessed the most horrifying sight of my life."

Jack noticed he was talking faster and faster, and he drew a breath to slow the pace of his words.

"We'd caught the barges mid-stream, and scores of men were diving into the water in a desperate attempt to escape the slaughter. To give you an idea of the extent of the devastation we caused, each P-47 carries eight .50-caliber machine guns that fire a hundred rounds a second. As I pulled off the target, the first plane was already making its second strafing pass. We emptied our ammunition in three passes, and the river ran red with the blood of those men." He squeezed his eyes shut and clenched and unclenched his fists several times before he could look up and continue.

"That abominable scene will haunt me till the day I die. Up until then, I hadn't witnessed the devastation wrought by my own hands. Flying high above my destructive wake, I'd never really suffered from much guilt—especially when I'd been aiming for inanimate enemy targets such as railroads, munitions depots, or factories. I don't recall giving much thought to the fact that innocent people might have been in the midst of those places. I fought the Germans machine to machine. Pilot against pilot, one-on-one. We even held to an unwritten code of conduct that we wouldn't shoot down any defenseless enemy personnel who had bailed out of their planes."

He looked to Caroline to measure her response. She offered a reassuring nod, but true to her word, she didn't utter a sound.

"That was only the beginning of my nightmare. With our mission complete, I'd just started to climb out of the target area when my engine took a hit from a 20-mm flak gun. That shot ruptured both my gas and oil lines, and my bird began to drop like a rock, trailing fire and a billowing cloud of black smoke. Knowing that I risked flipping the plane if I tried to lower my landing gear, I searched for a place where I could belly her in and spotted a freshly mowed field that I thought might work. Just before *Sweet Caroline* hit the ground, I jettisoned my canopy. Unfortunately, I misjudged my speed and overshot the field. The jug smashed into a stone wall surrounding a barnyard and she burst into flames no more than a split second after I hit the ground. Horses and chickens and pigs were flying everywhere. I figured the Germans would be hot on my trail. So I made the most of the smoke screen, fire, and general barnyard chaos and slipped away into a nearby grove of trees. I heard my flight buzz once over the crash site, but they didn't have enough fuel left to stooge around looking for me, and I couldn't give away my position. When the skies grew quiet, I knew I was on my own behind enemy lines."

He traced along the pattern of the faded green Formica tabletop with his index finger as he measured his next words.

"Evidently, my escape into the trees hadn't gone as unnoticed as I'd thought. While my attentions were still focused overhead, someone knocked me to the ground. I turned over to see a uniformed Nazi with his rifle trained to my chest. Glaring and grunting commands in German, he poked his bayonet into my shoulder and jerked his head to signal for me to stand. I don't know what came over me. Maybe after all the stories I'd heard, I figured I'd rather be shot and killed on the spot than to die in a German POW stalag. Whatever I was thinking, I grabbed the barrel of his rifle and yanked. The Hun recovered long enough to ram the blade into my left shoulder. Pain shot down my arm. I kicked his feet out from under him. When I did, his rifle flew out of his hands and he fell on top of me. Frantic, I fought to gain control before he could recover his gun. I managed to wrestle him into submission, and I pinned him to the ground with my hands around his neck. He looked at me with this desperate pleading in his eyes, but something inside me snapped. I don't know if fear or rage drove me, but I tightened my grip on his neck. His eyes grew wider and wider as my own blood dripped from my wound and into the ground by his head. I choked him until he went limp. I knew he was dead, even though his eyes seemed to look right at me."

Jack rubbed his forehead, trying to erase the abhorrent image from his memory. A shudder ran through him and he gulped a deep breath. Staring sightlessly at the stove behind Caroline, he forced himself to continue.

"I stumbled away and picked up the dead man's rifle, only to learn that the chamber was empty. He'd run out of ammunition."

Jack had to pause again. He filled his lungs and exhaled a slow stream of air before continuing his story.

"Exhausted, I thought I'd rest for just a minute before putting more distance between me and the wreckage. I must have fallen asleep. When I awoke, I found myself on the floor of a ramshackle hut deep in the woods. From what I gathered later, the farmer whose barnyard I'd just set aflame was a member of the Dutch Resistance forces and he'd smuggled me out of the area. The wife of a village doctor came every day to dress my wound and nurse me back to health. When I was well enough to travel on my own power, various members of the Resistance shuffled me through their network, from one place to the next under the cover of darkness, until I finally made it back into Allied-controlled territory. Before I knew it, I was boarding a boat for Boston to see you."

He darted a glance at Caroline, then lowered his head. He didn't dare look at her too long for fear of reading disappointment or disgust in her sweet, solemn face.

"I killed that man. And ever since, those eyes of his

have tormented my days. Kept me awake every night. I have no way of knowing the man's spiritual condition when he died. Still, I can't stop thinking that, even though the dictates of war say I had the right—even responsibility—I may have sent his soul to suffer an eternity in hell." Jack struggled to swallow around the hard lump forming in his throat. Not trusting himself to speak, he squeezed his eyelids shut and waited for his swelling emotions to subside.

He felt Caroline's light touch as she patted him on the arm. "How absolutely awful for you," she said. Her tender comforting gave him the courage to open his eyes and look at her. If his confession had repulsed her, she hid her feelings well. He saw only concern reflecting back at him.

"I'm sorry to burden you with all this. I know I can't change the past. I'll just have to learn to deal with it somehow."

He used his spoon to dig trenches in his long-cold stew.

"But I'm not only faced with what I did, I need to decide what I'm going to do. As I've told you before, my father expects me to follow in his footsteps and become a minister. Practically all my life I've felt God calling me into full-time Christian service. I should have listened to Dad. He tried to get me to file for conscientious objector status when I registered for the draft. But I wanted to learn how to fly. I told him I could be a good Christian example among the other guys." Another deep sigh filled his chest and he released it with a puff.

"Dad was right all along. No man who's called into the ministry has any business going to war, regardless of the noble cause." He shoved his bowl away and looked Caroline straight in the eye.

"I can't serve as a pastor now. Not after what I've done. I can't offer spiritual comfort and healing or point the way to eternal life—after committing cold-blooded murder with my very own hands. . . ." Briefly, he glanced at his open palms, then he grasped them together and hid them in his lap.

"I used to look down on the fellas for constantly drinking themselves into a stupor. Now I understand there are times that the only way to find relief is with a stiff drink or two." Caroline's face registered her surprise, and he raised a hand in protest before she could interrupt.

"I can probably guess what you're thinking before you say a word. You're going to tell me that I should turn all my burdens over to the Lord and He'll solve everything. I know that's what my dad would say." He slammed his fist onto the table. "I would have said the same thing too. Up until August 25. But it's different when something like this really happens to you. Those words are now nothing more than meaningless platitudes. I've taken a man's life. Regardless of how sorry I am, I know I can't bring him back again. I feel like I've let the Lord down in a big way."

His chair scraped across the linoleum as he pushed back from the table. He half-expected Caroline to send him packing back to the Bay View Inn, and he braced himself for a religious lecture now that he'd confessed everything. He felt a sudden urge to pace. However, she motioned him back down in his seat before he could fully stand. Her voice quivered when she started to speak.

"I can't and won't judge you. I know in my heart you're a good man who has always longed to serve God."

A warm sense of relief flooded over him when she sent him a small smile, and he nursed a flicker of hope that he might still stand a chance with her. He relaxed in his chair as she continued.

"I'm not schooled enough in theology to know whether or not killing as an act of war is a sin. I suppose that's something you'll need to work out between you and the Lord. I do know the Bible is filled with accounts of men who found themselves in a predicament similar to yours."

Jack imagined that she could recite the chapter and verse of several examples if he were to ask. He leaned in to catch her soft-spoken words.

"While you were talking, the story of Moses when he murdered the Egyptian jumped into my mind. Prince Moses had led a pretty blessed and sheltered life until then. He probably saw himself as better than other men." She paused to clear her throat, but Jack could already see where she was leading him.

"Only after experiencing the rage that drove him to kill was he able to come to terms with his own sinfulness and recognize his need for God's help. Only then was he able to become the humble servant that God could really use."

Caroline chewed at her bottom lip as though debating whether she should say what was on her mind.

"Don't take this wrong," she said, then stopped. After what seemed to Jack like an eternity, she began again.

"I think you know already, I've loved you for a very long time. . . ."

She lingered just long enough for her words to soak in, and Jack wanted to echo the sentiment. His heart pounded in his chest with love for her, but she didn't give him a chance to respond.

"However, I have a feeling you've never felt a real need for God's grace until this happened to you. I suspect you've prided yourself a bit because you've lived a holier life than most other men. Maybe you've taken too much satisfaction in the fact that you don't drink or smoke or chew or go with girls who do. Only after you saw what dark deeds and evil thoughts you were truly capable of could you realize your own desperate need of a Savior. Maybe, like Moses, you've not really been ready to be used by God until now."

His ears began to ring as if he'd been shaken real hard. He knew Caroline well enough to know she had only his best interest at heart, but her words still hit a bit too close to home. Although he'd asked for her advice, he wasn't sure now what he'd expected to hear. If he'd thought she would make him feel better, he'd figured wrong.

Even as he wished he had stayed near the bar at the Pirate's Cove, she seemed to read his mind. "Jack, you won't find peace in a bottle or by seeking counsel from me or the wisest of men." Caroline drew a deep breath and shook her head. "I've preached enough. Whether you want to hear it or not, you already know what you need to do. You said so yourself earlier. The only way you can come to terms with all this is to take it to the feet of Jesus and leave your burdens there. Pour out your heart to Him. God can use even this tragic circumstance for your good, if you allow Him to." She stacked the dirty dishes in a pile and stood, looking down on him.

"Every day, men come to the mission struggling with the same heavy consciences that you've just described. Christ can lift this awful weight you're carrying and transform it into a way to really minister to folks like them." She turned away to carry the load of dishes to the sink as if intending to leave him alone with his thoughts, but a commotion in the foyer brought him to his feet.

"Yoo-hoo! Toots! You home?" The warbling voice of an elderly woman filtered down the hall. "Did you find your long-lost flyer boy? If so, enlist him to help me drag this Christmas tree inside."

Chapter 5

"For unto us a child is born, unto us a son is given:
and the government shall be upon his shoulder:
and his name shall be called Wonderful, Counsellor,
The mighty God, The everlasting Father,
The Prince of Peace."
ISAIAH 9:6

Caroline led the way to the foyer with Jack close at her heels. When Grams spotted them, she dropped her hold on the trunk of a small pine tree where she stood, halfway over the threshold. "I know we weren't planning on decorating this year, but they were selling trees at the patch of ground on the Commons across from the State House that they'd converted into a victory garden last spring. I saw this cute little thing and just couldn't resist. Especially since we have a special house guest." She used her plaid scarf to wipe the sap off her hand. The wool stuck to her fingers, but she peeled it off and jutted her arm toward Jack for a handshake. "You must be Cap'n Jack. Pleased to make your acquaintance and glad to know you're not dead."

Her grandmother's bluntness made Caroline cringe, but Jack chuckled as he took her offered hand. "And I presume you are Grams," he said. "You're every bit as beautiful and charming as Caroline described you in her letters to me."

For the remainder of the evening, Caroline faced stiff competition for Jack's attentions. He and Grams hit it off instantly.

The two of them tromped to the basement to drag up the Christmas decorations while Caroline cleared a space for the tree in the parlor. As they clambered down the stairs, she overheard Grams prying him for details about his falsely reported death. He laughed it off by saying that, after he'd crashed the Air Corps plane, he figured they'd be hoppin' mad, so he decided to lay low for awhile. His voice dwindled to unintelligible murmurs, but Caroline knew by her grandmother's shrill cackles that he'd somehow managed to satisfy her curiosity and had moved the subject to a more light-hearted vein.

She put away the Cornish hens and other groceries that Grams had purchased at Sculley Square for their Christmas dinner, while Jack helped the eldest member of the Harrington clan string cranberries and pop corn for garland.

He replaced the burned out bulbs on the strand of colored lights as Grams supervised, leaving Caroline to fish the broken ornaments out of the box on the other side of the room.

At last, after Jack had placed the angel topper on the tree, Grams switched off the ceiling light and they all stepped back to admire their work. Jack stood between the two women, hugging each of their shoulders.

"Well, as Tiny Tim would say, 'God bless us, everyone.' " Grams broke the tender moment by dusting her hands, then perching them on her hips. "That's it for me. I need my beauty rest and we've got church tomorrow, so I'm off to bed. You two are adults. Don't need me to chaperone. But I'll sleep with my door open, just for my own peace of mind. Stay up as long as you want, but breakfast will be served at eight o'clock, and I expect you to be ready to walk out the door by eight-thirty so we can make it over to the Park Street in time for early services."

Jack reached out to thin and arrange a glob of silver tinsel that Grams had tossed on a lower branch. "If you don't mind, I think I'll stay behind and sleep in tomorrow morning. You two ladies go on without me, just like you've planned."

Caroline stared at the crown of his short-cropped hair. Obviously, her words hadn't phased him. With his back still to them, she shared a perplexed look with Grams and noiselessly shrugged her shoulders.

"Wh–wh–why, of course we mind," Grams sputtered. "What would your preacher daddy think of me if he were to hear I allowed his son to sleep through Christmas Eve Sunday services? Seems to me that you, of all people, ought to be prayin' a prayer of thanks to God for bringing you back from the brink of death and seeing you home from the war in one piece. No. I won't abide you kicking up a kerfuffle about going to church. Even a carnal old dame like me, who seldom darkens the church door, knows we all should go to services at Christmas. You can sleep the whole rest of the day when we get back, but unless you're incapacitated in some way I can't see, I'll hear no more of it. You're going to church with us. You be down here, dressed, and ready to eat breakfast by eight, like I said. You hear me?"

"Yes, Ma'am." Jack cowered like a schoolboy from Grams's sharp rebuke, and Caroline had to cover her mouth with her hand to hide a spreading grin. She could have kissed her unlikely advocate. She'd never once heard Grams insist on anyone going to church.

"Good. I'll see you both in the morning, then." Grams bobbed her head in a quick nod, scooped up Icabod, and walked out of the room. She paused at the parlor door long enough to add a cheerful benediction, all traces of her scolding voice gone. "Oh, and Cap'n Jack, we're glad to have you in our home. Aren't we, Toots?"

"Yes, Grams," she replied, trying to ignore her warming cheeks. "Sleep tight." While her grandmother climbed the stairs, Caroline moved to follow her. "We'd better call it a night as well," she said over her shoulder to Jack. "Midnight is fast approaching, and we've both had a pretty exhausting day."

"Wait. Before you go up." He stopped her at the base of the stairs. "I have a gift for you." He fished the small, bedraggled package from the deep pockets of his baggy trousers and flicked at the bow. "It's nothing much. Just a little something I found in a village second-hand store the night before my final mission. I've carried it with me from then until now, hoping that today would come."

Stealing quick glances at him, Caroline slipped the ribbon from the box and ran her fingernail under the cellophane tape to undo the gift wrap. "I feel just awful accepting this, when I don't have anything to give you in return."

"Seeing as how, up until a few hours ago, you still thought I was dead, I'll let you off the hook this once," he said with a wink. "Go on. Look inside and I'll explain."

Buried under a layer of cotton, she found a ring that featured a most unusual crest.

"It's a signet ring. When you press the face into a dot of melted sealing wax, you'll find an imprint of your initials, CAH. I could hardly believe my fortune at finding a ring with your same initials. So, I saw my discovery as a special sign—a seal to the promise of our future relationship, and I figured you could use it on all the letters you're going to send to me until my discharge from the service." He took the ring and slipped it onto her left hand. "I know that we aren't ready for a permanent commitment yet, seeing as how we're just now meeting face-to-face. You see, my sweet Caroline, I—I've grown to love you through your letters. . . . I hope after all I've told you this evening, you still feel the same way too." He took her hands in his and stroked them softly with his thumbs. "And I'm hoping that. . .maybe. . .someday. . .we can exchange this ring. . .for a different kind."

"Quit your gabbing and kiss her, you silly goose." Gram's voice floated down from her bedroom.

Even as Jack pulled her ever so gently toward him and guided her arms around his waist, a war raged within Caroline. She longed to melt into his arms. Stare into his sky-blue eyes. Lose herself in his kiss. For months before getting word of his death, she'd dreamed of just such a moment as this.

Yet the man whom she had grown to love through letters had shared her zeal for the Lord. Without a doubt, she sensed God calling her to a life of ministry. She could not allow herself to foster a deepening relationship with Jack, if they no longer shared the same future vision to serve Christ.

He brushed her lips with his and her heart began to pound. She had to garner every bit of inner strength to pull away from him. Jack's crestfallen expression made the pain of her withdrawal even worse.

She risked crying and losing all her resolve if she looked up at him, so she studied the ring on her hand. "I'll cherish this, and I look forward to corresponding with you in the days and months ahead." She cringed at the sound of her own cold words compared to his heartfelt ones, but she managed a weak smile and backed onto the bottom step. "Let's go out on Tuesday when the stores reopen and buy some sealing wax, okay?"

She backed up another step, looking past Jack, not daring to look him in the eye. "Please excuse me, I really must get to bed—" She spun around and raced up the remaining stairs, feeling Jack's stare on her back as she fled.

The next morning, Jack, sandwiched between Caroline and Grams, held onto the pew in front of him with a white-knuckle grip as the congregation sang "Joy To the World." He hadn't seen much joy anywhere on earth of late. Just war and hatred, suffering and death.

When the minister announced his text, "The Prince of Peace," Jack tried hard to focus on anything but the sermon. He certainly hadn't experienced any peace in months. He felt totally alone, unable to pray, and after late last night, snubbed by Caroline. No matter where his thoughts took him, they led to deeper turmoil and inner strife. This fierce battle raging in his heart was exactly what he'd hoped to avoid by skipping church.

At the last "Amen," Jack fought the urge to rush out of the sanctuary ahead of Grams and Caroline. As the crowd of exiting worshipers bumped and jostled past, he stood on the sidewalk and gulped deep breaths of the crisp December air. According to the morning paper's weather report, Boston was experiencing an atypically warm Christmas Eve, but the wind still hit his face with an icy slap.

"You young'uns don't need a dowdy old woman like me tagging along when you still have so much catching up to do." Grams pushed Jack into taking Caroline by the arm. "I'm going to run along home and throw us something together for lunch. You two come the round-about way. Stroll through the Commons. Take your time. I won't be cooking anything fancy until tomorrow night." She swept the tail of her scarf over her shoulder and shuffled off down the street.

Jack shot a sideways glance at Caroline. He grappled for something to say to break the awkward silence that hung between them like a frosted windowpane. "You'll need to lead the way. I don't know where to go from here."

"Sure. Follow me." But she stood stock-still until Jack looked into her eyes. "Grams is right, you know. We have a good deal yet to talk about. I think I need to explain my behavior of last night." Caroline's brown eyes crinkled, and the corners of her lips curled in a shy smile. Jack didn't know whether it was from the chilly air or embarrassment, but her cheeks pinked. Whatever the reason, her beauty sent an electrifying charge through him.

"I know of a quiet place where we can go to talk. Do you mind?"

"I'm right behind you," he said, nodding his head.

Crossing Park Street, they cut across the brown lawn of the Commons and passed through a row of shrubs to a small clearing. Caroline stopped short, causing Jack to trip over his feet.

"Ah, too bad. Some poor drunk is sleeping off last night's binge on my favorite bench. We'll have to find another spot."

Jack started to follow her back through the shrubs when a spark of recognition passed over him. The man sprawled across the bench appeared to be missing an arm. "Wait, Caroline. I know this guy. Name's Bob Landry. Remember? I was sharing a drink with him yesterday when you came into the bar. He looks like he needs help."

Ten feet from the man, the air reeked of liquor. Two large whiskey bottles lay empty on the ground by his one extended arm. Bob's head hung limply over the bench's wrought-iron armrest, his mouth open wide as he snored. "He's passed out cold," Jack said, meaning the words literally.

He wore the same clothes he'd had on when he'd left the bar—but with no coat. Either he or some kind passerby had tucked newspapers around his body in an attempt to keep him from freezing to death during the night.

Caroline looked up at Jack. "The best thing I know

to do is to get him to the mission, where they're equipped to help guys like this. Do you think you can carry him to the street so we can hail a cab?"

Jack scooped the drunken veteran, like a baby, into his arms, nearly stumbling under the weight. Together, he and Caroline delivered Bob to the downtown mission where she volunteered.

A man wearing the dress blue uniform of a Salvation Army officer greeted them as they climbed out of the cab. "Let me get that door for you," he said, rushing on ahead. "Caroline, I'll show these gentlemen to the men's sleeping quarters, if you want to wait in the chapel or the dining hall."

"Thank you, Major Stanton. We won't bother with long introductions now because my friend's struggling with a rather heavy load, but I'd like you to meet Captain John Johnson. He's an old pen-pal of mine."

"I'd prefer it if you'd just call me Jack." With his hands preoccupied, the best Jack could manage was a nod of acknowledgment to add to his salutation.

"Pleased to make your acquaintance. I'm Samuel Stanton, the guy they blame when things go wrong around here. Whadya say we get this gentleman put to bed?"

Caroline called after them as the major ushered Jack through another set of doors. "I'll be in the kitchen preparing the communion elements for this evening's candlelight service. You can find me there."

Jack eased his soundly sleeping bar mate onto a cot and pulled a moth-eaten blanket up over him. When he straightened to stand beside Major Stanton, they exchanged the handshake they'd postponed at the door.

The major looked down at his new charge and folded his arms. "No matter how many times I see guys like this, I'm still moved by the waste of human life and the tragic results their alcohol dependence brings to them." He slowly shook his head. "When they get to this point of alcoholism, their chances of returning to a life of sobriety aren't very good."

Jack gaped as the man he'd shared drinks and war stories with the day before began to moan. Bob's body trembled beneath the blanket, and his pale, haggard face contorted in pain.

"You may not want to stick around," Major Stanton said as he pulled a bucket out from under the cot. "Looks like our friend here's about to be sick."

He tried to will himself to leave the room, but Jack couldn't pry his gaze from Bob or the nauseating scene.

They'd only met the day before, yet a bond of kinship had developed instantly between the two of them. Jack thought of the chain of tragedies in Bob's life that had reduced him from a corporal in the Army infantry and a decorated war hero to a pathetic drunk who had to be carried to the local mission. He couldn't help but compare his own emotional battle scars to those Bob had elaborated on yesterday at the bar. They'd shared the same horrible reaction when they'd had to kill the enemy. They both bore an unrelenting burden of guilt.

For now, he only belted a few drinks to help numb his mind. He felt certain that he could control his intake of liquor, so as not to become totally dependent on the stuff. However, Jack was equally sure that Bob had had the same good intentions in mind. At first. He also knew that, over time, Bob had given up trying to deal with the loss of his arm and the emotional trauma of his war injuries. Instead, the drinking became heavier, consuming more and more of his life. Until his greatest and only worry was where he would get his next drink. Reducing him to this.

Is this what he had to look forward to? Jack saw, in stark clarity, his life spinning out of control, if he continued on the downward spiraling path he now traveled. The only difference between his situation and that of Corporal Bob's might be simply a matter of time.

As much as he hated the thought of himself, a grown man and an officer, shedding tears, Jack couldn't suppress the rising sob pushing up his throat. He dropped to his knees beside the foot of the cot and buried his face in his hands.

"He's going to be all right, Jack," Major Stanton called from his post near Bob's head. "We'll take good care of him."

Jack shook his head and muttered through his hands. "No. It's not that." He couldn't find it within himself to expound.

A desperate prayer sprang from the depths of his inmost being.

Oh, God, please help me. Forgive me. Take me back. Rescue me from this heavy load. He rocked back and forth with each plea.

Please, Lord. I'm begging You. I'm so sorry for turning my back on You after all You've brought me through. I'll do whatever You ask of me if You'll see fit to have me. Wherever You send me, I'll go.

When Jack had surrendered to God all the excess baggage of his guilt and shame, he whispered an amen.

He lifted his head deciding, in faith, to believe that God had answered his plea. As he looked up, an overpowering, unexplainable peace flooded over him.

Major Stanton came alongside Jack and embraced him with a strong arm around his shoulder. "Our client appears to have fallen back to sleep for the moment. Is there a spiritual matter I might be able to pray with you about, Friend?"

Jack couldn't keep from laughing aloud as joy soaked his soul. "I appreciate your offer, but this was something that had to be dealt with one-on-one between me and the Lord. God's already heard and answered my prayer." He gave the major a good-natured slap on the back. "I would like to ask another favor of you, though, after you've done what you can to make my friend, the corporal, here, comfortable. When you have a spare minute or two, I'd like a chance to sit down and discuss a few personal matters pertaining to my future and that of Caroline."

He rose to his feet, breathing another prayer—this time on behalf of Bob. If God would give him the opportunity, he'd do all he could to help his buddy recover from his war wounds without the aid of alcohol or any other crutch.

Jack turned back to Major Stanton. "Would you mind if I excused myself? I need to find Caroline immediately. You see, someone we've both been mourning is actually alive and well."

Chapter 6

FREE CHRISTMAS DINNER
Are you hungry and all alone this Christmas?
Looking for a friend?
We at the Central Boston Mission invite you
to share Christmas Dinner with us. Lunch of
turkey and dressing and all the trimmings will
be served from 11:30—1:00, followed by a
carol-sing and a brief inspirational message
from Major Samuel Stanton.
Experience the joy of Christ's coming.
Celebrate the birth of the Savior with us!

T he next day, overcast skies held the promise of a white Christmas after all as Caroline took her place in the serving line next to Jack. She hummed a glad carol as she took the first plate from Sister Grace. Snow or not, the Christmas of 1944 would go on record in Caroline's diary as her Christmas of miracles.

She plopped a mound of mashed potatoes next to the turkey and dressing that had been piled high on a pale green melamine plate. Then she passed it to Jack. He winked and rubbed his hand against hers when he received the extended dish. He added a spoonful of green beans and sent the meal on down the serving line.

When she offered him the next plate, his gaze met hers, and it seemed as though they were alone in the crowded dining hall.

"I've made a decision about my future." Jack leaned over and whispered so that only she could hear. "Want me to tell you my plans?"

"That depends on whether or not your plans include me," she teased, but her heart skipped a beat at his words. In light of the miracles this Christmas had brought, she anticipated what he would say. Still, she couldn't wait to hear the confirmation from his own lips.

"They do if you don't mind being seen with an enlisted man."

Caroline tilted her head to look at him and drew her face into a confused frown. "What do you mean?"

"When my current tour of duty ends, I plan to reenlist in another branch of the army. I'll face a demotion, if I'm accepted into the ranks of the outfit where I'm hoping to serve, starting all over in boot camp."

She passed another plate to him, unable to mask the disappointment washing over her. She thought for certain that, after yesterday, he would seek to enter the ministry and pursue a life of service to those in need—like Bob Landry.

"What branch of the service wouldn't recognize your current rank? I've never heard of such a thing." She struggled to think of something to say that would stem her welling tears.

Jack set down his plate and took from her the one she held. He seemed oblivious to the line of waiting, hungry patrons and the other volunteers who strained their necks to see what the hold-up was in the serving line. Taking her by the shoulders, he turned her to face him.

"According to Major Stanton, the Salvation Army requires all new recruits to start at the bottom and work their way up. You'll probably have to show me the ropes around here."

Caroline watched Jack's face split into a wide smile as the meaning of his words sank in.

"I'd be happy to take you under my wing." The restrained tears spilled down her cheeks, but they were tears of sheer joy.

She threw her arms around his neck. Thunderous applause resounded from their forgotten audience as she stood on tiptoe and they shared a long, sweet, Christmas kiss.

SUSAN DOWNS
Susan knows firsthand the power of misdirected mail. If a certain WWII fighter pilot's marriage proposal hadn't been lost in transit, Susan's mother would have never met and married the handsome guy who turned out to be Susan's father.

Today, thanks to God's divine guidance and that postal faux pas, Susan resides in Canton, Ohio, with her minister husband, David, and two teenage daughters. She also has three grown sons and two delightful daughters-in-law. She works as an editor for a Christian book publisher and snatches every other spare minute to write stories of her own.

The Missing Peace

by Rebecca Germany

Dedication

For my friends and family who answered the call of
their country and went to war to defend freedom.
Thank you.

*"Return unto me, and I will return unto you,
saith the LORD of hosts."*
MALACHI 3:7

Prologue

April 1943

"Wouldn't you like to travel and see the world?" Joy asked her best friend as she twirled in the bright sunshine and relished the first real signs of spring.

"I'm sure the world has plenty of interesting things to see, but I'm content living here in the valley," Rusty stated with his trademark assuredness. "This is a wonderful place to raise a family. Why, while the world goes crazy, we have safe, close-knit communities here."

She sighed at the young man, who hadn't yet laid down the fishing poles he had been carrying. "But don't you ever want to break out of the norm and do something. . .unexpected?"

Rusty chuckled. "Like what?"

So confident, so predictable. If only a robin would just happen to plaster the top of that gorgeous copper hair of his. Joy turned and strode to the river's edge, kicking at twigs and clumps of weeds in her path. She sent a stone plopping into the river. The muddy brown water ambled by on its monotonous course. She'd love to see its destination in New Orleans—a new, adventuresome place.

Spinning back toward Rusty, she stiffened her shoulders—and her resolve. "I'm leaving the valley." Her words fell blunt and harsh, yet she couldn't take them back. "When I graduate from college next month, I'll join the army as a nurse."

"Why do you need to do that? I'm not going to fight someone else's war, and I can give us—"

"That's just it! You're thinking of yourself. You're not *listening* to me. I wish I could find just one person who cared about what I want. I'll suffocate if I stay here any longer than necessary."

Rusty stared at the blond spitfire he had known most of his life, not recognizing this sudden determination for independence in her. He'd met his match on the grammar school yard when she'd worn braids and gingham dresses. She'd taught him arithmetic, and he'd taught her to fish. They were inseparable pals, but this sophisticated young woman was saying all the wrong things, going against his vision of the perfect future.

"Mark my words, Rusty. You'd do yourself a real favor if you'd leave here, too, and explore the possibilities beyond these crowded hills." She gave her wavy hair a toss. "I've played the obedient baby of the family long enough."

"But I have to—"

"I know. You won't leave because you are tied to your duty. It's honorable but boring." She picked up the bag containing their untouched picnic, took some cookies for herself, and left the rest for him. Then she abruptly left.

"Where are you going? We haven't seen each other in weeks," he called, adding softly, "and the fish are biting good."

Joy's stylish hair swung against her shoulders, and her long legs strained to pull her up the short hill at the steady pace she had set.

Rusty felt himself release a deep sigh, as if he'd been holding his breath for a long while, and he loosened the painful grip he had on two bamboo fishing poles. When Joy disappeared over the rise, he turned his attention to the river, glistening in the late afternoon sun. It calmed him to know the river would always be there. It was the spine of valley life, strong, though changeable.

This was the life Rusty knew and loved—a life that beat with the steady pulse of the river. He'd never leave it.

Chapter 1

London, October 1944

The thick fog moved in to encircle an American couple's private moment. She relaxed into his long, muscular arms as he embraced her. The weak glow from the pale moon cast his face into the shadows but illumined the droplets of dew settling on the shoulders of his army uniform.

Across the street rose the dark skeletons of once-grand Regency-era townhouses. One week ago, a German buzz bomb, bypassing the Allies' ack-ack guns, had laid the whole block to ruins.

The war seemed a million miles from Lt. Joyce Aldergate's Ohio River Valley roots. She wasn't the same naïve girl who'd left home seventeen months ago. This Joyce radiated in the glow of womanhood. She could be on the arm of a different officer each night.

She let this one kiss her while she remained under the spell of the lavish treatment she'd enjoyed all evening among a group of army officers in Piccadilly Circus. The wild carousing would raise the hair on the neck of her reserved father, and Joyce was glad to have had an escort through the throngs of pressing bodies. Their merriment rang at a fevered pitch meant to drown out all thoughts of war and remind them only of the joys of living.

Now on the quiet street in front of her hotel, Joyce found she could not yet drop her guard. A small fortress deep inside her stubbornly stood watch over a line she would not cross.

The officer's hands began to get rather familiar as they caressed her body, but her mind was busy replaying the satisfaction of being whisked around the London party scene on the arm of a dashing and popular major. Where else would a small-town girl with no special connections get such lofty treatment?

His kisses became hot and sticky along her jaw line. She knew where too much of this conduct could take a girl.

She leaned back, breaking the embrace. "Hey, Soldier," she crooned in honey-sweet tones, "we both have a load of duties to perform tomorrow. We'll have to do this again—another time."

"But," he breathed between continued kisses, "your leave is over." His hands groped. "You'll be heading back to the Continent."

She thrilled to see embers of passion glowing in his shadowed eyes. Joyce had rarely felt so much power. She was at the top of her world. Could life get any better?

If only there wasn't still a war to be fought.

"I could still work on a transfer for you," he argued. "Word is that the campaign in France is off to a good start, but you never know what is ahead of you." His arms tightened around her waist. "There are army hospitals here in England."

"I'm familiar with my unit. I'd just as soon stick to the company I'm committed to."

"Commitment! Now there's a word from the homefront. Isn't it grand how we can leave those roots behind us?" He gestured out toward the world, eyes flashing, and whispered, "No one ever needs to know where we come from or what we used to be."

Joyce raised an eyebrow at his odd choice of words. Perhaps he was a lot like her, trying to remake himself through the army and taking advantage of the distance from home.

Another stolen kiss was answered by a playful swat to the officer's burly chest, and the night was called to a close with half-hearted promises to write.

So many of the soldiers had a one-track mind. It was probably best that her leave was coming to a close. She was beginning to get labeled a tease. The line of willing dates hadn't gotten any shorter, but she preferred leaving while her pickings were good and loneliness remained an impossibility. Loneliness could be expected under the weight of her duties, but she would have none of it while on holiday.

Now what was this fellow's name? She shrugged. She'd remember him as Major Fire-Eyes. His passion for life blazed in his eyes, and Joyce liked that about a man.

She entered the long brick building and climbed two steep flights of wooden stairs to the first small room on the right. She hung her army-issued raincoat and went about her nightly routine, careful not to disturb the occupants of the adjoining room. She was used to being the last to turn in.

"Prudish" Patsy and "By the Book" Beatrice bored Joyce and made her feel so stifled—too much like back home. She wanted to embrace all the fun life offered, while her roommates were careful to follow orders and focus only on their work. Even on leave, these two stuck to sightseeing and book reading. Both were older than Joyce. They had been working in civilian hospitals before the war, and their experience far exceeded what Joyce had seen just out of nursing school.

She took off her bright blue party dress, the one full outfit of civvies she had with her, then removed the pins from her attractively coiffured hair. She peeled off the long nylon stockings, grateful for the special gift sent from her older sister Dot, who was living back home. Though, Joyce had not appreciated the accompanying note about choosing her dates wisely.

Dot had made her share of embarrassing scenes before getting hitched into marriage and motherhood and joining their parents and older brothers in cautioning Joyce's every move. Her family generally made Joyce feel invisible, as if her desires and opinions didn't matter. The unwritten rule seemed to be if she was good, everything would go well. But a girl had to have some freedom in order to enjoy life, right? Besides, Joyce set her limits.

As she faced the small mirror under the hanging bulb, a thick layer of makeup came off on her washcloth. Joyce stared at the girl in the mirror with mixed emotions. She couldn't ignore the changes within herself. She needed to cut ties with parts of her past. It was time to write a letter home.

"Hey look, ya'll! Mail's comin'!"

Pvt. James Russell DeWitt chuckled as his buddy ran past to greet the newly arrived jeep with energy James couldn't possibly find. He pushed the field pack off his shoulder and sat down against a large tree. Head drooping, he looked out across the fading landscape of farmland.

His feet ached. The company had been on the march all day, even part of the night before. The army appeared to have a precise plan for getting this new batch of replacements from New York to France, but no one on the Continent seemed to expect them. James would have loved to have seen a truck or train meet them. Did the army expect to march them clear to Paris?

He couldn't imagine where the army planned to quarter them when night fell. The only thing around was a small farmhouse where the COs were congregating. If James were in command, he could tell those officers a thing or two about organization. Up until spring he had been the assistant manager at a brick-making company near Weirton, West Virginia, and in charge of more than one hundred employees. He'd done well for himself and succeeded in making a good living away from the coal mines, which had contributed to his father's early death.

Pvt. Calvin Cookson, who hailed from somewhere deep in Georgia's swamps, came scooting back with a fistful of mail. "Hey, DeWitt! Three letters for ya! All from ladies too. Shame that two already bear the Mrs. badge. Wanna tell me 'bout this one?"

James came to attention and grabbed his letters.

One from his sister Annabelle, one from Aunt Cleo, and one from his sister's teenage friend who thought it her civic duty to write to any and all servicemen. Her letters were full of mundane details about small-town life. James saved them for particularly boring times, like waiting in never-ending army lines.

Once again, he'd received no letter from his sweetheart. He was learning how to bury his disappointment. Something had splintered in their relationship when the war started. They had been practically inseparable since age ten, and he had been eager to make her his bride. But suddenly their lives had begun going in very different directions, and he hadn't been able to get her to tell him how she was feeling.

He fingered the envelopes, looking at the travel stains that accompanied each one. He immediately opened the letter from his sister. As expected, her flowery handwriting conveyed upbeat reports about her life as a young bride. James had to smile. Her words assured him she could do fine without his protective watch, at least for awhile.

But as her letter came to a close, James couldn't squelch a sense of disappointment. He scanned the words again. She was his closest relative, and James knew he was looking for an assurance that she would be praying for him. There was none.

James's mother had been a mighty prayer warrior for their family, as well as for the community. Since her death, James had acutely missed the sound of her murmured prayers each morning and evening behind the pocket doors to the rarely used parlor. He knew that she lifted Annabelle and him up to the Lord at every opportunity, and he rested in the peace that knowledge gave him to face whatever confronted him.

Who would be praying for him now when he most needed the Lord's protection? He certainly didn't have the strength to labor through such petitions for himself.

Departure day arrived bright and clear. Kaleidoscopic fall colors gave Joyce and others embarking for the Continent a bright farewell. As the ship left dock, Joyce found a quiet seat inside the lounge to eat the doughnut handed to her by a cheery Red Cross girl. The contemplative mood that descended upon Joyce seemed perfectly created for pulling out her stationery and pen.

But the words were slow to come. Where could she start? She hadn't written her childhood friend in weeks, probably months. When his ardent letters about home and future plans had followed her into basic training, she'd responded casually with details of her new adventures, confining her comments to the space on a postcard. When she'd set sail for the United Kingdom last summer, the letters from home had changed tone, becoming cautiously supportive without including the usual words of love and assumptions about marriage.

Could placing an ocean between them finally give Joyce the space and independence she had struggled so long to achieve? Could geography send the message she couldn't find the voice to convey?

Joyce didn't know what love was. She needed to learn more about herself and what she wanted before she could plot a course for a lifetime. She'd had big dreams of working in veterinary medicine, but she'd adjusted her schooling to follow her doctor-father's dreams for her to pursue a career in human health care. Her mother's dream for her was marriage and family, but Joyce wanted to accomplish a lot on her own before settling down and thinking about marriage. Is that why she ran so hard when a perfectly good friendship started to turn serious?

She looked at the blank stationery in her lap, but in her thoughts she saw a familiar boyish scrawl. While in London three letters had finally caught up to her.

My Joy,

Your folks may have already told you, but Mother passed away. Though I know she suffered long and felt ready to go, it hasn't been easy. I wish you were here to talk things through. I see all these posters around town encouraging gals to write servicemen, and I think of my unanswered letters to you. I do hope your silence means you are busy and that my words still bring a lift.

Sis is happily married to Joe Wright, now that he's returned from the war. She doesn't seem to mind their life running his family's five-and-dime, and she is good for him too. She doesn't baby him at all. Treats him like a man and doesn't make an issue of his missing foot.

I've decided it is time for me to do something for the war. The construction business is slow. Steel and hardware are where the real efforts are focused. I know I said Americans should keep their noses out of other countries' business, but this war is going on too long. I need to do my part. Maybe I'll change

*companies or maybe I'll enlist, since a hardship
exemption doesn't really apply to me these days.
You still hold my heart, and I hope you are safe.*
                                          Love,
                                          Rusty

In a letter from Dot, Joyce had learned, *By the way,
Rusty finally signed up for the army. Rumor has it they
need troops in the Pacific and Rusty will go there. Remember Pearl Harbor! So maybe I had it wrong. Maybe he got
into the navy. That red hair of his would be striking in
navy blue, don't you think? Anyway. . .*

From her mother, Joyce had heard, *All the able-bodied
boys from town are gone now. Some, like Joe Wright, have
returned sadly changed. Your old friend Rusty left a few
weeks ago. Did I tell you his mother finally passed on?
Probably not, your father prefers I keep these letters positive.
Think I'll mail this one before he gets home from the hospital
to read and add his part. His days are long and the hospital is
short staffed, but the patients keep coming. . . .*

Joyce adjusted the pen in her hand. How could she
tell a man who had just gone off to war that she could
make no future commitments, she was releasing his
heart to find love elsewhere, and she didn't plan to
move back home after the war?

The youngest of six children and the second
daughter born to Dr. Frank and Eva Aldergate, Joyce
had always tried to please her parents and follow their
plans for her. But it was true; she couldn't go back
home. The older Joyce got, the more her parents' old-
fashioned faith and ideals suffocated her. There had to
be something better awaiting her.

Dear Rusty,
I was sorry to hear about your mother, but do
send wedding congratulations to your sister and Joe.

It sounded half-hearted, but she could hardly jump right into an "I reject your love" dialogue. Joyce knew if she had been home when Rusty's mother died and his sister had gotten married she would have been at his side. He always supported her through every trial and triumph, and she could do no less for him.

Taking a deep breath to clear her thoughts, she poised her pen over the paper again.

"Hello there," came a booming voice from in front of her. "Writing me a poem, my dear?"

Joyce looked up to meet the smile of a tall lieutenant flanked by two of his friends. The officer's hat was set at a snappy angle. All she had to do was smile in return and they took the seats beside her.

"What a welcome bit of sunshine you are," another said.

As their flirtations got going, Joyce glanced around the lounge. A few other army nurses and WACS were engaged in similar circles of conversation. She was reminded of the need for morale boosters whenever possible, and she folded away her writing materials.

Oh Rusty, you and my family wouldn't recognize me now, sitting here openly flirting with soldiers I just met. Mother would be ashamed. Dot would say "I told you so" and impart more warnings. Yet I cannot deny the change in me that keeps pressing for more out of life. I can't go back.

Chapter 2

Late November 1944

S niper!"
James and his squad dove for the ditch and fence line along a road just inside Belgium's border with France. James's face was pressed against the frosty mud in the bottom of the ditch as he tried to wriggle his rifle out from under his body. Bullets skidded above him, and he moved slowly, careful not to expose an arm or shoulder to the line of fire.

When the pauses between shots lengthened, he sneaked a peek. A lonely church hovered on top of the sloping hill, which stood out from the surrounding forest. A German sniper perched in the bell tower.

To his right, James could make out his CO and another officer creeping along the fence line of bushes and trees, advancing toward the church.

Orders rang out.

Two men broke away from the squad, crawling across the road under a renewed barrage from the sniper. Soon a bazooka shell was launched by the Yanks, and the church tower burst into flames with one last gong from its bell.

James breathed a relieved sigh, though his heart was heavy. Not even a church was sacred in war.

The troops resumed their march. James steeled himself to walk past Americans who lay dead or wounded on the road. Medics scurried to their duty, James's stomach heaved, and he was grateful not to be in that line of work.

Just over the hill, they entered a devastated village. It was the first area of mass destruction they'd seen in weeks of roaming the Belgian countryside. Their approach was slow as they looked for concealed Germans behind every pile of rubble. James's whole body was tense.

Though long past noon, they pressed on, not stopping for lunch.

The Germans had pulled their big guns out of town, but a few soldiers roamed in and out of the area, creating brief periods of havoc. Under gunfire, in fear of landmines, and through billowing smoke, the Americans advanced. By nightfall they controlled the village and were rounding up their prisoners, their wounded, and their dead.

Tramping through a virtually impassable street that was littered with crumbled bricks and jagged pieces of timber, an exhausted James halted in front of a shelled-out house near what once must have been a lovely courtyard. A squad of soldiers lounged in the last rays of a weak sun. A green recruit stood in the center of the circle, holding two German soldiers under the aim of his rifle. The captain spat nasty jokes while the kid, who was barely big enough to manage a rifle, shook with fright.

"Shoot 'em, Chicken!" the captain screamed in the kid's ear, and the other soldiers joined in jovial encouragement.

James was horrified.

The kid quivered like a leaf in a thunderstorm.

The captain screamed at him again, and suddenly the recruit's rifle discharged. There was general surprise when one German fell to the ground, clutching his leg. James backed away as the squad burst into laughter. He watched from a distance as the Germans were dragged away for transport to holding tanks for POWs.

When he finally stretched out on a bench in a dilapidated storefront, his head hammered and he covered his eyes with his arm. He was so tired and hungry, but the constant replay of sights and sounds tormented his mind and sent waves of nausea through him.

"Pray we don't have another day like this one soon," Cal said with a wry grin as he dropped to the wooden floor beside him. "Can I serve ya a cup of lukewarm instant coffee straight from my K rations?"

James snapped to attention. "You mean all you can talk about are petty prayers and blackstrap?" He wanted to scream at his buddy, but instead he dropped back against the hard wood, heart pounding. "What do God and good manners have to do with anything here? This is hell we're in!" he muttered bitterly.

Cal was unusually silent.

James took long, deep breaths to clear his mind.

"It may look like hell, sound like hell, smell like hell. . .but God is still in control," came Cal's quiet words. "He wants to lead ya through, walk alongside ya with His hand on yer shoulder. . .if ya'll let him."

"What kind of God puts idiots into leadership positions?" James asked in defeat.

"I know what ya saw. That CO had a mind to toughen the rookie and put fear in the ranks of the POWs. I doubt he intended murder. Those were the only prisoners rounded up."

"And is that God's idea of getting us through this?"

"Naw, I'm not saying that," Cal drawled. "I jes mean, we're all tryin' our own way to survive this thing. I prefer to pray through it."

"What are you. . .some kind of chaplain?"

Cal's laughter echoed in the sparse room. "Hardly! I'm jes the son of a farmer, planning to farm too someday. The Lord has been my best friend for a long time. I trust Him to guide me through this job I have to do. I'm prayin' He'll 'elp me ferget most of what I see and then learn from the rest. See what jes six Germans were able to do to us today? There's a lesson."

"So how do you stay so positive? I can't be like that," James said.

"Oh, it's a constant battle that takes constant prayer."

"And God hears you?"

"I feel He does. I have peace that He hears and guides me."

"I'll have to think on that." And James did as he tried to drift into sleep.

It had been a beautiful, sunny day in the countryside, even if chilly. Everything remained quiet, and the medical unit kicked back and rested again. Expected to handle hundreds of patients streaming through the evacuation hospital, personnel struggled with boredom when patients were few and extra hands went idle.

Joyce enjoyed the luxury of washing her hair for the first time in more than a week. She sat in the sun on a folding chair with her right foot propped on a box and brushed her light brown hair with its blond highlights, brought out by the sun. Her big toe still throbbed from a mishap two weeks earlier when they were setting up camp at this location along Belgium's border.

Two old milk cows had wandered across the open field, right into the middle of attempts to raise a large ward tent. Grown men made fools of themselves as they tried to corral the beasts. Even the mail clerk who knew a bit of French was called in to "talk" the cows into submission.

Joyce enjoyed being on the sidelines of such a show until the lieutenant colonel arrived and fumed at the disorderly spectacle. Her heart went out to the poor cows, moving in nervous circles and looking for an escape route. She found a rope from a pile of tenting supplies and quietly walked up to the first old Jersey. Joyce easily slipped the rope over the animal's head.

The second cow was much flightier. When Joyce approached her, the Jersey kicked back her heels and aimed for a row of reclining GIs. The men jumped and scattered, sending the cow back in Joyce's direction.

As soon as she was close enough, Joyce flung the rope around the cow's neck. Resisting the tug of the rope, the cow stepped back onto Joyce's right foot. Both cows were towed off and secured behind the mess tent where the cooks reportedly enjoyed a cup or two of fresh milk daily, even though army medical headquarters frowned upon using unregulated food sources.

Now Joyce admired her purple toe. No nail paint she had could achieve such a shade.

"Hey, Girlie, that's quite a shiner," Misty Jones remarked as she returned from the shower house with her hair hanging in wet raven ringlets, shirt untucked over her baggy combat pants, and a wool coat draped over her shoulders.

Joyce giggled with her.

"I see you've got your stationery out. I hardly ever see you write. Who's this to?"

Joyce sighed. "It's time I wrote back to that friend from home I told you about."

"Oh, the old shoe that could use a good toss? Toss away, Honey! He's probably out on skirt patrol even as we speak," Misty predicted.

"Hardly!" Joyce laughed. "I've never known Rusty to hound the ladies. And for all I know, he's in the South Pacific by now."

"Oh, all the better for the exotic beauties in grass skirts," Misty hooted.

Joyce felt her temper take a sudden lift. Surprised, she didn't comment further.

"What you need is a little night maneuvers like I've got scheduled with the new staff sarge in supplies." Misty related the sergeant's best qualities, then headed inside the tent barrack the two women shared with four other nurses.

Joyce couldn't imagine Rusty being anything but faithful to their friendship—their understanding. It irked her that she couldn't clearly define this stage of their relationship, yet it fueled her resolve that some action needed to take place.

How do you tell a guy that you can't stand to lose his friendship and closeness, but you can't go on being treated like his sister and chum when everything within you needs more? Needs to know she's valued. Needs more than he or their small town is offering.

The shadow of a cloud fell across her lap. It wasn't that she didn't care for Rusty or couldn't see them married someday. It was just she'd finally realized how much she wanted to be treated like a woman, and she couldn't ignore that discovery just because Rusty was compatible.

A girl needs to have her guy stand up and protect her, treat her like the gem she is, and guard her for himself. Does Rusty realize I could walk away from this relationship anytime? Would he miss me if I'm gone—I mean, miss me and not just old times? Wouldn't it be better to let him go now than live in the disappointment of a passionless marriage? And, oh dear, if I were to go home to him, well, he'd have to learn a lot about what I've done in the process of testing my new independence.

A new intensity took over her letter writing. Words poured forth, words more blunt than anything she had ever said to Rusty before. Her mother had always preached the importance of tact, but Joyce didn't think Rusty would understand unless she was brutally frank. She reread her words, amazed at how much more she could tell Rusty now that she felt ready to release him.

She folded the letter into an envelope, sealed it, and wrote Rusty's name on the outside. This she placed inside another envelope addressed to Rusty at his home in the States. If his family had to open it and forward the letter to his military post, then her words would remain private. Now, if the censors didn't tamper with it. . . .

Shortly before dawn, James rolled out to assume guard duty after being tagged by his CO. Outside a drizzling rain fell and the cold damp air cut through him. He picked his way toward the main street, only recognizable because it was slightly wider than the other streets. He kicked at the rubble littering the sidewalk and watched the moon occasionally peek through the clouds.

The conversation he'd had with Cal was still clear in his mind. He didn't have the time or place to go and telephone the Almighty. And why would God even care to listen to him? His mother had always taken care of the spiritual matters of their home. Funny how he'd never seen the need to be responsible for those things on his own. He'd kept his nose clean and obeyed the rules. Still he felt empty inside and detached from the faith he'd claimed on his enlistment papers.

On the ground near crumbling steps, something glimmered in a brief splash of fading moonlight, capturing James's attention. He leaned down. Pearl buttons! Two uniform pearl buttons stared up at him from the torn and stained face of a homemade doll.

James picked it up, examining every detail. What kind of little girl would have owned it?

An image of another girl and the sound of her bright voice entered his thoughts, so out of place in his surroundings. "Can you imagine? Daddy bought me a doll for my birthday. A doll! I'm too old for dolls. I'm fifteen now, you know." The little spitfire had tossed her dark blond hair and leveled her deep blue gaze upon him. "I can go to banquets now with escorts. I *don't* need dolls to play with when I can go on dates," she emphasized.

He had smiled at her display.

"Well, *Mr. DeWitt,* what do you have to say for your poor manners?" she'd suddenly asked.

"What?" he'd croaked.

"I can't believe you haven't asked me to the spring banquet!"

"Why did I hafta ask? You always knew we'd go together."

"Men!"

Even in her fury, James's best friend had been the stabilizing force in his young life. She'd been there through his father's death. Even though she was a year behind him in school, she'd helped him study his senior year and raise his showing a full grade point.

Those were the days when she'd prepare a basket of fried chicken and a bag of cookies, he'd bring the fishing poles and bait, and they'd while away a Saturday afternoon along the muddy banks of the Ohio River and discuss solutions to all the world's problems. His memory of her was so vivid, yet she was so far away and growing farther out of reach with each passed opportunity to write.

James tucked the little rag doll into the large pocket of his winter coat, trying to set aside painfully sweet memories along with it. Even at this point, a "Dear John" letter would be less distressing than his sweetheart's silence.

Chapter 3

December 17th

Joyce dragged her tired feet back to duty from a brief break at the mess tent. An unusual flood of wounded had started pouring in around mid-afternoon, and by evening two ward tents had already filled up. As she passed a shadowed area between ward tents, she heard a plaintive cry from out of the dark.

"*S'il vous plaît, Madame.*"

Startled by the plea, Joyce reached for the small flashlight attached to her belt. The first sweeping beam caught the reflection of large, glowing green eyes. She turned the light slowly back to the spot.

A shapeless form under a dark cape or blanket shivered in the cold against a backdrop of white snow and army-green tent canvas. Above the gleaming eyes of a cat, Joyce identified the face of a child.

"*Moi chat! S'il vous plaît!*" The child extended the cat to Joyce, and it let out a strange sound, something between a moan and a meow.

Joyce didn't know what else to do but take the cat.

Her hand around the animal's middle only brought renewed cries from the feline, and Joyce had a hard time juggling both the cat and flashlight.

"*Hâte! Hâte!*" The child pleaded for Joyce to act quickly.

"Where did you come from?" Joyce asked. It was a black winter night and the temporary hospital stood on the edge of a dense forest. Joyce wasn't aware of any nearby homes.

"*Docteur! S'il vous plaît!*" the child responded with agitation.

Joyce motioned with her flashlight for the child to follow her, then entered the end of a long ward tent where a string of bulbs lining the center provided dim lighting. She went directly to a worktable and eased the cat onto its surface, but she jumped back when the animal screeched and swatted with its extended claws.

The child rushed forward. The woolen cape fell back and Joyce recognized the small person as a girl, not more than ten years old. Her light brown hair was caught up in two messy braids, and her cheeks were chapped bright red from the cold.

"Shh, shh," the girl said, soothing the cat.

Joyce took a deep breath. "Let me see what the problem is."

The cat's energy was sapped, so the animal allowed Joyce's gentle exploration. Its belly was lacerated and the wound had obviously festered for awhile. She reached into a box of supplies for a wound cleanser and swab. To really treat the poor cat, Joyce would need stitching supplies and bandages from the surgical tent.

But how could she explain to the anxious child what

was happening? How could she work on the cat without extra hands to stabilize it? And who would lend a hand while they were busy handling their biggest onset of patients—brave, self-sacrificing soldiers who deserved all the care available?

Joyce was torn between her duty and the tear-filled gaze of the young girl. "Wait," she said with a gentle pressure on the child's shoulder and a gesture toward the table.

She moved away slowly, searching the tent for a friendly face. Her quest took her outside where the sound of arriving ambulances rumbled in the still night. Fresh snow salted the assorted tents, while cold nipped at her cheeks. She pressed on and entered the surgical tent, weaving around stretcher barriers, doctors, nurses, tables, and curtain dividers until she located the things she needed.

"Over here, Lieutenant Aldergate. Help the major hold this one down," a top ranking surgeon ordered. "We have to get him prepped for surgery before this wound drains him dry."

Joyce felt her chest tighten at the gruesome sight. Laying aside her bundle, she leaned across the young soldier's fidgeting legs and held firm to the mud-caked pants as the doctor administered morphine.

She kept her gaze riveted on the patient's boots. Boots could belong to anyone—young or old, brave or cowardly. When Joyce looked into a face, she saw a soul, an individual person, and it placed her emotions at risk. To keep going, she had schooled herself to focus on anything other than the faces of the hundreds of scared and hurting men who passed through the hospital.

When the GI relaxed, the head nurse directed Joyce to another situation that needed her assistance. A full twenty minutes passed before she was able to retrieve her supplies and make her way back to her feline patient.

There she found the little girl sitting on the bare ground against the canvas wall, rocking the mewing cat.

The morning of December 18 started like most others for James and Cal. They swapped their cigarette rations for chewing gum, candy, and French coins. James coughed from a touch of a cold, but otherwise he felt rather good as he tucked his booty into his pack. Suddenly a loud whistle followed by a shattering impact sent him rolling back into the slit trench where he'd spent the night.

The thick fog made it hard to tell from which direction the artillery fire originated. The men waited, not making a sound. Rifle fire sounded in the distance.

Cal wiggled into the trench beside James. "Guess someone woke up in a right foul mood," Cal whispered.

James looked at his friend. The guy's view of war never ceased to amaze him. "Yep. We're in the land of fairy tales. Maybe that was just the giant getting back at good ol' Jack for growing that beanstalk," he responded sarcastically.

"Now yer gettin' it, Buddy!" Cal's face fairly glowed.

They heard a call to attention and joined the other men leaving their trenches and foxholes to assemble for march. "The boys over that next ridge need our backup," the CO yelled. "Forward and alert!"

James clutched his rifle, ready for anything, and stamped his icy feet.

A heavy mist cloaked the area. As they wove around what must have been a hundred oak and pine trees, the men dodged repeatedly to avoid slashing branches that seemed to appear from nowhere. Approaching the ridge, the squad fanned out.

Rifle and artillery fire sounded much louder. A metallic ping pierced the dense air, and James instinctively dropped to his belly. A shell exploded nearby, sending dirt and bark flying. Another soon followed, and James felt pinned against the snow-covered hillside.

Joyce made another round past her tent home as morning tried to shed light through the mist that covered the encampment. She staggered and pressed on against intense weariness.

The wounded hadn't stopped arriving all night. Pressing duty had kept Joyce from doing any more than bandaging the distressed cat. After some efforts and miscommunication, she had finally convinced the child to lie down with the cat on Joyce's own bunk in the nurses' quarters.

Pulling the door open, Joyce saw the child sitting on the floor of the dark tent. The cat lay still in the center of the cot.

The girl looked up with tears in her eyes and wailed, "*Pourquoi?*"

Joyce knew immediately that the child's pet was dead, and she went to the little girl, wrapping her arms around the quivering shoulders. She had no answer to the girl's question of why. A jolt of intense grief hit her soul as they rocked and mourned together.

Why, God? Isn't there enough pain here? Why do this to

a child? Can't You do something to stop this?

If God couldn't take care of a soldier on the battle-field or keep a child's pet alive, why would He care about someone insignificant like her? And why should she care about Him?

Misty found her there, clutching the child tightly. "What happened, Joyce? Who's she?"

Joyce didn't know where to start. She wiped at her eyes, surprised at the flood of tears that had soaked her cheeks. "A child shouldn't have to see death!" was all she could say.

Misty's face clouded with confusion, and she leaned closer, waiting patiently for the story to unfold. Joyce finally managed to recount the events of the preceding night while the child rested quietly in her arms.

"Where did she come from?" Misty asked.

"I—I don't know." Joyce had forgotten that the child had no business being in the middle of an army hospital camp.

"Over here, James!" Cal's pain-filled voice penetrated the calm during a lull in fighting.

James's feet were numb with cold, but limping, he followed the sound of his friend's voice down the hill near the impact point of an exploded shell.

"Hold on there, Pal," James called. "I'll get a medic."

"No rush. I'm not going anywhere," Cal answered on an eternally positive note.

James dropped to the place where Cal lay, balled up in agony. His thigh was soaked with blood. "Lean back and let me apply pressure," James ordered. "You're gonna make it."

"Sure, I will. God's not done with me. . .or you."

Renewed fire could be heard from the ridge.

"Pray with me, James."

"I. . .here?"

"Don't ya feel like David? He prayed on the battlefield."

"Oh Cal, you're a better Christian than I'll ever be." James envied his friend's faith. Cal made it sound so easy.

"What an odd thing to say! It's not a matter of one Christian being better than another," Cal retorted as a medic rushed over and James moved out of his way. "It's jes askin' the Lord to come into your life and followin' Him as yer guide." He grimaced with pain. "Take my New Testament."

As James watched the medic strap Cal to a litter, Cal added, "Jes talk to Him like you've talked to me."

Two litter bearers jogged Cal away to a collecting station, and James shoved Cal's little leather book deep into his coat pocket. He had to force himself to turn back toward the ridge, knowing that his unit needed every able-bodied man. He fought for hours until a sudden pain stabbed his upper arm.

Plastering himself to the ground, forehead stinging against the dirty snow, he called out, "God, can you hear me through all this chaos? Can a person so unworthy as I talk to You straight?"

The only sounds were the screams of guns and men battling each other.

"God, You know me better than anyone, and if You can see fit to clean me up of all the selfish and foolish things I've done. . . Well, Lord, I just want to follow

You and view things through Your eyes. Do with this man as You will." Peace flooded his soul.

A medic rolled James over and seemed surprised when James blinked against the falling snow and smiled.

Joyce's heart felt as if it were ripped and bleeding as she led her new little friend through the staff housing section of camp. She tried to gain control of her emotions. Her behavior during the last twenty hours had not been professional. It had been decidedly feminine and, if noticed, would lose her respect among her male peers, who already had qualms about women in the ranks. She tried to disguise an attempt to flick away unbidden tears by brushing a hand through her hair.

In less than a day, Joyce had come to feel as if she knew the French-speaking child and her homeless plight. Although they couldn't speak each other's language, they had bonded. The child's loss of a dear pet had hit both woman and girl deeply, and they'd shared in mourning for several hours.

But Josie DuPree's father had come looking for her. The walk to the hospital headquarters, located in a small country house, seemed so short, and Monsieur DuPree was easy to pick out, sporting a long mustache, standing short and wiry in his dirty brown corduroy and tweed next to tall American officers in full uniform.

Josie rushed into her father's welcoming arms, and he peppered her with kisses and rapid questions in French. Joyce felt it would be best to slip away without a fussy good-bye, so she backed toward the door.

"Wait, Miss. . .ur. . .Lieutenant Aldergate," the camp clerk called out. "You'll probably want to know what I learned about this kid."

Joyce stopped and turned back.

The young clerk occasionally served as an interpreter, poor at best, and had managed to get some information from the father. It would probably remain a mystery how the child had found the army hospital camp on her own. Her family's temporary residence was in an area coal mine where they had been living since their home was destroyed.

"Well. . . ," Joyce managed to say, "at least she has a family, Corporal."

The young officer seemed chagrined, but he continued with the story about the family's pet. The cat was one of the few things remaining to remind the child of her life before the war. The feline had claimed a high ledge in the mine on which to birth her litter of four kittens, and it was from there that the cat had fallen down onto some metal equipment, mangling her side.

Monsieur DuPree had described how one kitten had died during the first cold snap and a second, the runt, died when the injured cat stopped producing as much milk.

Joyce glanced over and saw the father put his hands into large coat pockets and draw out two skinny kittens. One was gray, much like the mother had been, while the other was a striped brown calico.

Josie cuddled them both in her arms, then she brought them over for Joyce to view.

While Joyce petted the wiggling animals, Colonel Herndon, who had remained unobserved at his desk, stood and said abruptly, "Corporal, ask the man if he is Jewish."

"Non, non!" the Frenchman refuted.

"Corporal, ask him if the cave harbors any Jewish refugees," the colonel continued, his face unreadable.

"Ahh, non, non." The Frenchman chuckled nervously and waved his daughter to come to his side.

The colonel nodded. "Corporal, see that they are given one of those infernal cows from behind the mess hall. That will be all." He resumed his place at the desk. "Clear this office immediately!" he added with a bark.

Joyce helped the clerk usher the DuPrees out into the hazy daylight. Josie tugged at her sleeve. *"Madame,"* she said as she shoved the calico into Joyce's hands. *"Amour moi chaton."*

Joyce felt honored to be asked to adopt the kitten and reached out an arm to hug the girl. Tears threatened her composure, burning the rims of her eyes. As the clerk led the father and child away, Joyce hurried to her tent, cradling her new companion.

She had had many pets at home, and she'd always found ways to tend to other animals in the neighborhood. The feel of something soft and alive in her arms pierced her heart with memories of home.

At least she knew her home and family still existed. Josie had obviously been homeless for many months, maybe over a year. Joyce could only assume from the colonel's questions that he believed the DuPrees to be using the mines to hide Jews and other targets of Hitler's hatred. She knew Monsieur DuPree must be terrified after the colonel's questioning, but soon he would be thanking God for the gift of the cow and freedom to leave the army camp.

Thanking God for what? Joyce rubbed her forehead and wondered at her rambling thoughts. God could have stopped a monster like Hitler from ever being born—but He hadn't. Now thousands were homeless and living in fear. What kind of life was that for a child?

Joyce wept a second time that day as she sank to her cot, petting the warm wiggling ball of fur.

Chapter 4

I'll call him or her—I don't know what it is yet—
Rookie, seeing as how the kitten is our newest
recruit," Joyce told Misty as they teamed up to
clean battlefield mud from an unconscious GI.

Joyce's movements were slower and gentler than
usual. Instead of rushing through her work and thinking ahead to the next chore, she took time to study the
young man's face. He was so pale.

An artillery shell hit nearby and shook the lightbulbs
dangling overhead. Joyce ignored the rumbles of war
that had been heating up all afternoon. She sneaked
another peek at his face. This young soldier was someone's brother, someone's son. Maybe he was married and
had fathered a child. For once Joyce didn't chase her
emotions away. Instead she thought how important it
was to have family who cared. How pleasant it would be
to relax in her father's big hug or listen to her mother
hum while working over the ringer washer.

When Joyce had thought her parents weren't listening to her, perhaps they had been, and what had
seemed to Joyce like guilt-driven manipulations might
have been their way of trying to steer her away from

the painful things in life. Joyce knew she would never find peace until she was allowed to try things on her own—take those risks. But could her search have simply brought her full circle? Why did she long so for home when only days before she had still abhorred the thought of all things so familiar and predictable?

Another close hit made Joyce dive across her patient in fear that the lights, poles, and tent canvas would collapse on them. Misty was called away to help with another round of incoming wounded. Joyce finished their job, then tucked the bedding up to the chin of the young soldier.

"God bless," she whispered, surprising herself.

As she stood to carry her chipped granite bowl of supplies to the work area, the flaps to the ward tent opened and litter bearers entered, one right after the other.

"What are you doing?" she called to a private she recognized from ambulance duty. "Those patients haven't been reviewed by the doctors yet."

"Too many. They're coming in droves, and we gotta put them somewhere out of the cold," the private stated.

Another stretcher-carrying private called, "Hey, Nursey, this one got pipped in the nose and is bleedin' all over. Got any stuffin'?" He then launched into a series of rude comments, so like those that usually failed to ruffle her, but this time they clawed at Joyce as she moved through the ward, making room for the surge of new patients.

The shelling continued as light faded from one day, then rekindled with another dawn. Clouds and snow placed a thick veil over the new day. Joyce hadn't found a moment to check on Rookie all night. She'd missed dinner, and she'd caught maybe a fifteen-minute nap the one time she was able to sit down for a spell. Now she pulled herself to the mess tent for a breakfast of lumpy oatmeal and blackened bacon. She leaned her weary head in her left hand while ladling food to her mouth with her right. Her wool coat did little to deflect the cold in the drafty tent.

When a young, good-looking officer bounded into the mess tent and headed toward her table, Joyce wasn't feeling particularly attractive. For once, the desire to flirt had left her. She offered only a weak smile and continued to focus on the chore of eating. The corporal, looking fresh off the boats, plopped his tray down across from her without invitation. He started with the usual "where are you from" questions, and getting little response, he soon seemed quite content to talk on and on about himself.

Joyce watched the enthusiastic expressions on his face. Like her, he automatically stabilized his tray and cup on the table when a bomb exploding nearby shook the ground under them. But he didn't miss a beat in his one-sided conversation.

Joyce thought of all the dinner tables she had shared with handsome soldiers since she'd been in the army. There were many, but those dates had been easy to forget. The men were usually tall, attractive, and well respected, but they lacked something. She could hardly think of one who'd seemed genuine. She'd date one and quickly move on to another. The thrill was in the attention she got, and she ignored the burning desire for something more. After all, she wasn't in a position to want anything lasting.

She reminded herself of that fact again as she nodded politely and tried to appear as if she were listening to another self-centered rendition of heroism. Maybe she should give up dating until she figured out who she was and where life was taking her.

After delivering a shallow bowl of canned milk to Rookie in the nurses' tent, Joyce finally shook off the corporal outside the operating tent. The officer didn't seem to appreciate the sounds of pain-wracked comrades being prepped for surgery.

She checked the mail, hoping for Christmas packages from home, but nothing was getting through, so Joyce returned to duty. Thanksgiving had flitted by, and she barely had time to think about the fast-approaching Christmas—her second away from family. It would be nice to make the holiday feel special, but there wasn't much available for decorations. Gifts might be easier to put together. Her patients often gave her little trinkets, bars of soap, candy, pictures, and jewelry and watches that presumably came from fallen Germans. Just that afternoon, when she finally found a baby-faced private an extra pillow to elevate his throbbing, frostbitten feet, he'd given her a tiny flower shaped from gum wrappings.

Chaotic shouts erupted outside, and her ears recognized a high-pitched metallic whine that reminded her of the V bombs she had heard when she'd first arrived in England so many months ago. Her instinct was to crouch. Even the seasoned soldiers shouted when their beds rocked upon impact.

Every mobile man and women sprang into action. Joyce stumbled outside the large tent to survey the damage. A supply tent was flattened. Anxiety tore through the camp. A passing orderly shouted that the colonel was pulling up stakes and moving the hospital out of the way of the dueling armies.

Joyce went back to work, corralling her nervous patients. A section of the ward had yet to be seen by a doctor. She would need to see that those men were stabilized for transport.

She gave only passing thought to her personal belongings. Most things were kept in her footlocker in anticipation of just such an unexpected move. But where was Rookie, and who would see to him?

Misty rushed past, her hair in terrible disarray and dark shadows of fatigue underlining her eyes. "Help me, Joyce. Ward Three is full of fresh wounded who need to be stabilized."

"But there are a bunch of them here too."

"Ruby is covering it. Come on. . .and grab a few syrettes of morphine on your way."

Joyce rushed to find the necessary supplies and hurried to the ward. Her paper flower slipped from behind her ear, and she stopped in the miry road to catch it before it landed.

An ambulance driver slammed the rear doors of his empty vehicle open and yanked out a stretcher as another bomb rattled Joyce to the very core. "Where's the Air Corps backup when they're needed?" he bellowed, adding a string of curses and strong opinions about procedure as he prepared to fill his vehicle with wounded.

Joyce looked up at the thick, low-hanging clouds and clutched her coat against the sting of bitter cold. More than the cold was biting today, and Joyce was sure the Germans would love to see the mass disarray in the Allied ranks. Setting her shoulders, she moved on to her next task.

The smell of blood and infection greeted her inside Ward Three, but she pressed on. Averting her gaze from faces and trying not to let her heart get attached to any particular case, she moved down one row, then another, of tightly packed soldiers.

James bounced in the back of an army jeep. His bruised body ached all over as the driver zigzagged through smoky and scarred terrain. An officer drooping over the seat beside him appeared to be in worsening condition, but James didn't have the strength to help him.

Letting his head fall back against the seat, he saw a lone plane chugging through the low-hanging clouds. Was it friend or foe? Weather conditions were too adverse to expect much help from the air powers.

Father! James still hesitated to call out to God on such familiar terms, but his soul compelled him on. *You hold all things in Your hands, and You know just where and when to intervene in man's blunders. Guide these soldiers in their fight for peace, Lord. Help also this one who is looking after me. And Lord, if you plan to see me through this, please use me for Your honor, even as You used a simple Joe like Cal.*

James rested his free hand on his bulging coat pocket where his treasures still rode with him. His head pounded with every bump of the rough-riding vehicle. He stole a peek to see how the other guy was holding up.

Though he seemed unconscious, the officer coughed. *Was that blood?*

"Hey, Med!" James managed to choke out from his dry throat.

The driver suddenly swerved the jeep. The vehicle leaned far to the left, threatening to tip, then righted. But just a few yards ahead the driver shouted, whipped the wheel for a U-turn, and dumped the jeep on its right side. James's helmet met the muddy road and all went black.

"Attention!"

The colonel entered Ward Three, and Joyce and Misty flew to the center of the tent to stand at attention.

His gaze swung slowly over the full ward, then he came to stand directly in front of the two women. "At ease, ladies. We have a situation," Colonel Herndon stated. "The Germans have launched a major offensive and have broken through our lines. Night is falling and this. . .ur. . .foul weather is not letting up. We can get one more haul of guys out of here tonight, but. . ." He paused and lowered his voice. "Nurses are to go in the last truck. Be sure these men's immediate needs are met before you leave."

"Leave, Sir?" Misty asked. "You mean leave them behind, Sir?"

A bubble of panic caught in Joyce's throat. Leave wounded behind? The press of war was heavy. It could be heard, smelled, even tasted. They couldn't leave defenseless men in the path of two wrestling armies. A lone tent could be flattened by a charging tank or shattered by artillery fire. The camp had taken another stray hit just an hour ago.

"Sir," Joyce said, her voice sounding weak, "who will stay to help the men?"

The colonel's gaze circled the room, seeming to count feet along the ends of two long rows of cots. When he glanced back at the nurses, Joyce thought she caught shadows of sadness and possibly fear in his gray eyes.

"I'll leave an orderly and another man who we might spare."

"Sir," Misty squeaked, "I—"

"Sir, let me stay with them," Joyce volunteered with bravery she did not feel.

"Yes, Sir. Me too, Sir," Misty added.

Colonel Herndon stared at the young women for a long minute. "Corporal!" he shouted in a voice that reverberated through the tent.

Joyce looked around at their patients under the dim lighting. All who had strength focused their attention on the trio near the tent's center post.

The young clerk came skidding through the tent flaps to stand alert at the colonel's side. "Yes, Sir!"

"How many more can you squeeze into those last trucks?"

The corporal's shoulders took an obvious dip. "Um." His gaze darted around Ward Three. His voice lowered. "We may get another ten, Sir."

Ten! Joyce wanted to scream. *Only ten!* There were nearly fifty men who needed to be moved.

"And if two nurses stayed behind?" Colonel Herndon asked.

"Well, um, then one prone. Two if they can sit." The corporal fidgeted under the attention of the room. "Sir."

"Very well," the colonel stated, standing tall and turning to leave. "You soldiers are most brave," he spoke softly to Joyce and Misty. "Godspeed you to morning."

Resolutely he walked through the tent into the lashing winter wind.

Air whistled through Misty's teeth as she relaxed from her military pose. "Whatcha make of this?"

Joyce let her eyes scan the room, looking for what they had to work with and what they would need to round up. "We grab an orderly to help," she started. "We'll need a supply of fresh water and a case of rations. They'll take the generators. Besides, we can't afford to shed any light tonight."

Joyce risked a look at Misty. The other nurse's eyes were wide. They both knew it would be a long, long night. But plans in motion, they rushed off to secure the needed supplies.

Twelve men were moved out of Ward Three and loaded on the last truck. Joyce was at the tent flap when the convoy started out. The colonel's jeep wove past empty tents and bare lots where tents once stood. Joyce noticed him tip his cap in her direction, and she saluted.

She watched the dim taillights disappear into the encroaching darkness while gunfire cracked behind her. A glow, possibly fire, colored the eastern horizon. Just inside the ward, about forty men waited in hushed suspense. Never before had Joyce felt so alone.

Oh, God, can You hear our prayers? Fear pressed upon her. Why had she said she'd stay? *What do I do, God?*

Even the battle racket was suddenly silent. New snow drifted down around her, covering the footprints and tire marks of those who had just escaped the danger.

You've been so quiet in all this, God, her heart cried. *But only You can see us through this. I'm trusting. . . .*

Chapter 5

The tent was closed tight and darkened. Joyce, Misty, and the orderly carried small flashlights and used them guardedly only when absolutely necessary.

Joyce felt her way down the row of cots to where a voice beckoned her. "Cold," a soldier said, teeth chattering.

She felt the draft that cut through the tent. Exploring along the bottom of the wall, she found an area of loose canvas that had been pushed out of place by a box of supplies. She shifted the box and pulled at the canvas until it was taut and once again blocked the wind.

The soldier sighed his relief. "You're an angel. Can I look you up when we get home?"

"Sure," Joyce played along. "You can 'look up' to the North Star. I'll be the next brightest star to the right of it. And I'll be saying a prayer for you."

The soldier chuckled while a low voice from the next bed asked, "Will you pray?"

A chill Joyce couldn't explain raced through her. She shrugged it off in the darkness, and from her crouched position between cots, she leaned toward the new voice.

"I just say that, I guess, to maintain my angelic status with these guys," she said softly. *And to ward off romantic notions,* she added to herself. "My grandma used to say something similar."

"I'm so cold," the voice returned. "Is there a blanket?"

Joyce reached into the darkness until her hand found the wooden frame of the cot. Her fingers identified the scratchy, army-issue blanket. "Your blanket's here, Soldier."

"So cold," he moaned.

Many of these men suffered from overexposure to wind and cold. Their limbs showed signs of frostbite. But blood loss could also lower body temperatures. Joyce knew she must check to see if the man was bleeding.

Outside, the distant rumbles of what she guessed to be tanks made her nervous about using even the small light from her flashlight. She questioned the man first. "Any pains, Soldier?"

"My arm burns and my head aches," he croaked. "Guess you'd say my feet are numb."

She flipped the light on, carefully holding the cold metal torch low between the beds. Through the shadows, she found that one of his arms had been ripped by a bullet. A medic along the way had most likely dusted the wound with sulfa and bandaged it. The dressing seemed tight, and she didn't see any sign of fresh bleeding.

Another bomb jolted them and the flashlight fell from Joyce's lap. The light shot up toward her face and at the canvas overhead. She grabbed for it.

The soldier gasped. "Joy!"

Joyce's heart clenched and she held her breath. She

didn't know if she'd heard the voice right.

"Joy?"

Behind the pain-laced word, Joyce recognized the voice of a friend. Her heart leaped and began an erratic dance.

"Rusty?" She fumbled with her light, the need for care momentarily forgotten. She aimed the beam along the soldier's torso, past an outstretched hand, and to his face. Two welcoming blue eyes gazed back at her.

"Your hair's *so* short," she burst out, glimpsing his red hair cropped close to his head. Suddenly she was laughing and crying as she reached for her old friend. The flashlight went tumbling again when Rusty's good arm moved to embrace her. His hug was warm, even if it lacked the strength she remembered. It felt so good to let herself sink against his chest and delight in having him with her.

"How? Where?" they asked each other in unison.

Joyce pulled back to study him through her tears of happiness. He stared back with a look of wonder, and she let her hand trace his stubbled cheek. He looked older. Was it the cropped hair or the new lines carved by the unknown ordeal that had eventually landed him in her hospital?

She hated to turn off her flashlight, but the importance of concealing their location and the need to conserve power came first.

"Ah, do you have to turn that off?" Rusty asked as immediately they were enveloped by the black of night. "I wanted to enjoy looking at you. You're still pretty— even in army green."

Joyce reached for his hand and gave it a gentle

squeeze. "Who could have imagined we would meet here? Why, I thought you were probably in the Pacific. Poor Dot didn't even know if you'd gotten into the army or navy."

Rusty chuckled. "God does have a sense of humor. . . and timing." He pulled her hand toward his chapped lips, brushing her knuckles with a kiss.

A tingle danced through her even as she puzzled over his casual talk of God. In all their long conversations as kids along the banks of the Ohio River, they'd rarely mentioned God or given Him much credit for anything.

"Timing?" she whispered from a throat that was suddenly tight.

"I couldn't have asked for a better Christmas gift than seeing you."

His touch reassured her. She longed to read his eyes, yet she was glad for the darkness. It made her feel as if they were alone, even though she could hear the murmurs, moans, and occasional snores of her other patients—and even though she knew her reunion with Rusty was entertaining every soldier within earshot.

"Oh, Rusty, I'm so sorry about your mother's death." Fresh tears burned for release.

Rusty moved his hand up to rub her shoulder. "It's okay. She had really been suffering toward the last and was ready to go."

Joyce felt the damp tears on her cheeks and shivered.

"Dear Joy, it was so hard losing Mother and watching my little sister get married. I longed to have you there to talk with. You'd been there for every major event in the past."

She imagined a bittersweet smile on his face like the one she felt tugging at her own lips.

"Joy, I've got to tell you what the Lord has been able to do with—"

"What's going on?" Misty approached, her hand over the face of her flashlight to deflect its beam.

"This is Rusty. . .uh Pvt. James Russell DeWitt. He's my. . .he's my friend from. . ." Joyce suddenly remembered that Misty knew Rusty as the "old shoe that could use a good toss." She felt her face burn in humiliation as her two worlds began to collide. "From back home," she finished for Rusty's sake. "Private DeWitt, this is Lt. Misty Jones."

Rusty couldn't ignore the hesitation in Joy's introduction of him to Lieutenant Jones. He noticed the other nurse's eyes widen with some hidden knowledge before she masked her expression.

Joy was called away to help a soldier writhing in pain, and Lieutenant Jones faded into the darkness. Rusty pulled the blanket over his shoulders, suddenly feeling the cold again.

The easy way he and Joy had strolled back into their friendship had quickly met a barrier. Cool, impersonal letters and postcards from Joy came to mind. They had trickled in after she'd left for the war, then stopped. He didn't understand then, nor could he imagine now, what had come between two longtime friends who used to share everything.

Was he assuming too much when he expected to pick up where they had left off their last day by the river? He had allowed himself to take for granted a lot in his life. He'd assumed his mother's faith and guidance would always be there for him, his sister would always need him, his course in life would remain clear, and Joy would join him along each step.

The eighteen months since the day he'd watched Joy board a train out of Steubenville had been filled with many changes. His life had radically altered. He could only guess she had gone through experiences that had affected her as well. But for the first time since childhood, he hadn't been able to share them with her. He wasn't able to reach her, and she didn't seek to connect with him.

Had she found what she seemed to be looking for? Did she have someone like his buddy Cal to help her sort out the answer to her questions?

Rusty shivered and gave in to the pull of fatigue.

Joyce felt actual relief when the orderly's request gave her an excuse to leave Rusty's side. Her head swam just thinking about what it meant to be near Rusty again, and her hand still radiated from his touch. It had been so easy to slip back into the camaraderie they had always shared.

It was so easy to forget the letter.

But the deed was done. The letter had been written and mailed. Surely he hadn't received the letter yet, or he would have. . .

What did you expect? To sever old ties and never see him again? Did you think he'd beg you to take the words back or turn on you with hatred?

The reasons she'd had for writing the letter seemed so fuzzy now that geography and war no longer separated her from her childhood friend.

Women's voices pulled Rusty from his restless sleep. Joy and Lieutenant Jones stood near the foot of his bed, arguing.

"I have to go out and at least check on him while it's quiet."

"No. You can't! You don't know what's out there."

"I have to go. I can't leave him."

Rusty recognized the last stubborn statement as coming from Joy. He struggled to sit up in the sagging cot. "Joy. . .Lieutenant Aldergate, what are you thinking? You can't go out there! Who is so important that the orderly can't go and help him?"

He felt someone bump into the end of his bed, then he sensed her at his side.

"Lie down. There's nothing to get worked up about. I'll be right back. Just promise me you'll rest." Then she was gone.

He heard Lieutenant Jones hiss, "Joyce," and felt a distinct draft as the tent flaps parted.

What could have driven Joy to leave the security of the tent? Soldiers needed to stick together. One-man missions were irresponsible. Who was this guy who was worth such a stupid risk?

Chapter 6

Joyce crept along the sides of the camp's remaining tents, empty shells offering no warmth or refuge. The cloudy night afforded little light to guide her, and she didn't dare risk using her flashlight.

She easily recognized the main road through camp. She followed it until a branch led to the quartering area. Most of the small housing tents still stood as dark mounds in the snow. It took awhile to determine her bearings and find her tent.

Inside was complete darkness, but she could tell that most of the contents had been removed. She felt for the first bunk. It had been disassembled, yet it remained in a pile on the floor. She shuffled to where the second bunk still stood. A quick exploration found bedding piled on the bottom bed.

"Rookie," she called softly and waited. The night was blissfully calm—for the moment. "Here, Kitty."

Joyce finally discerned a tiny meow, and she dug through the pile of blankets until she found the shivering kitten.

"Oh, you poor little thing. How lonely and scared you must have been."

She scooped the cat into her arms and turned toward the door. Suddenly she thought of how useful extra blankets would be. Balancing Rookie in one hand, she draped several blankets over her shoulder.

Awkward under the weight of her burden, she headed out of the tent and slowly made her way back toward the ward. Just as she thought she had reached her goal, the *rat-a-tat-tat* of machine guns caused her to screech and nearly trip. The gunfire was probably quite a distance away, but the night air made it seem much closer. She rushed into the large ward tent, panting for breath. "Misty," she whispered.

Silence. The room was so cold and dark. She took a step back, and her foot caught on something large. Down she fell, landing hard on her backside. Tangled in blankets and trying to hold onto her frightened kitten, Joyce couldn't get up. *Oh God, please help. I'm so scared. And yes, I do believe You hear my prayer.*

"Tell me where she went." Rusty stood in the middle of the ward tent, hanging onto the middle post.

Lieutenant Jones's hand clutched his forearm below the bandages. "You're in no shape to follow her. She knows the camp layout and will be right back." Her words lacked conviction.

"What on earth was so important to make her fly out into the night in the middle of war?" he barked.

"Well. . ." The nurse hesitated.

A blast of cold air whirled around Rusty, nipping at his exposed skin. Lieutenant Jones's flashlight came on and glowed red through the barrier of her hand.

"Oh, Misty!" Joy's soft voice brought a deep sense

of relief to Rusty's heart. He wanted to reach out to her, but his feet were numb and useless and his good arm was holding him up.

Joy stumbled to them under a bulky load. Did she carry her patient?

"What took so long?" Lieutenant Jones asked.

Rusty detected Joy's irregular breathing and waited anxiously for her response.

"I got turned around and entered another ward." Joy dropped the blankets from her arms and something wiggled in her hands.

"You found him!" Lieutenant Jones exclaimed.

Two small eyes reflected the minimal light.

"What *is* that?" Rusty asked.

"Rusty! Private DeWitt, what are you doing out of bed?"

"What is that?" he repeated.

"My kitten."

"What!" His bellow surely woke some soldiers.

"Shh!" Joy soothed. "Please get back in bed."

"You went out alone. . .when the enemy. . .is breathing down our necks. . ." Rusty fought to control his anger, then hissed, "Just to get a *cat!*"

Joy touched his arm and tugged him toward his bed. "It's okay."

"No—it is not! You could have gotten yourself killed."

Misty kept her filtered light on, but she said nothing.

Joyce could not understand why Rusty was so worked up. She pulled at his arm again. "Please sit down, Private DeWitt."

He sighed and seemed to relent. As she stepped with

him toward the side of the cot, she noticed his limp.

"What's wrong?" she asked. "Was your leg hit too?"

"No," he grunted. "My feet are numb like big cinder blocks."

"Oh." Joyce suspected frostbite.

Misty moved closer with her light, offering unspoken assistance. But Joyce caught her gaze and frowned. There was no use trying to do much under such conditions.

"Let's get them propped up," she soothed in her formal nursing tone.

Rusty gave a disgusted snort. "If you're going to treat me like a child, then the least you can do is sit beside me and hold my hand."

The statement caught her off guard. That he even wanted her presence brought a strangely satisfying warmth. Misty faded away with her flashlight, and Joyce pushed Rusty gently down onto his cot, pulling the blanket around him and reaching for one of the extras.

The kitten wiggled for freedom, so she plunked it down at Rusty's side.

"Hey!" He intercepted it as it jaunted across his stomach. "I can't believe what you'd put yourself through for an animal."

"He's special," she said, whispering again.

"Okay, tell me."

The request wasn't demanding. Joyce recognized the tone Rusty used when he wanted her to open up and confess to him. And she did. It was easy to tell him about Josie and how Joyce wanted so very much to help the little girl who had seen so many horrors.

"How special that God used you to help her through

that loss," Rusty said. "Your caring touch probably brought more comfort than her parents would have been able to express to her. I mean, in their daily struggles a pet would be the least of their worries. You would have been like an angel sent to brighten that one dark moment."

"Her father seemed quite loving when he came and brought the kittens," Joyce assured him. "But thanks for saying so."

She shifted uncomfortably. *Me, an angel. Ha.* She pulled an extra blanket from the neglected pile and put it on the tarp-covered ground beside Rusty's bed to sit on. Under the cloak of darkness, protocol seemed easy to forget.

"Rusty, tell me why you've mentioned God so often and see Him in such small things," Joyce prompted. "This war is so big, but I don't see Him doing anything about it."

"I had a comrade teach me to see God in the little things and focus on the positive."

"How does that help?"

"Instead of looking for major things—like the war ending and the Nazis changing their stripes—we find God in the little miracles. . .like friendship."

The simple word "friendship" pierced Joyce in a deeply buried spot. She felt like a hypocrite, soaking up the joy of his timeless devotion when she knew that somewhere a letter existed that could easily sever any good feelings between them.

Joyce rubbed her cold hands together and pulled her coat tighter. From the back corner of the ward came a soft humming noise. Rusty's words about God circled through her thoughts. She knew God existed; she called out to Him whenever she was in real need. She couldn't deny that she believed God would hear her—could answer her. But could she trust Him to give her hope and strength to go on? She would like the peace she heard in Rusty's voice. He seemed to have hope.

The humming had turned to soft singing. Joyce soon recognized it as a Christmas carol.

"See, there He is now!" Rusty whispered.

"Who? Where?" Joyce sat up straight, focusing once more on her dismal surroundings.

The carol had picked up singers. Bass, tenor, and baritone united to create a soothing harmony.

"Only God could orchestrate such a choir," Rusty said with a smile in his voice.

He's right! "Silent Night" had never sounded sweeter to Joyce's ears than when surrounded by the blasts, cries, and moans of war.

Joyce heard Rusty join a stanza in his gentle baritone. He stopped, coughed, then picked up the melody again.

Tears filled her tired eyes. She leaned back against the cot's frame and soaked in the sweet music as the men began singing "I Heard the Bells on Christmas Day." No tanks rumbled in the background, nor could she hear artillery blasts. For a moment, Joyce could almost believe that peace was not too far in their future.

Joyce woke with a start and her body screamed in pain. The darkness told her it was still night. She tried to unfold her stiff legs, while Misty stood over her, detailing the current needs of their patients. The words made little sense to Joyce's clouded mind.

She reached her hand out to the nearest bed to pull herself up and felt the warmth from Rusty's body. Misty's dim flashlight revealed his pale face against a white pillow, and alongside his good arm, Rookie nestled in a deep sleep.

Joyce willed her body into motion as she stood and checked Rusty's breathing. When assured that he breathed normally, she turned to follow Misty, but something caught her eye. At Rusty's side, near the kitten, a face stared up at her—a face made of cloth and pearl buttons.

She reached down and pulled a small rag doll from the tangle of blankets. She studied the toy in the dim light from her flashlight. Why would a soldier have a doll? Her gaze swung to Rusty's face, and he smiled back at her through the shadows.

"I know you are rather old for dolls, but you may have it," he murmured.

"Where did it come from?"

"Well. . .you've collected things along the way," he murmured as he petted the head of the tiny cat, "and I've collected a few things too."

She didn't think he was going to explain further.

Finally he said, "I found it in a small village after a very trying day. It's another reminder of hope."

"But this obviously belonged to a child. If you found it in this condition, then the child is probably dead or had to flee her home." Joyce thought of her sweet friend Josie. "I just see it as a reminder of all the hurting children who have been displaced by war."

"Okay," Rusty said and reached out to take the doll.

"You can look at it that way. I guess I did too. . .at first. But it makes me remember that innocent young children have seen the effects of war, and I can hope that when they grow up they'll do everything in their power to see that such needless bloodshed and destruction are not repeated."

He tucked the doll back beside the kitten and turned his head on the pillow.

Joyce's hands seemed so empty. Feeling dismissed due to her limited perspective, she moved down the row of cots to get a bowl of fresh water. As she checked her patients' wounds, she forced back the need for a good cry.

Why couldn't she see things like Rusty did? He'd been out in the thick of battle, and still he had the ability to find hope—and God—in the remnants. *Oh God, why can't I see and feel You here?*

Rusty tried to ease back into sleep. It was so quiet, too quiet. The soldiers felt a sensation of waiting for something, and fear nibbled at the edges of sane thinking.

He watched the glow of two flashlights as Joy and Lieutenant Jones moved among the wounded. He'd been short with Joy when she'd questioned his views. It wasn't always easy to look on the bright side when there was every reason to let fear and doubt take over. The renewed press from Hilter's Panzers in the last few days had started the Allies questioning their confidence about ending the war in Europe quickly.

Just a couple of days ago he had been like Joy, questioning God's place in these circumstances. He couldn't blame her when even now he let doubts creep in. On the battlefield, he'd felt he had no time to talk with God. But being flat on his back, there seemed to be little else to do.

He let his eyelids slide shut and focused on the Lord. Just as when he'd had his face in the dirt on the front line, he felt a heavenly peace. Rusty silently told the Lord about his doubts and felt his strength renewed.

Awhile later, Rusty opened his eyes to find Joy hovering over the neighboring bed. She checked the soldier's pulse and adjusted the blankets. Her actions were smooth and professional. He respected the way she worked among these men. He felt proud of her bravery, tact, and level-headedness. If only she could curb sudden impulses to rescue kittens and the like. He smiled.

"How is he?"

She jumped as though startled and turned toward him. "Fine and sleeping," she whispered. "Few have been able to get more than a snatch of sleep tonight." She rubbed a hand across her brow.

Rusty wished he could do something to ease the exhaustion she must be feeling. Her dark blond hair, cut shorter than he remembered, was mussed and tangled. He doubted she'd had any time to herself over the last couple days.

"Sit down a moment," he invited.

She stared at him awhile, then eased herself onto the edge of his cot. He knew balancing herself on the narrow board couldn't be comfortable, but their accommodations were sparse.

She flipped off the light.

"I wanted to ask you to read to me," he said, worming Cal's New Testament out from under the kitten, which seemed to have adopted him. Rusty hadn't had any chance to open the Bible since Cal had given it to him.

"Read what?" she questioned softly.

"Did you know King David talked to God on the battlefield?"

He felt her shrug. "I guess. . ."

He placed the little book in her hands. "I think the back of this has a section from the Psalms. Can you see if Psalm 18 is there?"

Joy snapped her flashlight back on, flipping reverently through the thin pages. "Did you do all this underlining?"

"No. The Bible belonged to my friend Cal."

She looked at him, and he could guess her question.

"He was wounded at the front and gave this to me before the medic took him away. I don't know where he is."

She turned her attention back to the book. " 'The Lord is my rock, and my fortress, and my deliverer; my God, my strength, in whom I will trust; my buckler, and the horn of my salvation, and my high tower. I will call upon the Lord, who is worthy to be praised: so shall I be saved from mine enemies.' "

Her gaze sought his. "That sounds too easy—call on God and be saved. I know a lot of these guys called on Him while being hit by bullets, and. . ." Her eyes brimmed with tears. "That GI who was moaning a few hours ago—he mumbled about God, and still he bled to death. Misty and I tried packing his wound with snow, but the bleeding wouldn't stop. God didn't save him."

Rusty felt tears choking his throat. She was right.

It wasn't always easy to trust in God's promises. "Joy. . . I certainly don't have all the answers, but I've been learning that God responds in His own way. If that guy was meant to die now and went to the Lord's arms, then think how he must be praising God."

Joy didn't say anything. She stared at the book, then she started to flip the pages. Her voice was subdued when she read, " 'Teach me thy way, O Lord, and lead me in a plain path, because of mine enemies. . . . I had fainted, unless I had believed to see the goodness of the Lord in the land of the living. Wait for the Lord: be strong and take heart and wait for the Lord.' "

She closed the book and placed it on his chest. "Hope is a good thing, but only good people can really expect God to be there in the end." Her downcast face reflected deep hurt. "Rusty, you just don't know. . ."

Lieutenant Jones came running up to them. "Joyce," she said eagerly. "I heard trucks. The orderly thinks they're ours. That means we may have made it through." She laughed with relief as the room began to buzz with the news.

Joyce snapped to attention and followed the other nurse as they tried to keep the men from getting too loud. Rusty pulled himself to a sitting position and set the cat on the floor.

He released a pent-up breath. *Dear Lord, I do believe she is hurting. Please help her past whatever is bothering her and show her that You love her completely. . .as I do.* He shuddered. He'd always known he loved Joy, but he'd never felt it so intensely.

Chapter 7

The orderly peered out through the tent flap at the haze of a new dawn. Joyce paced behind him, impatient to know what he saw. Nearby, Misty tried to keep a restless soldier on his cot. Tension filled the air.

Large trucks roared nearby, and the orderly bounced up and down. "They're ours, all right!"

Joyce looked toward the men in the gloomy tent and gave her best smile. *Hope!* It was always welcome.

The orderly stepped outside to greet the convoy, complete with a jeep with a military police escort. Joyce pulled the tent flaps back and secured them open. The morning breeze was bitterly cold, but the fresh air lessened the tang of blood and infection that filled the tent.

Everyone snapped into action, working frantically to get the remaining patients evacuated. Rumbles from the war front underscored the need to move quickly. Joyce and Misty helped to oversee the process of crowding the men into two large trucks and two ambulances. The soldiers in need of immediate care went to the ambulances at the head of the line. When it came time to load Rusty, Joyce had to convince him not to walk. He grumbled about being a burden to stretcher barriers, but he reluctantly cooperated.

Joyce moved on to other patients. A loose bandage needed to be retied. Someone demanded a drink of water. A few of the patients seemed in no hurry to be moved, but Joyce urged them along.

Rusty leaned back against the wall of a large truck. His feet throbbed, and he wished for a place to prop them up, but everyone who could sat along the sides. Four men on stretchers were then laid out at their feet.

Rusty had a seat near the rear with a view of the dilapidated camp. He watched the activity around the ward tent and judged the proximity of the smoke billowing from somewhere beyond the tree line. The Germans were very close.

The trucks rumbled to life. Leaning around another private, Rusty noticed that the nurses had yet to be loaded. Joy and Lieutenant Jones were gesturing over the contents of a trunk. Apparently deciding to leave it, Lieutenant Jones marched off to the first truck, but Joy suddenly whirled around and headed back into the tent.

The jeep began moving out. Rusty leaned out over the tailgate. Had anyone noticed that Joy wasn't on a truck?

The vehicle shuddered under Rusty as the driver put it in gear. Rusty shouted over the din for Joy to hurry. He watched the tent opening for any sign of her.

The MP jeep circled the convoy of trucks, and while passing between the last truck and the ward tent, it knocked over the corner support. A quarter of the tent collapsed.

Rusty sprang out over the tailgate. Hitting the ground sent knives of pain up his legs, but he plowed into the sagging tent and into blackness.

"Lieutenant Aldergate," he shouted. "Joy! Joyce! Where are you?"

"Oh, Rusty, over here!" she cried. "I can't find Rookie!"

"Who?"

"My kitten!" she shrieked. "I can't. . .I *cannot* leave him."

Rusty couldn't see her, but he recognized her panic. He stumbled deeper into the tent, banging against empty cots. The relaxed canvas swung overhead. A beam creaked. The truck engines roared. At least two sounded as if they were moving.

"Joy, come to me! We've got to go."

"Rookie!" she called.

Rusty's uncoordinated feet tangled and sent him sprawling. A loud screech met his fall, and he shot a hand out to catch a scurrying ball of fur. A tiny heart hammered against his hand and claws tore at his skin, but he kept his hand firmly clasped.

"I've got the idiot cat!" he bellowed. "Can we go?"

"Oh, Rusty." He recognized the sound of tears.

"I'm sorry," he called out in the dark. "I understand the cat is important to you." He breathed deeply to gain control and tried to pull himself to a sitting position while batting the canvas that dipped over him.

Outside artillery fire split the air, while inside a loud crack was followed by a downpour of tent canvas and a scream from Joyce. Weighted down in a tangle of tent material, Rusty shoved the kitten deep into his coat pocket and swam under the heavy canvas.

As soon as he reached daylight a large hand pulled him to his feet. Men were shouting commands. Horns were honking.

"Joy, the nurse. . .get her out!" Rusty screamed.

The man nodded and pushed Rusty ahead of him.

At the sound of the crack, the tent and its center beam came crashing down on Joyce. She landed on the ground in a twisted tangle and knew immediately that her right leg was injured—probably broken.

She screamed. The weight of the tent was suffocating. She thrashed her arms about, looking for a way to pull herself toward freedom.

Suddenly large hands grabbed her under her arms and tugged her out into the open. She drew in a deep breath of the cold air and sighed, "Rusty."

Expecting to see her friend, she looked up. A large soldier held her. He picked her up with ease and ran toward an ambulance. Unceremoniously, he tossed her to the vehicle's floor and slammed the heavy doors closed.

Almost immediately, Joyce felt the ambulance speed out of camp, rocking her back against the cold hard floor. She heard machine gun fire outside, the clanking tracks of tanks, and the snap of falling trees. Fear tore through her body, and she lay motionless until the sounds of the enemy faded.

Where was Rusty? Could he and Rookie still be encased in the monstrous tent? Horrid visions of what could be raced through her mind.

Joyce bounced on the floor of the ambulance. Pain ripped through her leg with every jostle.

"Look out there," a soldier in the truck said, pointing through the small, hazy window at the rear, which from Joyce's viewpoint only revealed cloudy skies. "We don't get white Christmases like that in New Mexico."

"I'll bet," the other guy responded, "but this ain't my idea of Christmas. I say, where's the holiday cheer? Mail call hasn't caught up to me in weeks, but I'm bound to be due several packages. Hope they get here before Christmas Day."

"Well, don't get your hopes up. The news is that the Nazis have been intercepting mail. They're probably eating your fruitcake and wearing your new red mittens."

Joyce didn't appreciate the men's laughter. She longed for mail from home. But. . .if mail was truly being seized by the Germans, Rusty's letter might never be delivered. The thought brought a measure of comfort.

Oh, I'm so selfish! Thoughts screamed through her aching head. *I'd wish a thousand soldiers didn't get their Christmas mail just so I wouldn't have to face the contents of that one stupid letter. How can You stand to look at me, God?*

She fidgeted, trying to find a semi-comfortable position on the hard floor.

How I wish I had never written that letter. My feelings— or at least my understanding of them—have sure taken a change. I know now that Rusty does care for me. He loves me in his own special way. But I tossed away a good thing with a few cutting words.

The ambulance dipped into a hole in the road and threw her against the steel stretcher frame, causing her to wince.

Okay, Lord, I know if You can see Rusty and me through this war, You can also give me the courage to talk to him about the letter and explain what I wrote. But then, I don't know if I'll ever see Rusty again.

At the thought, Joyce succumbed to unchecked tears.

"It's a good clean break of the fibula," the doctor said in a cheerful tone.

Joyce smiled up at the kind captain, whose round face was framed by graying temples. "When will you have me back to work?"

"Oh," he chuckled, "I suppose the army will find something for you to do within a couple weeks, even if it's just medical reports." He patted her shoulder, then left the women's ward.

Joyce wrapped the clean sheet and blanket around her, enjoying the pristine atmosphere. This orderly room was what a hospital was supposed to look like. Six iron beds lined the small area. Five were full, and Joyce guessed from the constant coughing she heard that one of the women suffered from bronchitis or pneumonia.

Joyce stared at the cracked ceiling. What a way to see Paris. When she'd landed on the shores of France, her greatest dream had been to see the famous city, but her assignments had kept her out in the field. The occasional view of a village cathedral or country manor was her only taste of Parisian artistry.

Now that she thought more about her dreams, she realized seeing Paris had meant being *seen* on the arms of influential officers. She had wanted to make a splash on the city. GIRL FROM NOWHERE IN PARTICULAR BECOMES THE HIT OF PARIS, the headlines of her dreams might have read.

She shook her head. *What foolishness! What does fame have to do with anything of real value?*

Joyce's heart no longer desired to be dazzled by men and pleasure. She could only think about a little girl living in a cave and a brave soldier whose whereabouts were painfully unknown to her.

Oh, God, you see all things. Josie and Rusty don't deserve to be hurt anymore. Please protect them.

She rolled onto her side and cuddled her pillow. A noise at the door made her turn. A Red Cross girl carrying a large basket of books headed for Joyce. "You're a new one," she said with a beaming smile. "Can I get you anything?"

Joyce eyed the basket curiously and noted a particular book. "Is that a Bible in there?"

"Yes, it is."

"Could I borrow it?"

"Certainly!"

Joyce took the offered book and shifted so she could open it on the bed. Flipping through the pages, looking for the Psalms, she barely noted the departure of the Red Cross volunteer. She scanned many Psalms, then came to the one numbered 139. "O lord, thou hast searched me, and known me. . .art acquainted with all my ways. . . Whither shall I go from thy spirit? or whither shall I flee from thy presence?"

It was comforting, yet intimidating, to know the Lord was always there, seeing all things. How much she'd like to hide. But talking to Him about her sin seemed somewhat easier since He already knew what she did, saw the reasons why, and was just waiting for her to acknowledge her mistakes.

She sighed and continued to page through the book. Someone had penciled in a reference to a verse in Malachi, so she jumped to the end of the Old Testament and read, "Return unto me, and I will return unto you, saith the Lord of hosts."

Tiring, she let the Bible drop onto the mattress and relaxed against the pillow. If she turned things over to God, would she just be binding her life once again to the traditions and expectations that had driven her from home in the first place?

She closed her eyes, willing the answers to come. Slowly a picture of Jesus came to her mind—not as a judge at a court bench but as a friend and comforter, a friend she could trust to love her unconditionally. He gave guidance for living that really was the only path to true happiness and peace.

Joyce could finally relax.

Chapter 8

Joyce struggled to maneuver the crutches and propel herself down the long hospital corridor. A frown of frustration pulled at her mouth. The crutches wouldn't cooperate, and she couldn't seem to find anyone with clear information about Rusty's whereabouts. While the most seriously wounded soldiers had been shipped directly to Paris, the last truck and the MP jeep had fallen behind and apparently taken a more westerly route into Normandy. Rusty was probably at an evacuation hospital in a village somewhere west of Paris. At least, he should be if the rumors she heard were true and he'd gotten out of the collapsed tent.

"Hey, Nurse Aldergate!"

She looked up to see a familiar face from Ward Three sitting in a wheelchair outside the X-ray room. She smiled.

"The army should give you some sort of honor for staying with us soldiers through that night. It was mighty brave of you. . .then getting injured and all. . ."

She blushed. "No. . .I don't know any nurse who would have abandoned her patients." She struggled to move farther down the hall as quickly as possible, not wanting any accolades for what she considered to be simply doing her duty.

Suddenly she stopped, realizing she could ask the soldier if he knew anything about Rusty. She swung her crutch out, preparing for an awkward rotation. The wooden leg smacked into the uniform-clad shin of an officer. Joyce looked up in surprise.

"I'm so sorry—" Her voice broke as she recognized the immaculately dressed man from her last night in London. "Major Fire—uh"

"Lieutenant Aldergate, how nice to see you again." He flashed a big smile.

A similarly dressed officer stood beside him. "Nurse, you know Major Ferris? He's just been transferred to the Continent, and we couldn't have found a better supply officer for our hospital." The man beamed, and Major Ferris seemed to grow taller under the compliment.

"Uh. . ." Joyce struggled to find words. "Yes, we met while in London. You're in meds, Major?"

"Of course—don't you remember that I tried to talk you into joining our hospital in England?"

Her memory of the conversation was hazy, but she distinctly remembered her last date while on leave in the U.K.

"We must find time to catch up," the major was saying. "Looks like you have been having a rough time of it."

Joyce flashed a bright smile and felt her feminine charms switch on. It couldn't hurt having friends in high places when she was in need of help and information.

⌨

Rusty closed his eyes and enjoyed the stable surroundings

of the hospital. Since being whisked away from the tent hospital in the MP jeep while under enemy attack, he hadn't seen anything of Joyce and the others from Ward Three. For the last three days he had been shifted between jeeps, trucks, ambulances, and trains, and into and out of temporary army hospitals. He felt that he must have seen most of Belgium and France while lying on his back.

It felt so peaceful to lie still.

"Why, Private DeWitt! There you are!" a feminine voice fairly sang.

Rusty opened one eye and peered around the large ward.

A raven-haired nurse, dressed neatly in formal uniform, rushed toward him and dropped a pile of packages on the foot of his bed where his frostbitten feet were elevated. Rusty guarded his feet doggedly. Just that afternoon doctors had removed two small toes from his right foot.

"Nurse. . .uh, Lieutenant Jones," Rusty said, finally recognizing the nurse from Ward Three.

"I saw these packages in a pile and just knew I had to see them delivered." Her enthusiasm was especially bright, and she fluttered her hands as she talked. "It's Christmas Eve, you know."

Rusty just stared at her. He hadn't given the holidays any real thought.

"It's just amazing that these got sent to the right hospital." Her words finally started to slow down. She held up one box with his name boldly written in black letters across the brown wrapping. "A hero shouldn't go without Christmas mail." She smiled.

"Hero?"

"Sure!" she declared. "The way you dove into that falling tent was the only way anyone would have known Joyce was still in there."

"Joy." Rusty sat up. "How is she? *Where* is she?"

"Oh, she's fine. The doc said the break was a good one."

"Break?" Rusty felt his impatience rising.

"She broke her leg, but it was a clean break and will heal fast."

"And. . .where is she?" he prodded.

"Oh, she's here!"

Rusty sank back against his pillow with relief. His Joy was alive and safe. *Thank You, Father.*

Suddenly the nurse's words caught his attention. ". . .Being nervous about seeing you."

"What?"

"I think you're a swell guy, Private DeWitt, and Joyce clearly thinks a lot of you," she continued. "Do yourself a favor and know that this war gets to women just like it gets to the men. Don't take everything Joyce wrote to you to heart."

"She wrote to me?"

"Under the influence of the war, a girl can do things she regrets, but you shouldn't let her go without a fight," Lieutenant Jones added. "I've got to scoot. There's so much to do before they send me back to the fields. Merry Christmas!"

"What. . .where. . .?" Rusty stammered, but the nurse had zipped away and out the double doors.

Joy was here, but she hadn't come to see him.

Joy wrote to him, but she might have regrets.

Joy cared for him, but he might have to fight for her. Rusty's head swam with unanswered questions.

Oh, Lord, please bring Joy to me. Did we meet in the middle of war and survive the enemy only for me to be back to not knowing how the love of my life feels for me? I just don't understand.

While the army had been transporting him back and forth across the countryside, Rusty had had a lot of time to converse with God. He couldn't pinpoint when the thoughts started, but he felt that God might be calling him to be a pastor. He wanted to help others to meet the Lord on a personal level like Cal had been able to help him.

He could no longer assume he and Joy would pick up their old friendship and make a marriage out of it. He had changed a lot. He sensed she had too. And a pastor would make a whole lot less than a factory manager.

Was it fair to fight for her affections when he had so little to offer?

Christmas was a time for good cheer and praising God for the blessing of His Son, but the setbacks on the European front placed a cloud over the day. Joyce went to the early morning chapel service. Worshiping with other believers brought tears to her eyes and added to the peace her heart was finally finding.

She had considered seeing if Rusty could be released from his ward for the service, but she hadn't been ready to see him yet. She had gone to great lengths to renew her friendship with Major "Fire Eyes" Ferris and get Rusty transferred to Paris in time for Christmas. She could have allowed the war to come between them again, knowing that eventually her letter would catch up with Rusty and he would move on with life.

But he had taken a great risk chasing after her on frozen feet into that tent. Just the sound of his voice had calmed her. She knew he could understand her motives. Any girl would be proud to have a guy like Rusty care for her. Somehow she had to find a way to erase the impetuous words she'd penned to him. She had already tried intercepting the mail for him, but she found nothing with his name in the room where mail was sorted. Guilt nagged at her for even attempting such a maneuver.

She pulled the ward door open and immediately saw Rusty sitting by a large window. He had a good view of the bustling street and a small park across the way. Faint sunlight picked out the gold in his short red hair and highlighted his chapped cheeks. Joyce's heart went out to him. He looked lonely. She shouldn't have stayed away so long.

"Those feet should be elevated, Soldier."

He hadn't noticed her slow progression across the ward and jumped at her voice. His look carried a guilty glint, but as soon as he recognized her, he sprang out of the chair and grabbed her in a tight hug.

"Oh, I missed you!" he said.

"I missed you too." She sniffed back a threat of tears. His arms wrapped her in warmth, but she reluctantly broke the embrace. "Please sit down and put those feet up."

She pulled another chair closer for his feet to rest on, and he slowly sat back down. Pain darted across his face.

"I heard you lost a couple toes. I'm sorry, but it

could have been worse."

"Yeah. It'll be fine, but they'll probably be mustering me out and back home soon."

"Oh. . .yes, probably." *Separation again.* Suddenly she couldn't think of anything to say, and he looked just as uncomfortable.

"Merry Christmas," she finally said, giggling nervously.

He smiled, revealing his dimples. "Yes. Merry Christmas to you. You still look good, even with an encased leg."

Her face burned, and if it weren't for the obstructing crutches, her hands would have covered her cheeks.

He gestured at the chair where his feet rested. "Will you sit?"

"Oh!" She patted her wooden crutches and shook her head. "No thanks."

He shrugged. "I received some packages from home."

Joyce's heart started a tap dance. "You did?"

"Aunt Cleo sent homemade chocolate fudge. The box was passed around the room. Not sure if any is left."

"That's okay." She stared at the legs of his chair.

"Sis also sent a box."

"Ohh!" She couldn't bring herself to ask if it contained a letter. "How is Annabelle? Dot wrote that she married Joe Wright." Joyce swallowed against the rising pressure in her chest.

"She seems to be enjoying married life." Rusty smiled with a faraway look in his eyes. "She's all grown up and probably enjoying not having me around to baby her."

"I'm sure she misses you, though," she assured him.

"I know she always looked up to you."

Rusty caught her gaze, and she couldn't look away. His blue eyes contained a deep reminder that he knew her very well, but there was more. This was not the look of a man who thought of her as a sister. Joyce shivered at the awareness.

"Ah, Lieutenant Aldergate." Someone walked up behind her. "Do you realize I've been searching all morning for you?"

Joyce looked over her shoulder. Major Ferris stood with arms crossed and looked down at her over his regal nose.

"You're not on duty and don't have to fraternize with the enlisted." His words held the punch of insult.

Joyce looked at Rusty and saw the glare he leveled on the major.

"Major Ferris, this is Private DeWitt. . .a very good friend from back home."

"Ah, yes, your paperwork and I have met." The major's handsome face suddenly hosted an ugly smirk as he returned Rusty's silent glare. He didn't offer a handshake. "I'm sure you'll understand that the lady and I have made plans for today."

"Plans?" Her voice squeaked.

"Certainly." His charming tone was back as he looked at her with that passionate fire she had encountered before. "We could do a repeat of Piccadilly Circus, but the sticks would be a nuisance on the dance floor. So I've found an exquisite little restaurant I know you'll love."

Joyce stiffened. "I'm afraid I'll have to—"

"Now." The word came as a growl from the major's

throat. "I do believe you have a favor to return."

From the corner of her eye, Joyce noticed that Rusty had become rigid with anger.

She tried again. "Umm, I don't think I'd be up to an outing today."

The major drew himself up to his full height and glanced at Rusty. "Perhaps we should take our conversation outside, Lieutenant. No sense in bothering the boys with our mundane plans."

Joyce didn't want to go anywhere with the major and regretted anything she might have done to lead him on. But if it hadn't been for the major's efforts on her behalf, Rusty would still be in some unknown hospital, perhaps even back in London.

The air was tense. She chewed at her lower lip.

"Come." The major placed a painful vise on her arm.

"Excuse me!" Rusty shot to his feet and stood gripping the back of his chair. "The lieutenant doesn't appear to want to go with you."

Joyce couldn't believe her ears. Fear knotted her throat. What was Rusty thinking to challenge an officer?

"Who says?" Major Ferris was clearly insulted.

Rusty stood his ground, but his tone softened. "I mean no disrespect, Sir. But the lady is not free to accept your invitation."

Joyce knew her mouth had dropped open, but she was powerless to control her expression.

The major's face darkened with bottled rage.

Rusty continued. "You see, the lady is engaged. . . to me."

"What!" Color quickly drained from the major's face.

Joyce couldn't believe what she was hearing. Did

Rusty just lie to an officer? She watched as a nerve fluttered below his temple, but he stared at the major with a blank expression.

"Lieutenant?" The major wanted an explanation, but she couldn't stop looking at Rusty.

Would he say such a thing if he'd read her letter?

If he hadn't read her letter, then his statement could hold some truth. Nothing had ever been declared or promised, but Rusty and their families—even Joyce herself at times—had always assumed she and Rusty would eventually marry. But how could he speak for her in such a way?

Rusty finally turned his steady gaze to her. His look was so different from those of her dates who had leered over her outward appearance or her patients who had viewed her presence as angelic and motherly. Rusty's eyes reflected a warmth that stirred an untouched part of her. It was a connection she had longed for—a connection she wanted to hold on to.

"Lieutenant, is this true?" Major Ferris pressed, his face contorted in anger and embarrassment.

Joyce dared time for another look at Rusty. His expression was open, offering his heart to her.

"Yes," she heard herself say.

Chapter 9

Major Ferris stormed from the ward. The room buzzed with murmurs from the men, and Rusty experienced the first acute awareness that they had just put on quite a display.

He leaned conspiratorially toward Joy who was staring out the window in stunned silence. "You'd better leave, Joy," he said. "We need to continue our conversation when we have more privacy." He tried to give her an encouraging smile, but his insides fluttered nervously and his limbs felt limp.

She nodded, glancing at him and blushing prettily. Her retreat from the room was painfully inhibited by the crutches, and she kept her eyes downcast. At the door she glanced back, but he couldn't read her expression from that distance.

As soon as she was gone, Rusty dropped to his chair, shaking with weakness and the weight of the confrontation. What had he done? Where had such resolve come from?

He'd known immediately that the major was not to be liked or trusted. He didn't like the implication that the major and Joy had either a past or present understanding.

But could he be sure she wanted his interference?

He and Joy weren't ready to go back to talking commitment. Hadn't he recently told himself that he had no right to impose upon their past when the future was an ever-changing canvas?

The door slapped shut behind Joyce as she left the ward. Before she could continue down the hall, she noticed Major Ferris slumped against the wall. The crutches pressed painfully into her arms, but they couldn't cover the humiliating burn in her chest brought on by the memory of her actions. She had led the dashing major along while she still had an unresolved attachment to Rusty. Now that she understood where her heart wanted to be and she could trust God to guide her future, Joyce knew she had to make a difficult apology.

She approached the major with caution. He looked up, but his expression was empty of anger. In fact, she detected grief.

"Major Ferris, I'm—"

"Lieutenant, I was just handed a telegram from home. My son is very sick."

"You have a son?"

"I'm ashamed of myself." He stared at the floor. "I have a son. . .and a wife. . .and I've used this war to escape from my responsibilities to them."

Her breath caught.

He slowly turned to her with agony in his eyes. "You don't need to explain about the private. We both have a lot to regret."

She looked away as a wave of embarrassment washed over her. Then she snuck another peek at him.

She noticed he fingered a piece of paper. "I'm sorry."

He shook his head and started to walk away.

"I'll pray for your son."

He stopped and turned to her with surprise. "Thank you."

Joyce waited nervously in the hospital lobby by the small Christmas tree. The lone pine was the only indication that the day held anything special to celebrate. The high ceiling and imposing doorways of the grand foyer muted the Christmas cheer. She closed her eyes, trying to envision what Christmas at home would look like.

Mother had special decorations she brought out each year and treated with particular reverence. Joyce thought of the dainty, hand-blown glass bulb that always hung near the top of the family tree. She had never dared to touch it, fearing she'd damage its rare beauty.

She sighed. Christmas was blissful at home, but it was also holy.

Father would read the Christmas story on Christmas Eve. Then Christmas morning he would tell how the magi brought the first Christmas gifts. Each child received one lavish, love-filled gift from their parents, then exchanged hand-made presents with each other.

Joyce thought about the large package she had received just two days before from home. Each of her family members had included a small gift, but her parents had sent a beautiful white sweater. The luxury of it surrounded her now, reminding her of their thoughtfulness.

"Dreaming, my dear?"

Her heart took off on wings, and she turned to see

Rusty balancing on crutches that matched her own and favoring his right foot just as she did. He wore a large overcoat and apparently had agreed to the suggestion she'd sent by note through a Red Cross volunteer.

She smiled, suddenly feeling shy. "It's Christmas," she managed to say. "I can't help but think of home."

"Yes." His face reflected a whimsical look.

"I've arranged a taxi for us. Do you mind going out for a short while?"

He raised his eyebrows but put his hat on his head. "Shall we?" He indicated the door as he shuffled his way toward it.

Rusty held the door open for her, and they struggled to keep from tangling their crutches. Outside, a car waited for them. The driver got out and opened the back door, staring openly at the odd twosome.

Joyce gave in to a fit of giggles at the ridiculous juggling they had to do to get situated in the car. She couldn't seem to get herself over any farther than the middle of the seat before Rusty dropped in beside her. The driver kindly deposited four crutches in the trunk.

Joyce made a halting attempt at giving directions to the Frenchman, then sat back and waited to see if they'd end up where she hoped. They were both quiet as they took their first look at the city.

Paris seemed to glow at twilight. As requested, the driver took them past the Arc de Triumph, the Eiffel Tower, and the Louvre before stopping near an ornate bridge along the Seine River.

The couple struggled out of the car and onto their crutches. Night descended and the air cracked with cold, but they pressed on to the middle of the bridge.

Joyce pulled a small bag from her coat pocket. "Our usual riverside picnic would include fried chicken and chocolate chip cookies. I hope you don't mind these French pastries."

He laughed. "You thought of everything."

She offered the bag to Rusty, and they had it emptied in a jiffy.

She dusted flaky crust from her hands and sighed, watching her breath crystallize in the air. It was time to confess.

He broke the silence first. "You haven't asked about Rookie."

"Oh. . .well, honestly I was so consumed with finding you and getting you transferred to Paris that I didn't think about my kitten."

Rusty gave a knowing grin. "He's here in Paris, being cared for by a hospital custodian."

"You looked out for him all this time? Oh, that's wonderful." Her heart warmed to think that he would care about her cat. She had to take a moment to refocus.

"Uh, Rusty, I have something to confess."

"So do I. Can I go first?"

She nodded, pushing aside the burning need to voice her rehearsed words.

"I shouldn't have said what I did to the major today."

Hope plummeted in her chest.

"I know you haven't appreciated people speaking for you, and I know I've assumed a lot about our friendship. I've loved you since grade school and supposed we would eventually marry. And when the major starting making demands of you, I was consumed with a jealousy I've never known before."

She wanted to reassure him, but all she could do was place her hand over his where it rested on the stone structure.

"I shouldn't have made claims on you. We are both adults and have changed," he added.

"I'm sorry," she said. "I was searching for my own identity and didn't know what I wanted out of life." Just a few words helped her to open up. "I shouldn't have written that letter. I was taking my frustrations out on you. It wasn't until I started turning to God that I could understand my feelings. . .and, oh Rusty, how my feelings have changed."

"Do you mean this letter?" He pulled out a white envelope from inside his coat.

Pain pierced her at the sight of it. She turned her face away.

"It arrived in Annabelle's Christmas package. Something told me not to read it."

He held it out where they both could view it.

It was a sickening reminder of how low her priorities had sunk and how confused she had let herself get. She stared at it—wrinkled, slightly soiled, and perfectly sealed.

"I'm so sorry."

"Well. . . " His voice held a new lilt. "If there is something in here that you regret and would rather forget, then we should throw it away." His tone was soft. "There's no use opening the past when we can start fresh from today."

The letter slipped from his fingers. She gasped. They both leaned over the side of the bridge and watched as the letter fluttered on the breeze and landed on the water. It was still visible as the current carried it under the bridge.

Joyce turned, intending to cross the bridge to see it emerge on the opposite side. Rusty stopped her with a hand on each shoulder. She looked into his face. The unguarded look, holding no judgment, reassured her. She reached out and wrapped her arms around his waist, the crutches forgotten.

"Thank you," she whispered into his neck. No one had ever put aside their own desires and considered her feelings like that before.

"I know we both have been doing a lot of changing, and I'd like us to start our friendship afresh. I know I can't ask—"

"Oh yes you can! It's about time you go ahead and ask. We get in trouble assuming."

"But you don't understand. I can't ask you to marry me."

She pulled away from him. "Why?" The word came out as a squeak.

"I do love you. . .still and always. But I don't know where my life is going right now. I can probably go back to the brickyards, but I feel God is calling me to be a pastor or work in some kind of ministry. I can't make any promises to a wife."

"No one can be sure of the future," she reminded him. "But I've become very thankful for having a solid background. When I floundered, I had my parents' love and teachings to return to."

His gaze caressed her face, and she read longing in his eyes. But something still held him back.

"What more could I ask for," she asked, "than a man who wants to follow God's will? I can feel safe and secure knowing that God will provide for our needs."

He smiled. "Oh. . .well then. . .I can't really get down on one knee."

"So."

"I don't have a ring."

"So."

"Besides, we're both still in the army and Uncle Sam owns our time. I can't promise when we can marry. It's not like the army will release you to get married."

"But none of that matters to me. Will I have to freeze to death before you just ask?"

He chuckled. "If you can accept what little I have to bring to you and tell me you wouldn't mind claiming a lowly private. . .uh, make that soon-to-be *civilian*. . .as your fiancé, you'd make me the happiest man alive."

"Yippee!" she shouted across the expanse of river. "You finally asked and my answer is most definitely yes."

He pulled her into his embrace. "May I kiss you?"

"Now you shouldn't have to ask that."

"Nope. Your deep blue eyes and pouting lips are already begging me."

He leaned closer, hesitating, and she realized this was probably his first kiss. She felt a moment's regret that she hadn't saved her first kisses for him—*what a waste*. Placing her hands alongside his cheeks, she encouraged him closer.

The gentle brush of their lips was sweet. She yearned for his touch like she had never yearned for any man before, and he responded by deepening the kiss. Joyce experienced a deep sense that this was right. She had come home.

Epilogue

Aldergate-DeWitt

Joyce Elaine Aldergate and James Russell DeWitt were married in a small wedding ceremony at Grace Community Church in Steubenville, Ohio, on May 5, 1946. Mrs. Joe Wright attended the bride, while Mr. Calvin Cookson stood up with the groom. Also in the wedding party were the bride's two nieces and a nephew.

Mr. and Mrs. DeWitt took their wedding trip to Niagara Falls. She works as a nurse at Steubenville Hospital. He is employed as a manager for River Clay Corporation. Both served the U.S. Army in France during the war. The couple plans to move to Indiana, where Mr. DeWitt will enter seminary in the fall.

REBECCA GERMANY

Rebecca considers herself an old-fashioned kind of girl who loves old-fashioned kinds of romance. She was hooked from a young age, and it was a natural progression that she chose to devote her life's work to books and writing.

Heartsong Presents inspirational romance series and book club started in October 1992. Rebecca joined the Heartsong team exactly one year later and was named managing editor in 1995. She has written several things, and her first work of fiction was a novella published in a collection from Barbour Publishing. She now has four novellas in print.

Single, but contentedly enjoying life on the old family farm, "Becky" has several hobbies (like reading, singing, gardening, crafts, quilting, and so on) to keep her very busy.

Christmas Always Comes

by Darlene Mindrup

Chapter 1

Butte Camp Relocation Center
Casa Grand, Arizona
November 1944

Mitsu Yakamura stood poised, hands on hips, head thrust back, chin out. Her slanted almond eyes gleamed like molten copper when she smiled at the little girl standing at her feet.

"What is this? What are you saying?"

The child dipped her head in obeisance, but her shoulders were thrown back mutinously.

"I do not believe in this Santa Claus," the child whispered defiantly.

Mitsu dropped to kneel beside the little girl. Taking her by the shoulders, she lifted her chin until their eyes, so similar yet so different, met.

"Tell me, Emily, what has made you decide this all of a sudden?"

Emily pressed her lips tightly together before suddenly bursting into speech. "Jimmy says there is no such thing as Santa Claus! He says it is stupid to believe in

179

such things, things you cannot see."

A sheen came to the little girl's eyes, and Mitsu realized she was about to learn the true reason behind Emily's sudden bout of tears. Slowly Emily lifted tear-drenched eyes toward Mitsu's face.

"He says there is no Jesus, either. He says that only a fool would believe in such a man."

Mitsu sighed. It was the way with most of the people here in Butte Camp. A small army of relocated Japanese lived here, but for the most part, they were followers of Buddha, with a sprinkling of believers in the Shinto faith. Very few were Christians. Even her own parents worshiped the false image of Buddha.

Mitsu sat on the cold, dusty ground and pulled Emily down beside her. Leaning back against the guard tower, she took the six year old into her arms, brushing her straight, dark braid back with one hand. She buttoned the little girl's winter coat to protect her against the biting cold wind.

"And do you believe everything that Jimmy says?" Mitsu asked softly, spreading the skirt of her own wool coat over Emily's cold legs.

Emily hesitated, then shrugged her shoulders slightly.

Mitsu knew what that gesture meant. The afore-mentioned Jimmy was at least two years older than Emily, and the little girl saw him as a much wiser person. From Emily's perspective, it would never do to disagree with her best friend.

"Emily."

The child looked up reluctantly.

"Lift your hand," Mitsu commanded.

Frowning, the little girl slowly did as she was asked.

"Do you feel the wind?" Mitsu asked her.

Emily nodded, her face scrunched in bewilderment. "Yes."

"Do you see it?"

Emily glanced across the compound at the United States flag blowing in the breeze. Sage bushes lightly bent their sturdy branches in the stiff wind.

"Yes, I can see it."

Mitsu smiled, hugging the child closer. Her gaze followed the same path as Emily's.

"Do you really see the wind, Emily? You see the flag moving, and the bushes, but do you really see the wind?"

Emily lifted her hand again, feeling the breeze blow against her outstretched fingers. Her forehead puckered.

"I *feel* it," she argued.

Mitsu laughed lightly. "How can you feel something that you cannot see? Surely it is a figment of your imagination."

Emily's almond eyes grew large. "A *what?*"

Mitsu tapped the child's forehead lightly. "It is all in your mind. Up here."

The little girl's face darkened. "It is not! I can feel it!"

"And I can feel Jesus," Mitsu told her, pointing to her own chest. "Right here, in my heart. I can't *see* Him, but I can feel Him."

Emily paused for a long moment. She glanced at the azure blue sky overhead, then returned her look to Mitsu.

"Do you feel Santa Claus too?"

Mitsu leaned back, her eyes avoiding the child's intense look. She felt thoroughly trapped. There had been so much disillusionment in Emily's life already, she couldn't bear to add to it. But although she didn't want to destroy the little girl's fantasies, she couldn't bring herself to lie, either.

Mitsu spread her flowing pink skirt around her, pleating and unpleating the fabric with nervous fingers. She couldn't bring herself to look at Emily.

"I think maybe I am too old," she finally told her.

Emily's face grew solemn. "Will you get too old to believe in Jesus?"

Mitsu grinned. "I will *never* get that old," she laughed.

Emily glanced away, and Mitsu saw that the child had noticed a car entering the barbed wire gate beside them. Someone within the cab was looking at them, his almond eyes dark and mysterious. He took a pair of sunglasses from a container and placed them on his face. Only for a moment was he there, then the car flashed by. Emily looked back up at Mitsu with resolve, returning to their conversation.

"I think maybe Jimmy is too old too." She sighed heavily, getting to her feet. Her sad face was slightly above Mitsu's reclining figure. "I suppose one day I will be too old too."

Mitsu's lips twitched. Since Emily's mother, Mayumi, was American born and bred, she had passed on to Emily many of the American philosophies and customs that she had grown up with. Christmas was one of them, though Mayumi was also a Christian and had taught her daughter the true meaning of the holiday.

"I'm going to go find Jimmy," Emily stated firmly, interrupting Mitsu's thoughts.

Mitsu had no idea what the impetuous child might

say to her hero, but from the firm set of her chin, it didn't bode well for Jimmy's persistence in trying to demolish Emily's beliefs.

"I'll see you later," Mitsu said.

Emily took three steps, then stopped and ran back to Mitsu. She threw her arms around her neck, almost strangling Mitsu with her hug.

"I love you, Mitsu," she whispered.

Mitsu felt a lump form in her throat. Returning the hug, she slowly put the child away from her.

"I love you too, Emily."

In a flash, the little girl was off and running. Her thoughts far away, Mitsu watched after Emily long after the child had disappeared from sight. Mitsu found herself faced with the same struggles that Emily faced daily. For Emily, though, there was an ally. Her mother, and her grandmother before that, were both Christians. Even Emily's father had been a Christian. When he had been killed in a battle in Europe, Mayumi's faith hadn't wavered. Mitsu had been awed by Emily's mother's strength at such a time.

For Mitsu, however, there was a daily battle with her parents. It was a wonder that they hadn't thrown her out a few months ago when she had professed her belief in Christianity. Still, she was an only child, born late to her parents. They had doted on her for years, and it hurt her more than a little to cause them such grief now. She couldn't for the life of her see why her parents didn't embrace the Christian faith. Probably it had more to do with tradition than anything else. They were firmly Japanese: *Issei*, first-generation Japanese who had immigrated from Japan. She, on the other hand, was *Nissei*, a second-generation Japanese born in the United States.

She heard someone approaching through the crunching sand and lifted her face to the intruder. Briefly blinded by the bright Arizona sun, she raised a hand to shade her eyes.

Her gaze traveled upward over black shoes, black jeans, a black turtleneck, and on to a face topped by straight, black hair. The young man who stood before her was unusually tall, and his powerful shoulder muscles bunched when he removed the dark sunglasses covering his eyes. She recognized him as the person she'd noticed driving by earlier.

"They told me in the administration house that you were Mitsu Yakamura."

Surprised, Mitsu nodded. She stared at the stranger for some time before she realized what she was doing. Embarrassed, she quickly got to her feet, brushing the clinging sand from her skirt.

"Hai," she agreed, the affirmative Japanese word sounding more like a whisper. She cleared her throat. "I am Mitsu Yakamura."

The stranger held out a large hand, and Mitsu hesitantly placed her own hand within it. His fingers engulfed hers in a brief handshake.

"My name is Kenshin Takano."

Mitsu jerked her head up in surprise and felt her stomach twist. This then was the brother of the man she was engaged to. Though she had never met him, she had heard much about him from both her parents and the brief notes she had received from her absent fiancé.

Her heart began thundering in her chest. Surely Shiro hadn't decided to move the marriage ceremony forward. Having met the young man only once at their betrothal ceremony, she had foolishly believed that she could pretend the engagement had never really happened. Seeing Kenshin brought back all kinds of frightful possibilities.

Dark almond eyes studied her face, then drifted slowly over her small form. She pressed her too full lips tightly together, knowing that he must find her rather dull to look at.

"I was hoping to speak with both you and your parents," he told her, his deep voice triggering butterflies in her stomach.

Mitsu bit her bottom lip apprehensively. She had a sudden wild idea to lie to this overpowering man and tell him that her parents had changed their mind about her marriage. Knowing that such action would accomplish nothing since the truth was bound to come out, not to mention that she couldn't betray her Lord in such a way, Mitsu sighed heavily and motioned with her hand.

"This way. They are in the barracks."

Kenshin walked at her side, matching his usually long strides to her smaller ones. He glanced at her silent figure periodically. Eventually he broke the silence.

"This camp is a lot different from ours."

Mitsu peeped up at him, then quickly lowered her lashes. "You are from Topaz in Utah?"

He nodded, one dark eyebrow raised. He must wonder at her lack of interest in his brother's affairs. Still, she had no desire to know anything at all about Shiro or his family. She had agreed to this arranged marriage partly because she was used to being a dutiful daughter and partly because she didn't really believe it would happen.

Not in this day and time and certainly not in the United States of America.

"It was already snowing at Topaz," he told her conversationally.

Mitsu looked around her at the cold bare desert. Though the nights had grown progressively colder, the days were still fairly warm for November. Topaz must be very different from Butte Camp.

She didn't bother to answer his statement, her mind wholly occupied on trying to decipher the reason for his journey. The closer she came to her barracks, the more agitated she became. Suddenly she stopped, placing a detaining hand on his arm. She felt his muscles tense beneath her slight touch.

"Look," she said, swallowing hard. "Could you tell me why you are here?"

He looked down at her, his brown eyes gleaming. "I will tell you at the same time that I tell your parents."

"If it's about the wedding—"

"I would prefer to speak with your parents at the same time that I speak with you."

His chin jutted out inflexibly, and Mitsu knew she would get no further response from him. Angrily she stormed ahead.

Kenshin watched Mitsu's retreating figure, her angrily swaying hips a sure indication that she was upset. A small smile tilted the corner of his mouth. He was unused to hot-headed women, and he wondered if his brother had had any idea what Mitsu was really like.

A familiar pang of loss ripped through him. His hand closed over the sheet of paper in his pocket, a suffocating lump coming to his throat.

The words of the letter still filled his mind:

Dear Kenshin,

This is probably the hardest letter I have ever had to write. I love you and Mama-san and Papa-san. I want you to know that. I never wanted to hurt any of you. But the time has come for me to tell you something that will, in all probability, bring shame to all of us.

I met a woman at the USO almost a year ago. I have seen her from time to time, and we have grown to love each other very much. I tried not to, but I couldn't help myself. I find that I can't live without her. She is white, and her name is Elisa. When I get back from my assignment, we intend to marry here in France.

I can't break the news to Papa-san and Mama-san, so like the coward I am, I am leaving that to you. I will send a letter to Mitsu breaking our engagement. I know Papa-san and Mitsu's father had an agreement, but I can no longer go along with their plans. Please don't hate me.

Love, your brother,
Shiro

Hate. That was a strong word, and one which hardly applied to Kenshin's feelings. He loved his brother, in spite of his failings. Now he was faced with a dilemma. Two days before he had received the letter, his parents had received a telegram from the War Department telling them that Shiro had been killed in action some-where in Europe. The particulars were still confidential, but the message was not. His brother was dead.

His father had made plans to come and inform Mr. Yakamura of his youngest son's death, but the letter that Kenshin had received had forced Kenshin to con-vince his father to let him go in his stead. Kenshin still hadn't told his parents about the letter. At first, he thought he would never have to, but his brother had said that he was writing Mitsu. If that were the case, then something would have to be done. He knew his father. Honor was honor, and Shiro's act would bring disgrace to them all if Mr. Yakamura ever found out what his future son-in-law had done.

Kenshin's reflections were brought to an abrupt end when Mitsu stopped in front of one of the barracks. Though it was an exact replica of the others that stretched out for as far as the eye could see, it still had differences that reflected the uniqueness of those who lived within.

Purple, red, and white petunias bordered the door-way, giving a burst of color to the otherwise drab exterior. The color stood out starkly against the dark, tar-paper walls.

All around the compound individuals had placed their mark on the surrounding landscape. Desert sage had been planted and carefully tended. Small trees struggled against the hostile environment.

Mitsu opened the door, peeking her head inside. She rattled off something in Japanese that Kenshin could not hear through the barricading portal. Standing back from the door, Mitsu motioned him inside.

Kenshin took the door from her, opening it wider so that she could precede him. She swept by him, and for a brief instant, he felt his pulse accelerate at her nearness. Frowning, he followed her into the small cubicle.

Mr. and Mrs. Yakamura were seated at a small wooden table. Apparently the occupants of Butte Camp had made use of the scrap lumber to be found in the area, as at Topaz.

The elderly people got quickly to their feet, bowing low before Kenshin. He returned their bow with marked formality.

"*Hajimemashite,*" he said quietly.

They returned the greeting with equal formality. Mrs. Yakamura motioned for Kenshin to take a seat while she prepared tea.

Kenshin seated himself across from Mr. Yakamura. The older man's quizzical eyes peered at him over the rims of his glasses. His gray hair was pushed back from his forehead, giving him an elfin look.

"It is an honor to meet you, Kenshin-san."

Embarrassed, Kenshin didn't quite know what to say. When he had first suggested the trip to visit with the Yakamuras, he hadn't expected Mitsu's open hostility. Though she tried to hide it, it was quite evident that she had no feelings for his brother.

"And you, Yakamura-san."

Mrs. Yakamura set a cup of tea before him, giving him a shy smile. The color of her hair perfectly matched her husband's, but whereas her husband's eyes were a solemn brown, Mrs. Yakamura's bird-like eyes were alive with humor. She reminded him of his own mother. He returned her smile with a reassuring one of his own.

When Kenshin looked across at Mitsu, he found her watching him with unnerving intensity. He turned back to Mr. Yakamura.

"I have come with news of my brother," he told them without preamble. They stared at him expectantly. Swallowing hard, he pulled the telegram from his pocket and handed it to Mr. Yakamura.

The old man read the note quietly. When he lifted his eyes to Kenshin, they were full of sympathy.

"I am sorry, Kenshin-san."

He glanced at his wife and Mitsu, then read the telegram aloud. As the words resounded through the still room, Mitsu slowly sank to a chair.

She lifted troubled eyes to Kenshin. There was sadness in her eyes, but the relief couldn't be disguised either. Kenshin's eyes narrowed.

"I received a letter from my brother just two days after the telegram. He said that he planned on writing Mitsu a letter." His looked again at Mitsu. "I wondered if you had perhaps received it."

Mitsu exchanged looks with her father. She shrugged her shoulders and shook her head no.

Relief surged through Kenshin. It was possible Shiro had never completed his letter before he was killed. Then again, the letter might have been lost if it hadn't arrived after all this time. The likelihood of hiding his brother's dishonor was much greater than he had at first imagined.

He looked at each member of the Yakamura family in turn. Taking a deep breath, he told them, "I have come to offer myself in my brother's stead as a husband for Mitsu."

Chapter 2

Mitsu stared in horror at Kenshin, who steadfastly avoided her gaze. She opened her mouth to protest, but at her mother's fierce glare, she settled into morose silence.

"That is a very honorable thing for you to do, Kenshin-san," her father said, then turned to look at her. She couldn't read what was in his face, but she noticed his slight hesitation. He looked back to Kenshin.

"Your offer is acceptable to us, if it is acceptable to Mitsu."

Three pairs of almond eyes focused on Mitsu huddling in her chair. She wished heartily that the ground would open and swallow her whole, her embarrassment was so great. Besides that, Kenshin's intense look was doing funny things to her insides.

"I. . .I. . ."

What could she say? If she said no, her parents would lose face with Kenshin's family. She had no idea what the debt was that her father owed to the Takano family, but it was a longstanding one. Her Issei parents were totally Japanese in their beliefs on such things. She had always tried to be dutiful, but this was something else entirely.

"Mitsu?" her mother prompted.

Mitsu forced herself to look at Kenshin. "May I think about it?"

Kenshin's knowing look made her want to disappear. She felt her cheeks grow hot.

Kenshin nodded. *"Hai.* I will be staying here for another three days. Would you have your decision by then?"

Three days! Mitsu swallowed the huge lump in her throat. She nodded her agreement, and Kenshin rose to his feet.

"Then if you will excuse me, I will return to the single men's barracks." He held out his hand to Mitsu. "Perhaps you would walk with me."

Mitsu's stomach felt as though she had suddenly gone down a steep hill. She reluctantly got to her feet in response to a stern nod from her father.

Taking a deep breath, she followed Kenshin out the door. He adjusted his steps to her smaller ones.

His voice filled with curiosity, he asked, "You would prefer not to honor our parents' commitment?"

She cut him a scathing glance. "This is hardly feudal Japan."

His face seemed suddenly carved in granite. "Honor is honor, no matter the time or place."

Mitsu gave an exasperated sigh. "The whole world is at war. What is there to honor?" she asked sarcastically.

He glanced at her wryly. "All the more reason for those of us with rationality to adhere to the ways we know best."

Mitsu stopped, forcing Kenshin to pause with

her. She placed her hands on her hips, glaring at him defiantly.

"Do you even know the reason behind our parents' bargain?"

"*Hai.*"

Mitsu slowly slid her hands from her waist to her sides. Her eyes opened wide. "You do?"

Kenshin frowned at her. "*Hai.* Don't you?"

Mitsu shook her head slowly, wrestling with a jumble of emotions. "No. My parents have refused to tell me."

Kenshin took a deep breath and let it out slowly. "I see. That explains much." He turned and started walking.

"Wait!" Mitsu hurried after him. Grabbing him by the arm, she pulled him to a stop. She studied his face hopefully. "Tell me about it."

He opened his mouth slightly, his dark eyes giving her a thorough inspection. Closing his lips tightly, he shook his head. "It is not for me to tell. You should ask your parents."

Frustrated, she unthinkingly placed both hands on his forearms, her eyes beseeching. "They will not tell me. Please. . .I would like to know."

His glance went from where her hands rested on his arms, back to her face. Something flickered briefly in his dark eyes but disappeared before Mitsu could put a name to it.

"I don't know," he said, his voice full of doubt.

"Please."

His eyes met hers once again, and Mitsu felt the force of his look all the way to her toes.

"We can't talk here," he told her, searching the compound for some place suitable to talk.

"We can go to the mess hall. There won't be many people there at this time of day."

He agreed, and Mitsu practically held her breath the whole way, certain that he would change his mind about telling her. For years, she had tried to find the reason behind her parents' agreement with Mr. Takano, but they had steadfastly refused to tell her. Her questions came from more than idle curiosity; she wanted to understand how her parents could force a loveless marriage on their only child when they had lived in the United States for so long. Surely the traditions of their past should have been modified during that time.

The long, dark mess hall echoed with the sounds of clanging dishes. Few people milled about, because the evening meal was still some time away. Mitsu took a seat on one of the benches beside the picnic-style tables. Kenshin seated himself across from her. Already she could see his hesitation to divulge what he knew.

"Surely your parents had a reason for not telling you."

She gave him a scorching look. "I'm a girl. That's reason enough."

He took his time studying her petite form. Her face grew warm under his scrutiny.

"You are that," he told her quietly.

Mitsu stiffened her shoulders and made no response, waiting for him to reveal the secret she so longed to know.

"Very well, but it's not a happy story."

Mitsu frowned. It had never occurred to her that there might be a tragedy involved in her parents' decision. She had always thought that it had to do with

Japanese tradition. She held her breath, waiting for Kenshin to continue. He stared off in the distance and began to speak.

"A long time ago, in Japan," he said, his voice taking on a fairy tale-like quality, "your father worked for a man who sold produce."

"I know that," she interrupted, wanting him to get to the point of the marriage. He fixed her with a steely eye, and she subsided back into her seat. *Fine, let him do it his way.* She tried to curb her impatience.

"Every day, your father drove an oxen cart to my father's house to deliver produce. I was only two at the time." He stopped.

Mitsu fixed her eyes steadily on his face.

Taking a deep breath, he continued. "I had an older sister. She was three then."

The din from the kitchen increased steadily, but Mitsu had no trouble hearing Kenshin's low voice. She noted the past tense of the verb he used, and suddenly her heart started to thump erratically. Her eyes widened, yet she refrained from speech, willing him to continue. He did.

"One day, my sister was playing in the yard when your father made his delivery." His voice grew eerily quiet. "He didn't see her until it was too late."

Color drained from Mitsu's face, and she leaned heavily against the bench. "My father killed your sister?" Her hoarse voice echoed strangely in the vast chamber around them, combining with the noise of the workers preparing for the evening meal.

Kenshin shrugged. "It was an accident. No one blamed your father, but he blamed himself. In his guilt he made a pledge to my father to replace his daughter with one of his own."

Mitsu was appalled. So, she was a guilt offering, someone to relieve her father of the burden for his past offense. She stared into Kenshin's eyes, unable to speak her indignant thoughts for fear he would think her totally without feelings or the honor he seemed to hold in such high esteem.

Kenshin's eyes met hers. "At first my father wouldn't accept the offer, but after my brother was born, he found out that my mother could not have any more children. My mother was devastated. She loved my sister and missed having a daughter." He smiled slightly. "She would love you."

Mitsu rose slowly to her feet. She shook her head slightly. "I don't think so. You see, Kenshin, I have lately accepted Jesus Christ as my Savior, and I serve the true God of heaven. I don't believe in Buddha."

Kenshin studied her from where he sat. She grew flustered under his prolonged stare. Finally he got up and stood beside her. When she searched his eyes, she found them unfathomable.

"While I agree that your beliefs will affect my mother's opinion, it will not influence my own. Frankly, I don't care who you believe in, because I don't believe in anything myself."

Mitsu felt her face harden. "And that's exactly why I can't marry you. It would be wrong to marry an unbeliever."

A brief flicker of anger passed through his eyes. "Haven't I heard somewhere that children in the Lord should obey their parents?"

Mitsu flushed with guilt. Many years of training were hard to forego overnight.

"You heard wrong. The Bible says for children to obey their parents *in the Lord*. My parents are not in the Lord."

He crossed his arms over his chest, giving her a hard stare. "So that nullifies your duty to your parents?"

Mitsu bit her lip anxiously. She had been wrestling with this very issue for the past several months, ever since accepting Christ for her own. She stared at Kenshin helplessly, and suddenly he relented.

"Never mind. Just think about it. As I said, I will be staying here for three days, so you can let me know what you decide before I leave."

Mitsu swallowed hard. "You mean you are actually willing to go through with this arrangement?"

He nodded briefly, and something suddenly occurred to Mitsu.

"Why was Shiro chosen first instead of you?"

He shrugged. "My father needed me to care for our farm in California."

Mitsu placed her hands on her hips, suddenly suspicious. "And he doesn't need you now?" she asked sarcastically.

The look on Kenshin's face caused Mitsu to take a hasty step back.

"There is no more farm."

Instantly Mitsu regretted that she hadn't thought before speaking. Like almost all Japanese in America, the Takanos had lost most of their possessions when they had been forced to relocate by the government during the spring of 1942.

"I'm sorry," she murmured, feeling her words were inadequate.

Again, he shrugged. His dark eyes scanned her face, stopping briefly on her lips. When his eyes met hers again, something shimmered in their depths that she didn't understand.

"Will you consider my proposal?"

Mitsu had no intention of agreeing to his suggestion, but she thought now was hardly the time to say so. For both his sake, and her parents', she would bide her time.

"I'll think about it."

He relaxed. "That's all I ask."

Later that day, Mitsu sat down in the wooden chair across from her friend Mayumi. She noticed her friend's pale, tired face.

"What's wrong, Mayumi?"

The other woman wrinkled her nose becomingly, her beautiful face contorted slightly. She lightly rubbed her swollen stomach, pulling her sweater closer. Even with the small potbellied stove working, the room was cold. Frigid air blew in between the cracks of the barrack's walls. The hastily erected structures had been built with green wood, and when it dried it had left cracks everywhere: floor, ceiling, walls. After more than two years of living at Butte Camp, it still amazed Mitsu that a desert could be so cold.

Mayumi shifted on her hard chair, smiling slightly. "This child has been harder than Emily. For some reason, I can't seem to find any energy."

Mitsu grinned. "It must be a boy, then."

Mayumi smiled in return. "Must be. Probably he'll be like his father." Instantly, all humor fled the woman's face. Sudden tears sprang to her eyes. She brushed them away in embarrassment. "I'm sorry. I would give anything to hear John again, even if it was in argument."

Mitsu reached across the small table and gripped her friend's hand. She could never understand why John Ishiyama had volunteered to serve in the U.S. Army when he and his family had been locked up in an internment camp without so much as a trial to determine if they were guilty of any crime. The government had superceded the Constitution and given no redress to its Japanese citizens. All in the name of security. She knew that John and other men like him believed that joining the army would prove their loyalty, but it was a decision she could never have made.

"It must be hard for you, Mayumi. If there is anything I can do, you know I'm here."

Mayumi squeezed Mitsu's hand, then let go. "I know, Mitsu. I thank God that He sent you to me just when I needed someone."

Mitsu smiled without mirth. "It was the other way around. God sent you to me to teach me about His Son. I am the one who will be eternally grateful."

And that was the truth. It had been through little Emily that Mitsu had first encountered Mayumi. Mitsu had been drawn to the child's bright face from the moment she had first seen her playing in the compound. The same brightness filled Mayumi's face, and even through such excruciating grief as the loss of her husband, her faith in God had held strong. It was that, most of all, that had drawn Mitsu to her friend.

"How about if I take Emily with me tonight and let you get some rest," Mitsu suggested.

A sudden crash from the cubicle next door startled both of them. Mayumi shrugged wryly. "It's not little Emily that keeps me from rest."

Mitsu smiled sympathetically. These small rooms with their paper-thin walls did nothing for privacy.

Mr. and Mrs. Goto, who shared the small room with Mayumi and Emily, entered the small compartment. Mitsu rose to go, patting Mayumi's shoulder.

"Don't get up," she told her friend. "I'll see myself out, but you let me know if there's anything I can do for you."

"I will."

When she reached the door, Mitsu bowed deferentially to the Gotos. They returned her bow, their dark eyes shining with disapproval. Both of the Gotos were devout Buddhists, and they were thoroughly displeased with both Mayumi and Mitsu.

As she closed the door behind her, Mitsu felt a sudden sense of dread. Shaking off the feeling, she hurried home out of the November cold.

Chapter 3

Mitsu was playing ball with Emily when Kenshin joined them. He smiled at the little girl, and she readily grinned back. Emily never met a stranger, which was sometimes very disconcerting. She tucked the ball under her small arm and strolled over to where Kenshin stood leaning against the barrack wall. The chill wind ruffled her black bangs, and her long, dark braids bounced merrily behind her. She came to a stop, giving Kenshin one of her most congenial smiles.

"Hi! My name is Emily."

Kenshin dropped to his jean-clad knees so that he might be more on the child's level. His brown almond eyes gleamed with amusement.

"Hello. My name is Kenshin."

Having received a favorable response, Emily's smile grew. "Are you new here?"

Kenshin glanced at Mitsu and noted her sudden embarrassment. One dark eyebrow shot upward.

"I am here to see Mitsu and her parents."

Emily's mouth rounded into an O. She turned her look upon Mitsu. "You know each other?"

Mitsu wanted to deny the fact but thought better of it. *"Hai,* we know each other."

Emily turned back to Kenshin. "Do you like to play ball?"

Kenshin placed one elbow on his bent knee and stroked his chin thoughtfully with his hand. He pushed back his sheepskin jacket, shoving one hand into his jeans pocket. "Well now, that depends."

Without hesitation, Emily leaned her little body against his shoulder. "On what?"

Kenshin placed an arm loosely around her back. "Why, on what you're playing of course. I'm not very good at football."

Mitsu's gaze moved over his lithe form, and she seriously doubted his words. She smiled at Emily's giggle.

"Silly! This isn't a football."

Though Kenshin's face was serious, his eyes sparkled with mischief. "No? But I saw you kicking it with your foot."

Emily giggled again. "But it's not a football. It's a kickball."

"Ohh!"

Kenshin glanced again at Mitsu, bringing her into their conversation. "So when you throw it, does it become a throwball?"

Emily burst into peals of laughter. She finally comprehended that Kenshin was joking with her. She threw a small arm around his neck, grinning into his face.

"You're silly!"

Kenshin chucked her under her chin. "And you're cute."

Mitsu felt a warm glow at the exchange between Kenshin and the child. He wasn't merely pretending to like Emily; it was obvious that he truly enjoyed spending time with children.

Emily looked up at Mitsu seriously. "He's very good looking, Mitsu. You should marry him."

Mitsu squeezed her eyes shut, wishing that she could suddenly disappear. When she opened them again, she found Kenshin grinning. She opened her mouth to rebuke the little girl, but Kenshin interrupted her.

"I agree, Emily."

Mitsu felt her anger rise. Her voice was harsher than she intended when she spoke to the child.

"Emily, take your ball and go see if you can find someone to play with."

The atmosphere became suddenly tense. The smile slid slowly from Emily's face. She glanced at Mitsu uncertainly.

"Mitsu?"

Trying to control her temper, she steadied her voice, but the tone was filled with annoyance. "Go, Emily! I will see you later."

Emily retreated from them slowly, her look going from one to the other. Only when Kenshin gave her a brief wink did she finally turn and hurry away. The look he fixed on Mitsu wasn't friendly at all.

"She's only a child," he rebuked Mitsu.

Feeling guilty, Mitsu nonetheless snapped back at him. "But you're not. You shouldn't fill a child's head with such nonsense." Perhaps the fact that she had been so instantly attracted to this handsome stranger had something to do with her irritation. No man had ever given her more than a glance, and now here was Kenshin suggesting marriage. For the sake of honor, no less.

Pulling her blue wool coat tightly about her, she turned and quickly walked away. She passed the washhouse, noticing that the line of people waiting outside to do their laundry wasn't nearly as long as usual. Probably the dropping temperatures had something to do with it.

When she turned, she found Kenshin right beside her. Startled, she jumped back.

"You scared me half to death," she reprimanded, her heart thumping wildly in her chest. "I didn't even hear you!"

His smile didn't quite reach his eyes. "I was wondering if we could talk."

Mitsu sighed. "About the marriage?"

He nodded. *"Hai,* about the marriage."

"Look, Kenshin—"

"You never had any intention of marrying either my brother or me, did you?"

Though his face was devoid of emotion, Mitsu sensed his tightly controlled anger. She moved one hand deprecatingly, uncertain what to say. Looking into his eyes, she knew she owed him the truth.

"No," she finally agreed. "I didn't."

His nostrils flared, and his eyes darkened to obsidian. "And what of our parents?"

Mitsu's anger matched his. "What about them? This is *our* lives we're talking about, not theirs. People should marry for love."

"Love," he snorted.

"Yes, love," she returned angrily, not able to look him in the eye. He suddenly reached out and took her by the chin, forcing her to meet his gaze.

"There are other reasons just as sound for a couple

to marry. Probably better ones," he told her softly.

She pulled her chin from his hold, disturbed by her reaction to his touch. "Such as?"

He folded his arms across his chest in that forbidding way of his. "Honor, for one."

Mitsu angrily blew out a breath. "Honor!"

"Yes, honor."

"And just what am I supposed to honor?" she asked quietly, her voice edged with sarcasm.

"Did you agree to marry my brother?" Kenshin asked.

Glaring at him, Mitsu snapped, "This conversation is pointless." She would have walked away, but he took her by the arm, his hold gentle but unyielding.

"Answer me."

She fixed an icy look on his offending fingers. Seemingly undaunted, he exchanged glare for glare, and Mitsu knew that she would have to answer him.

"Yes," she hissed. "I agreed to marry your brother. But I *did not* agree to marry you."

The look he gave told Mitsu that she had succeeded in frustrating her adversary.

"You said you would think about it," he ground out savagely.

"And I did. I won't marry you."

Kenshin released her. "And what of your parents? Have you no concern for their feelings?"

Much of Mitsu's anger drained away. In fact, she *did* care about her parents' feelings. She knew that they would in all probability be disgraced by her rejection of their pledge, but she simply couldn't tie herself to a man for life just to fulfill a thirty-year-old contract. Could she? The old feelings of guilt surfaced, and she tried to push them away. They refused to be budged.

Mitsu stared up at Kenshin. Something about the man attracted her. She would be lying if she tried to deny it. Still, what they were all proposing for her was wrong. It had to be.

"I can't," she told him quietly.

Kenshin took a deep breath, his look never wavering. "So be it," he finally told her, taking a step back. "I will be here another two days if you should change your mind."

Mitsu watched him walk away, his anger evident by his set shoulders and rigid back. For an insane moment she was tempted to call him back, but she quickly quashed the thought.

She decided to visit Mr. Kim, her minister, and see what he had to say about all this. Maybe he could make things clear to her confused mind. She found him digging dead flowers from the bed beside his barrack's door. He glanced up at her in surprise, his face lighting with a smile. Getting quickly to his feet, he brushed the dirt from his hands, pushing his dark hair from his eyes.

"Mitsu! Welcome."

Mitsu was suddenly full of misgivings. Mr. Kim was young, a Nisei who had lived in this country all his life. Would he understand her dilemma?

"Mr. Kim, may I speak with you?"

Recognizing the seriousness in her voice, the smile suddenly left his face. "Of course, Mitsu. Come in and I will have my wife fix us a cup of tea."

He opened his door and motioned for Mitsu to precede him inside.

Though the room's temperature was cold like the others of this compound, Mitsu still felt surrounded by a warm atmosphere. Love reigned in this home. Mrs. Kim had used her sewing abilities to add touches of color to the small room, and the drab interior took on a warm glow from the pink shade covering the hanging bulb. The woman had used everything at her disposal to turn this prison into a loving home.

Ann Kim met her with a ready smile, taking Mitsu's coat and pulling out a chair for her at the small table that they used for their visitors. Though Ann was Caucasian, she loved her Japanese husband with a fierceness that Mitsu envied.

Mitsu slid into the chair, suddenly unsure of herself. Ann busied herself at the back of the room while her husband took off his coat, seating himself across from Mitsu. He studied her face, waiting for his wife to place the teapot before them. He smiled at her with affection when she did so, then focused his full attention on Mitsu.

"Something is bothering you, Mitsu?"

Mitsu's cheeks colored hotly. She slowly related her dilemma to the minister, her eyes fixed on his face, seeking any hint of censure. He remained silent until she had finished her story.

Lifting his cup, he blew softly to cool the tea within, appearing to reflect on what she had just told him. He finally looked at her. "That is truly a dilemma, Mitsu, and one I am not certain that there is an answer for."

Disappointment flooded through Mitsu. She leaned back in her chair and regarded him with unhappy eyes. "Is there nothing you can tell me that will help me make this decision?"

Mr. Kim folded his arms on the table in front of him, leaning forward to fix her with a steady gaze.

"You want to honor your parents, but you also want

to honor your Lord. If you honor your Lord, then you dishonor your parents. If you honor your parents, then you dishonor your Lord. Is that about the size of it?"

Mitsu nodded, relieved that he seemed to understand. He fingered his chin, then frowned at her.

"Mitsu, did you agree to marry Shiro before, or after, you became a Christian?"

"Before. I would never have done so now."

He settled his cup back in its saucer, frowning. "The Scriptures say much about keeping vows, Mitsu. There is some debate about whether we do so *before* or *after* we accept Christ. All I know is that the Scriptures say that if we make a vow, we should do all in our power to fulfill it."

Mitsu had thought this all out in her mind. As she had told Kenshin, she had agreed to marry his brother, not Kenshin himself. She told the minister so now.

"I see. Well that *would* make a difference, of course. So you actually agreed to marry Shiro himself, not Mr. Takano's son."

Mitsu set her cup slowly back into its saucer with suddenly shaking fingers. Had she agreed to marry Shiro, or had she said she would marry Mr. Takano's son? Mr. Kim saw the uncertainty in her eyes. He sighed softly.

"I have to tell you, Mitsu, that my own Japanese upbringing causes me to think differently about certain things. There is one Scripture passage you might consider when making your decision." He got up, retrieving his Bible from the cabinet beside him. "In Romans, chapter fourteen, Paul talks about causing a brother to sin. He ends in verses twenty-two and twenty-three by saying: 'Hast thou faith? have it to thyself before God. Happy is he that condemneth not himself in that thing which he alloweth. And he that doubteth is damned if he eat, because he eateth not of faith: for whatsoever is not of faith is sin.' " He looked up at Mitsu, who struggled to comprehend Paul's words.

"Here the Bible speaks of foods that were offered to idols then eaten by believers, but the point is the same: Whatever isn't done with faith is sin. You have to have faith that what you are doing is true and right."

"But how can I be sure?" Mitsu whispered.

Mr. Kim returned to the seat across from her, and reaching across the table, he squeezed her fingers gently. "Pray that God will make it clear to you. Ask for the wisdom you need."

Mitsu got to her feet, more dejected than ever. Mr. Kim smiled with understanding. He rose to his feet and took her by the shoulders, his eyes meeting hers with full assurance. "I will pray for you."

"As will I," Ann interjected softly.

Mitsu turned to find the minister's wife watching them sympathetically. She thanked her, then hugged her before leaving the apartment.

Her feet dragged as she contemplated returning to her own barracks. If anything, the minister had only added to her feelings of guilt.

Whatever isn't done with faith is sin.

Sighing, Mitsu began to pray as the minister had suggested. She remembered the Scripture that said that anyone who needed wisdom should ask of God. Well she certainly needed wisdom now. Lifting her face to the cold, blue sky, she stormed the ramparts of heaven with her silent cries.

Chapter 4

Mitsu sat at the small table in their barrack apartment, waiting for her parents to return from dinner. She herself decidedly lacked any appetite, so she'd refrained from going to the mess hall.

She pushed around the delicate china cup sitting before her, a gift from some white friends who had been kind enough to visit them here at the camp. The tea, long since grown cold, sloshed over the sides, spilling into the matching saucer.

Scuffling steps outside the door let Mitsu know that her parents had returned. She watched them take off their coats, warming their hands by the small pot-bellied stove that the government had provided for heat. Her father's bent frame caused her a sudden pang of alarm. He wasn't getting any younger, and suddenly, she was hesitant to speak her thoughts aloud. Still, she had better do so now before Kenshin had a chance to tell them of her decision.

"Mama-san, Papa-san, I wish to speak with you."

Her father frowned, and realizing that her voice had sounded arrogant, Mitsu hastily contrived to fix her features into a more submissive frame. She bowed her head slightly, awaiting her father's reply.

When she heard the scraping of the other two chairs, she looked up. Both parents were seated, watching her expectantly. Mitsu cleared her throat, swallowing twice before she could finally speak.

"I. . .I wanted you to know that I cannot marry Kenshin Takano." At her father's sudden frown, she hastily added a qualifying statement. "At least not yet."

Mr. Yakamura wearily rubbed a gnarled hand against his forehead. "What are you saying, Mitsu?"

What *was* she saying? When it came right down to it, she just couldn't let her parents down. She lowered her eyes.

"I'm. . .I'm saying that I *will* marry him, but not right now."

If that didn't sound a bit wishy-washy, she didn't know what did! Seeing her father's shoulders slump with relief, she felt the old feelings of guilt flood through her.

Her mother smiled. "That is good, Mitsu-chan. We can tell Kenshin when he comes this evening."

Mitsu jerked her face up in surprise. "Kenshin is coming here? But I thought. . ." Her voice trailed away to silence. She had hoped that Kenshin had already left to return to Camp Topaz in Utah. She should have known that he would stop by to say good-bye. Sudden butterflies filled her stomach. She just couldn't bring herself to face him with such news. She had to get out of there somehow.

Getting to her feet, Mitsu reached for her blue wool coat hanging from a nail on the back of the door.

"Mitsu, where are you going? We told you that Kenshin was coming by this evening."

Mitsu continued shoving her arms into the sleeves of the coat, avoiding her father's gaze. "I. . .I wanted to check on Mayumi. She hasn't been feeling well."

"But Mitsu—"

"I'll be back soon."

She shut the door behind her with finality, turning her face into the brisk November breeze. In just a few weeks it would be Christmas, and what did she have to show for it? She knew without a doubt that her parents would not accept a Christmas gift from her, nor would they allow any display of Christianity in their devout Buddhist household.

She passed the Kims' apartment, noting the wreath hanging on the door. Ann had created it from some of the green broom bushes that grew so prolifically in the surrounding desert. She'd scattered little red bows across its surface then placed one larger bow to flutter from the bottom. Sighing, Mitsu continued on until she reached the barracks where Mayumi lived. Here also, there was no sign of the coming season. Though Mayumi had the right to worship as she pleased, she refrained from forcing Christmas on her Buddhist roommates.

Mitsu knocked on the door and it opened almost instantly. Little Emily peered out at her, her little face pinched with worry. Mitsu frowned.

"Emily? Is everything all right?"

"Mama is sick."

Concerned, Mitsu pushed past the child, searching until she spotted Mayumi lying on her cot. Mr. and Mrs. Goto were not at home. Relieved, Mitsu knelt beside the cot, pushing damp tendrils of hair away from Mayumi's flushed face. Her relief was short-lived.

"Mayumi, you're burning up with fever!"

Mayumi's fever-bright eyes stared at her vacantly. Mitsu got quickly to her feet, glancing down at Emily, who had attached herself to Mitsu's side like a limpet.

"Emily, I'm going for help. You stay here with your mother."

Emily's normally laughing eyes were dull with worry. She nodded glumly, and Mitsu bent to give her a quick hug.

"Now don't you worry. Your mama's going to be all right."

As she rushed through the compound, Mitsu wished that she felt as confident as she had just sounded. She hurried to the hospital, bolting through the end doors of the open barracks used as a hospital facility.

A young nurse looked up from her desk, her almond eyes widening at Mitsu's harried expression.

Mitsu hurried to her side. "Please, I need help. My friend is burning up with fever. She needs to see the doctor."

The nurse looked past her, lifting delicately shaped brows. "Where is she?"

Aggravated, Mitsu frowned. "She's not with me. She's lying on her bed."

"She'll have to come in," the nurse replied calmly, going back to her paperwork.

"She can't! I don't think she can even walk."

Frowning, the nurse stared at Mitsu. "Well, the doctor isn't here right now. You'll have to wait."

"Where is he?"

The nurse would have ignored her, but Mitsu

reached down and snatched the papers from the table, flinging them across the room. The nurse rose angrily to her feet but hesitated when Mitsu glared at her.

"What the dickens is going on here?"

Mitsu whirled to face the older man standing in the doorway. He was looking from one woman to the other, his dark eyes flashing behind his horn-rimmed glasses.

"Nurse Furitani?

Clenching her fists, the woman glared at Mitsu. "Dr. Magai, this woman—"

"This woman needs your help!" Mitsu interrupted.

The doctor entered the room slowly, one eyebrow lifted at the disorderly mess of papers on the floor. Mitsu blushed, realizing how her rash action must look.

"I'm sorry. I'll pick them up." She rushed forward, clutching his sleeve with a firm grip. "But first, my friend Mayumi needs help."

The doctor focused his full attention on Mitsu. Adjusting his glasses, he asked, "Mayumi Ishiyama?"

Mitsu's eyes widened. "Yes."

Dr. Magai began buttoning his coat. "I take it that since she isn't with you, she must be at home."

"*Hai!* She is burning up with fever. I don't think she even knew who I was."

The doctor turned to the nurse. "Get the ambulance truck over to the barracks where Mrs. Ishiyama lives." He grabbed his bag from the desk. "And make it snappy."

Nurse Furitani hastened to obey. The doctor took Mitsu by the arm. "Come with me. I may need you."

They hurried through the gathering dusk. Mitsu

214

glanced around the compound. Soon it would be dark. As if they had heard her thoughts, the outside barracks lights came on, casting their glow on the area.

When the doctor and Mitsu reached Mayumi, they found her exactly as Mitsu had left her. Emily sat by her side, holding her hand. Dr. Magai smiled at the white-faced child. "Hello, Emily. How about if I take a look at your mother?"

Emily moved to the side, still retaining her grip on her mother's hand. Dr. Magai pulled the stethoscope from his bag and began his examination. Mitsu and Emily watched in silence. Finally, Dr. Magai turned to Mitsu, his face grave.

"I need to get her to the hospital. If I had time, I would see if I could get her into Phoenix, but. . ."

He didn't finish the statement. Mitsu opened her mouth to question the prognosis but was interrupted by the ambulance's arrival. The orderlies brought a cot, quickly loading Mayumi onto it.

When they disappeared out the door, Emily suddenly cried out, running to the truck. Mitsu quickly followed her, taking the child into her arms. For the first time that Mitsu could remember, Emily wanted no part of her. She squirmed, fighting to be set free.

"No! Let me go! I want to go with my mama! Let me go!"

Mitsu held on, turning the distraught child to face her. "We will go with her, Emily, but we can't go in the ambulance."

The child fell still, lifting tear-drenched eyes to Mitsu's face. She watched the doctor climb into the back of the truck, then the vehicle roared away.

"May we go now?" she asked, her voice barely a whisper.

Mitsu brushed the tears away with gentle fingers. "Right now. Get your coat."

It took some time to make it back to the hospital. By the time they arrived, Mayumi had already been partitioned off from sight by screens, the only means of creating privacy.

Emily wanted to go to her, but the nurse wouldn't allow it. When the child started to argue, Nurse Furitani turned serious eyes to Mitsu. The message that flashed from one adult to the other was missed by the child. Mitsu shivered, but not with the cold.

She turned Emily to face her. "The doctor needs us to wait, Emily. How about if we sit over here?" She glanced at the nurse for permission and received a nod of approval.

Mitsu seated herself, but instead of taking the chair beside her, Emily crawled onto her lap. They sat for some time, the silence disturbed only by the whispered comments coming from behind the screen.

When the doctor appeared, his blood-covered gown brought a cry of alarm from Emily. The child yanked herself free from Mitsu's hold and rushed toward the screen. Only Nurse Furitani's quick reflexes kept Emily from reaching her goal.

Emily fought frantically and her banshee-like screams filled the almost empty ward. Her tear-ravaged face brought the tears to Mitsu's eyes as both she and the nurse struggled to calm the child.

Nurse Furitani's soothing words finally penetrated the child's hysteria, and Emily slowly calmed down.

The nurse hesitantly released her fierce grip on Emily's shoulders.

"Your mama is alive, Emily. The doctor had to perform surgery, but your mother is alive. You can see her soon."

Mitsu sighed, closing her eyes in relief. Tension drained from her body, leaving her as limp as a noodle.

Just then Dr. Magai knelt before Emily. His stern features demanded attention, and he got it. "Now listen to me, Emily. You may see your mother tomorrow, not tonight. As the nurse said, I had to do surgery, and it's not a pretty sight in there right now. Your mother is fine, and you can see her tomorrow, but not if you put on another display like you did just now. Do I make myself clear?"

Emily regarded him soberly. She finally nodded her head.

"Promise me, Emily," the doctor demanded.

The clock on the wall ticked off several seconds before Emily finally answered. "I promise," she murmured.

The doctor watched her several seconds before he finally nodded his approval. "Fine." He glanced up at Mitsu. "Will you take her with you?"

Mitsu nodded. "Of course."

The doctor got to his feet. He was watching Mitsu but spoke to his nurse. "Nurse Furitani, would you get that information from Emily for me?"

Doctor and nurse exchanged looks of understanding. The nurse smiled at Emily. "Come, Emily. I need you to give me some information."

They walked to the other side of the room, and the doctor turned to Mitsu. "Mrs. Ishiyama lost the baby."

Mitsu's face paled. "How?"

The doctor shrugged. "I'm not certain. The fever perhaps." He turned away, unable to meet Mitsu's eyes. "It was already gone when I got there. That's why I had to do the surgery."

Mitsu felt the room reeling around her. She hoped and prayed that she would awaken soon and find this all just a nightmare. "And Mayumi?"

The doctor's grave look was hardly reassuring. "I don't know."

Their conversation halted when Emily returned. She lifted her pinched white face to Mitsu. "May we come first thing in the morning?" she asked.

Mitsu's heart went out to the child. Her expression softened with love. "Of course we can. As soon as the doctor will allow it."

They both looked at Dr. Magai. He smiled briefly, telling them when visiting hours were, then the two left, both wishing they could stay.

Eerie shadows from the lights fastened to the corners of the barracks buildings reached out to them. For the first time, Mitsu realized just how late it was. She hurried their steps, anxious not to be caught out after curfew.

A lone figure stood in their way, his identity hidden by the night. Mitsu stopped, her heart suddenly pounding in fear. She could feel Emily's hand clutching hers, the child's terror equal to her own. When they refused to move farther, the figure approached them. Mitsu was trying to decide her best course of action when she suddenly recognized Kenshin. She sighed in relief.

"I take it you didn't want to tell me good-bye your-self," Kenshin said, his voice filled with barely controlled anger.

Mitsu's anger rose to match his, the fear and tension of the last several hours combining to take her to unprecedented fury. She jerked Emily forward, just as the child cried out Kenshin's name. Mitsu would have walked past, but he reached out a hand, pulling her to a stop. She tried to pull away, but his hold was relentless.

"I would like an explanation," he told her through gritted teeth.

"Not now, Kenshin," she snapped, her composure beginning to buckle.

"Now," he disagreed.

Suddenly it was too much. Mitsu crumpled against him, burying her face in his chest. She felt Kenshin wrap his arms tightly around her while tears poured from her anguished heart.

Chapter 5

Mitsu awakened to leaden skies and the persistent tapping of rain on the tar paper outside her small window. She rubbed gritty eyes, wondering what had awakened her. An elfin face peered into hers. Emily sat beside her on the bed, bending forward until her long braids touched Mitsu's face.

"You're awake," the child said in relief.

Events of the night rushed back upon Mitsu, and she sat up abruptly. Remembering how she had practically thrown herself into Kenshin's arms, she felt her cheeks grow hot.

"Can we go see my mama now, Mitsu?" Emily's face still held traces of her ordeal from the previous night. Mitsu had held the weeping child until, exhausted, they'd finally fallen asleep together on the small army cot.

Mitsu's mother pushed back the curtain separating their sleeping quarters from the front room. They were fortunate to have the apartment to themselves, small though it was. Before last week, the little ten-by-twenty-foot room had housed another family as well. They had been allowed to leave when the son procured work in the

Tooele Ordinance Depot in Utah. The American government still had to explain how someone considered dangerous enough to be locked up in an internment camp could be allowed to work in a munitions factory, but that was the story in many parts of the country. It seemed the longer the war continued, the more freedoms interned Japanese-Americans were being given.

Mrs. Yakamura glanced from Mitsu's haggard face to Emily's solemn one. She smiled at the little girl. "Emily, Yakamura-san is waiting for you to go with him to get breakfast."

Emily pulled back, leaning against Mitsu's chest. She shook her head vehemently. "No. I don't want to eat. I want to go see my mama."

Mitsu leaned down until her face was even with the child's. "Remember what the doctor said about visiting hours? We cannot go until it's time. So you have time to eat breakfast."

Emily tilted her head, studying Mitsu. "And are you coming too?"

Mitsu met her mother's eyes and realized that her parent was waiting to discuss something with her. Very much afraid that it had to do with Kenshin carrying her home in his arms last night, Mitsu sighed. "No, not right now. I will come later."

She pushed Emily off the cot gently. "Now go with my papa-san, and I will meet you there. Then we can go to your home and get you something pretty to wear when you visit your mama."

Emily smiled broadly, nodding her head in acquiescence. Mitsu watched her father take Emily's hand. After opening a small umbrella, together they exited the little room. Mitsu's mother seated herself on the cot across from Mitsu. She smiled as the sound of Emily's chatter was cut off by the closing of the front door. "She's a beautiful child."

"She is that," Mitsu agreed.

The smile left her mother's face, and she studied Mitsu, who felt warmth rush to her cheeks.

"Kenshin-san told us that he had to leave today. His pass will soon expire," her mother stated.

Mitsu nodded. She didn't know what to say. When Kenshin's arms had wrapped around her so tightly the night before, she had felt truly safe for the first time in more than two years—ever since the government had issued its relocation orders. She hadn't wanted him to release her and had clung unashamedly to him until he had finally lifted her in his arms and carried her home. Her parents had been astonished by the couple's arrival, to say the least, but not more so than Mitsu. It had taken some time before she could, through her choking tears, relate the day's happenings to both her parents and Kenshin. She had watched the anger in Kenshin change to contrition.

Her mother's voice came to her softly, interrupting her reflections.

"Mitsu, Kenshin-san still wants to marry you."

A dull thud started in her temples, promising to become a full-fledged headache before the day was done.

"Mama," Mitsu begged. "Please, not now." She pushed back the covers, shivering in the morning chill. Quickly dressing, she listened as her mother continued to talk about Kenshin. Her feelings on the subject were so obvious that, were the situation not so serious,

Mitsu would have laughed.

Her mother's next words brought her up short. "Kenshin-san will be by to get you in a few minutes."

Mitsu stared at her, blinking rapidly. "Get me?"

"To take you to breakfast," her mother said, frowning over Mitsu's lack of understanding. "He has to leave today, and he wanted to talk to you before he left."

Heart dropping, Mitsu pondered whether she could escape before he arrived. There was no way she could face him after her actions of the night before.

A tap sounded on the front door. Rolling her eyes, Mitsu passed her mother, taking note of the hopeful expression on the older woman's face. The familiar feelings of guilt overcame Mitsu.

She opened the door and looked up to see Kenshin's unreadable face. Whatever he felt, he was keeping it well hidden. Not so Mitsu. She felt the warmth rise to her face, and she hastily averted her gaze.

"Are you ready?" Kenshin asked.

She didn't really want to go, but she doubted if she had any choice. Looking over her shoulder, she noticed her mother smiling hopefully at the two of them. Gritting her teeth, Mitsu grabbed her coat, buttoning it while they crossed the compound to the mess hall.

The rain had changed from a steady downpour to a slight mist. Mitsu took her scarf from her pocket and wrapped it securely around her head, tying it beneath her chin.

Before they reached the building, Kenshin reached out a hand and pulled her to a stop. When he turned her to face him, she couldn't lift her gaze above his sharply pressed white shirt collar.

"Mitsu," he said softly, "we need to talk."

Finally she lifted her face to be met by his glowing brown eyes. Water beaded on his carefully styled dark hair. The force of his look did funny things to her midsection, and she had to swallow hard before she could speak. "Not now, Kenshin. My best friend in the whole world is in the hospital. She just lost her baby, and her daughter is distraught. I can't think right now."

He cupped her cheek with one large palm, and Mitsu's heart stopped beating altogether, then thundered on in response to his soft touch. She placed her palms against the front of his black coat, for the first time realizing that it was a valuable garment. Even his shoes spoke of wealth. Surprised, she glanced up into his face. His attire fitted him. Dark hair parted on the side and neatly in place, black business suit; he looked every inch the dapper businessman.

"I'm truly sorry," he told her quietly. "And I understand how you feel, but I really need to talk to you before I leave. I haven't much time."

"Emily's waiting for me," she hedged.

"This won't take but a moment."

Sighing, she capitulated. He moved her to the side of the building, away from prying eyes and the force of the wind and rain.

"I want to leave here engaged to you," Kenshin told her firmly.

Mitsu tensed against his restraining fingers. She lifted frightened eyes to his. Although she had been angry and defiant at the thought of being engaged to Shiro, the idea of being committed to Kenshin garnered no such feelings anymore. It was as though she were slowly becoming used to the idea.

Kenshin studied her face, remembering the previous night. There had been no sleep for him after holding Mitsu in his arms. When she had thrown herself into his arms, her weeping had brought out every protective instinct within him. Her warm body and soft scent had been hard to dislodge from his mind, and he had spent a restless night tossing and turning, trying to decide exactly what was happening to him.

There was nothing even faintly beautiful about Mitsu, except maybe her loving personality. Although he hadn't known her long, it hadn't taken him much time to realize that. She wasn't ugly, but then neither was she exactly attractive. But there was *something* that kept her on his mind for much of the time.

Now, staring into her shimmering brown eyes, he knew that this woman had touched a chord deep in his heart that had never been touched before.

"I. . .I told you that I couldn't marry you," she whispered.

He lifted his chin with determination. "But you told your parents that you would."

She shook her head vehemently. "But I didn't say when."

He took a step toward her, and she stepped back, bumping into the building behind her. Kenshin placed one hand on the building beside her right shoulder, leaning forward until his glittering eyes were mere inches from hers. She seemed unnerved by his closeness.

He brought his face even closer. "You promised to marry my father's son, and you told your parents that you would marry me."

She glared back at him. "I don't get it. Why are you so determined to marry me?"

For a moment, Kenshin said nothing. His tenacity surprised even him. Although what he had told her about family honor was true, was it all that spurred his interest or was there something more? He wasn't sure. But whatever it was, he couldn't let his father down, and he was determined that this marriage go through.

"I owe my father much," he said with resolution. "And I think you feel the same."

He watched contrary emotions fight for control of Mitsu's face. He knew she had been taught from birth to obey her parents wishes, but he also sensed her reluctance to take this step. She chewed on her bottom lip. At last, she spoke. "You don't share my faith," she said, her voice quavering slightly.

"So, teach me."

The soft challenge of his words seemed to stun her. "Now?"

He moved back from her. "No, I haven't the time right now." He glanced at his gold wrist watch. "I have to leave in twenty minutes to catch my bus." He smiled slightly. "But you can write." He paused to gauge her reaction to his words. She looked as if she had never considered such a possibility. "But I still wish to leave here engaged to you," he told her, his voice suddenly hard. "It would be best for our parents."

Mitsu's shoulders slumped wearily. "Very well."

Kenshin quickly masked his triumphant expression. He pulled a black box from his pocket, opening it before Mitsu's astonished eyes. "I intend to do this differently from my brother," he said, reaching for her hand. He slid the cold metal onto the ring finger of her left hand, pretending not to notice when she jerked her hand away.

Mitsu glared at the diamond, then curled her hand in a fist and shoved it into her coat pocket. When she looked up at him, her expression was not encouraging.

Kenshin took her by the shoulders, pulling her slowly toward him. He smiled slightly when he noted her startled expression. "We have to seal the bargain," he murmured just before his lips closed over hers. The kiss was over as quickly as it had begun, but if he were any judge of expressions, it had lasted long enough to challenge Mitsu's aloofness.

"Now," Kenshin said, taking her by the arm, "let's go tell your parents."

Later that morning when Mitsu stood with Emily, staring down at Mayumi's colorless face, everything that had transpired between Kenshin and herself was completely obliterated from her mind. Terrified by her friend's condition, she looked up at Dr. Magai.

The doctor squeezed Emily's shoulder and smiled, but his eyes remained sober. "Emily, you can sit with your mother if you want to. I would like to speak with Mitsu," he said quietly.

Emily nodded absently, reaching for her mother's hand. She seated herself in the chair beside the hospital bed.

Dr. Magai took Mitsu by the arm, pulling her some distance away so that the child couldn't hear them. His grave face sent Mitsu's heart plummeting to her toes. "It doesn't look good," he told her without preamble. "I am trying to get her to Phoenix or Tucson where they have better medical facilities, but it might take some time." His gaze rested on his patient momentarily. "Time I'm very much afraid we don't have."

Mitsu had to swallow twice before she could speak. "Is it that bad?"

He nodded, taking off his glasses and rubbing his tired eyes. "I'm afraid so. She's hemorrhaging, and I haven't been able to stop the bleeding."

"What are you going to do?"

He shook his head. "There's nothing that I can do. Except maybe pray."

Relief flooded through Mitsu. She had forgotten that Dr. Magai was a believer. He was right. They should all pray.

When they returned to the bedside, they heard Emily's softly spoken words. "And please God, make my mama better. And you can tell Santa Claus that all I want for Christmas is for my mama to get better. He can give all my presents to my friend Jimmy, even if he doesn't believe in either one of you."

Mitsu's heart twisted. How poignant a child's prayer. How beautiful. She laid a hand on the girl's shoulder. "Emily, it's time for us to go."

The child's body tensed under her touch. "I don't want to go," she growled defiantly, looking at the two adults over her shoulder.

"Your mama needs her rest," Mitsu argued quietly, although, since Mayumi had fallen into a coma, that was a moot point.

Emily tried to argue, but when Dr. Magai threatened to have her removed and not allow her to return if she didn't comply, she finally acquiesced. She followed Mitsu home in utter silence.

When they reached the barracks, Emily hurried to the cot she shared with Mitsu, throwing herself onto it. Her shoulders shook from her sobs, and Mitsu's heart went out to her. Mitsu's mother smiled understandingly and went to Emily, who allowed the woman to take her in her arms. The older woman rocked the child gently, singing a Japanese lullaby that Mitsu remembered from her own childhood

Mitsu's heart overflowed with love for her mother. She had heard the same song as a child whenever her mother wanted to heal Mitsu's hurts. It brought warm feelings of being loved back to her now. She really did owe her parents more than she could ever repay. Tears clogged her throat.

Mitsu seated herself at the table across from her father. His sad gaze met hers. "She is no better?" he asked quietly, so that the weeping child could not hear him.

Mitsu shook her head, glancing apprehensively at Emily. "Dr. Magai says that it doesn't look good. If something isn't done soon. . ." Her words trailed off into silence.

"*Shikata-ga-nai*," her father intoned softly, *Whatever will be, will be*. Mitsu felt her anger rise. She didn't want to believe that. Surely there was some way to influence the Lord to allow Mayumi to live. Mr. Kim and the rest of the Christian community were praying for Mayumi already. With so many voices lifted in petition, surely the Lord would hear.

For the rest of the day, Mitsu prayed for Mayumi. She knew that Emily was doing so as well, because every so often she would notice the girl's closed eyes and her lips moving silently.

Mitsu took Emily to lunch, but both of them left their food untouched. Mitsu pushed her food around on her plate, remembering the meals they'd received when they'd first arrived. The food had been awful. After more than two years, and with the addition of the crops the internees raised, the food had decidedly improved. But even that wasn't enough to induce her to eat.

Mitsu's engagement ring glittered on her finger, and she was sorely tempted to pull the thing off and throw it away. She felt branded, somehow. Although she had agreed to the engagement, she had thought that it would be like the one she had had with Shiro. This visual token bothered her more than she would admit.

Kenshin's kiss had bothered her, too, but in a much different way. If she felt branded by the ring, her lips felt seared by Kenshin's possessive kiss. Aggravated, she wondered how she was going to get out of this whole situation. When a little voice in her head wondered whether she really wanted to get out of it, she firmly stifled it.

Later, Mitsu and Emily returned to the hospital. Dr. Magai met them at the door, his face tense and white. Before he could say anything, Emily noticed the empty bed where her mother had been. Her wide eyes looked up at Dr. Magai's face.

"Where is my mother?" she asked hoarsely.

Dr. Magai's sympathetic gaze settled first on Emily, then on Mitsu.

"I'm sorry, Emily. Your mother is gone."

Chapter 6

itsu held tightly to little Emily's hand three days later as they loaded Mayumi's coffin onto the army truck. Her request to be buried in her home state of Washington was being granted. A smaller coffin was handed up to the soldier in the truck, and Mitsu cried in her heart for the little brother who Emily would never know.

Emily stood stoically by her side, her slanted almond eyes devoid of emotion. Ever since she had learned of her mother's death, the child had walked about like a zombie. Mitsu was truly worried about her. Dr. Magai had said that all she needed was time, but Mitsu wasn't so certain. She glanced down at Emily, frowning at the child's blank stare.

"Come, Emily. Let's go home."

Emily didn't argue. She allowed herself to be led away after the truck disappeared through the barbed-wire gate.

Mitsu's mother glanced at them both when they returned. Her understanding look settled on the child before turning to Mitsu. "The administrator would like to see you."

Believing that it must have something to do with Mayumi and Emily, Mitsu nodded. "Will you watch Emily for me?"

Her mother smiled briefly. "Of course. Come with me, Emily-chan." She held out her hand, and Mitsu was relieved to see Emily place her own in it. That small spark of awareness was reassuring after days of watching zombie-like actions.

When Mitsu reached the administration building, she tapped lightly before entering. A soldier rose from behind a desk, motioning her forward. "Come in, Miss Yakamura. Have a seat," he told her, indicating the chair in front of the desk.

Mitsu complied, lifting enquiring eyes to his. His sudden unwillingness to look at her caused her a sudden pang of trepidation.

The soldier shuffled some papers on the desk. "I understand that you have been caring for Emily Ishiyama."

Mitsu's heart rate accelerated. "That's correct."

He glanced at her briefly. "You understand that she is an orphan now."

Mitsu's face paled. "Yes, but we are willing to care for her, my parents and I."

He shook his head. "That's not possible. The army has strict orders, Miss Yakamura. All Japanese orphans must be sent to Manzanar Relocation Center. There's an orphanage there for Japanese children."

The anger that Mitsu had tried so hard to subdue surfaced quickly. "But we are friends of her family. We are willing to care for her. Surely something can be arranged."

He was already shaking his head. "Orders are orders, Miss Yakamura. We have made arrangements for the child to be taken to Manzanar day after tomorrow."

Kenshin smiled briefly at the woman sitting behind the desk before taking the receiver of the phone that she handed him. His heart pounded with dread. Who could be calling him here in Utah?

"Kenshin Takano." There was silence on the other end. "Hello?"

"Kenshin?"

He recognized the voice immediately. "Mitsu?"

"Yes."

The throaty reply harbored tears. Kenshin frowned, his stomach tightening into a knot. Icy fingers of dread threaded their way through his body.

"What's wrong?"

The silence lasted longer.

"Kenshin, can you come?"

"Tell me what's wrong. Did something happen to your parents?"

Kenshin had to relax his hold on the phone for fear of crushing it with his grip. He listened as Mitsu slowly explained her situation to him. He was trying to think rapidly, but his emotions were interfering with his normal calm reason.

"Can you come?" she repeated, and Kenshin felt only surprise that she would call on him for help.

"I'll see what I can do."

There was another brief silence. Kenshin could hear Mitsu struggling with her tears, and he suddenly wanted more than anything to take her into his arms and offer her his protection and care. She'd seemed so helpless the last time he had talked to her. He knew that he had worn her down with his persistence, aided by her own fluctuating feelings of grief and duty. If he hadn't felt the need for speed, perhaps he could have wooed her slowly, but for some reason, he had been determined to make her his before he left Butte Camp.

"Thank you."

The line went dead, and Kenshin slowly hung up the receiver.

Mitsu handed Emily the crayons and coloring book that she had purchased at the canteen. The child took them, laying them to the side on the table next to her. Three more days had passed, and still there was very little change in the child's demeanor.

Although Emily was supposed to have been sent to Manzanar on the truck that had left the previous day, the administrator had told Mitsu there had been a change of plans. He glanced knowingly at Mitsu, and she had wondered at his secret smile.

Her mind snapped to attention as Emily lifted her head, her dull eyes focusing on Mitsu. It surprised Mitsu to see the spark of anger that lit the child's eyes.

"Jimmy was right."

Confused, Mitsu tried to remember what Jimmy had said. "About what, Emily?"

The six year old pressed her lips together, her eyes growing darker with increasing fury. "There is no God or Santa Claus."

Remembering their earlier conversation, Mitsu sighed. "Oh, Emily. That's not true."

"I prayed," the little girl refuted. "I prayed and prayed and prayed, and nothing happened."

"Emily, come here," Mitsu commanded softly, seating herself in the chair next to Emily's. The little girl reluctantly obeyed. Mitsu took her on her lap, brushing her dark bangs from her eyes. Emily relaxed against her.

"God said no, Emily. I don't know why, but He knows best."

The little girl glared at Mitsu in silent rage. "He took my daddy then my mama. He's mean!"

Mitsu wasn't certain what to say. Pastor Kim had told her that anger would be the next step in the child's recovery, but she wasn't prepared for Emily's anger at God. Her own faith was so new, she didn't know the words to convince the child otherwise.

Setting Emily on her feet, Mitsu rose and retrieved her coat, handing Emily hers. Emily looked up at her in question.

"We're going to see Mr. Kim."

Emily's face darkened, but she dutifully obeyed. Mitsu wondered if perhaps the child was hoping the minister could shed some light on her mother's death.

They found Mr. Kim once again working in his flower beds. He glanced at Mitsu, then rested his attention on Emily. Taking off his work gloves, he brushed the dirt from his pants and motioned them inside.

Mitsu stated her problem rather succinctly. The minister nodded, still looking at Emily. He turned to Mitsu.

"I wonder if I might speak to Emily alone."

Mitsu's glance flashed to Emily. The little girl looked frightened, but she also seemed hopeful. "Certainly. I'll go see if there has been any word from Kenshin."

Mr. Kim smiled at Emily. "My wife is at the laundry right now, so I guess I will have to fix us some tea."

Mitsu left them, uneasy at abandoning Emily. She only hoped that the minister could reach through Emily's growing wall of anger.

She walked into the administration building, stopping short at the sight of Kenshin's figure standing next to one of the desks. Her mouth dropped open in surprise, and if she hadn't caught herself, she might very well have thrown herself into his arms again. She was amazed at the sheer relief that flooded through her.

He looked up, saw her, and smiled slightly. "I was just coming to see you."

"I. . .you didn't say you were coming."

Kenshin shrugged. "I told you that I would try." He frowned, looking concerned as he studied her face.

Mitsu stared at him, feeling hope for the first time in days. "Can you help?"

Kenshin's glance flicked quickly around the room full of people. He took Mitsu by the arm. "Come, what I have to say is best said in private."

Mitsu allowed him to pull her along until they were far enough away so that there was no chance of being overheard. She drew to a stop.

"What can you do?"

Kenshin sighed heavily. "Is that how you always are, right to the point?"

Frustrated, Mitsu dug her fingers into his coat sleeve. "Kenshin!"

His eyes darkened with quick anger. "Fine. Have it your way. I've come here to marry you."

Her mouth dropped open in astonishment. She backed slowly away. "Of all the. . .where did you come up with *that* crazy idea?"

"Look," he said, pulling his leather gloves from his hands. "I tried, but the army is adamant. The only way to keep Emily is for you and me to marry and then adopt her."

Mitsu opened her mouth several times to speak, but words failed her. She needed to think about this, but her thoughts were too chaotic to make sense.

Kenshin took her arm and started walking forward again. "I tried everything, Mitsu. My father even has a considerable amount of clout with a few government officials, but they believe it is in the best interest of the child; it's either Manzanar or a settled home."

"But to marry!"

He shrugged. "We're already engaged."

Mitsu's head spun with conflicting thoughts. Yes, she had agreed to an engagement, but she had hoped that somehow the marriage would be diverted. "And did the government say that it would be all right to marry and adopt Emily?" she asked.

"I contacted President Roosevelt and told him that you were the fiancée of my brother who was with the 442nd. I reminded him that my brother was awarded the bronze star, which is actually one of the reasons I was even able to talk to him."

Mitsu stared at him in amazement. "You talked to the president?"

He nodded.

Mitsu headed them toward Mr. Kim's barracks, her head whirling. Kenshin had talked to the president of the United States on her behalf! How had he managed such a thing?

When Mr. Kim opened his door, Mitsu was surprised to see Emily sitting at the table, happily munching on store-bought cookies, the drawn look gone from her face.

Mr. Kim grinned broadly at Mitsu, and she gave a hesitant smile in return.

Emily looked past Mitsu to Kenshin. She smiled widely. "Hi!"

Mitsu and Kenshin exchanged puzzled glances. They looked to Mr. Kim for some explanation. He shrugged. "Emily and I had a long talk."

Emily bobbed her head, her face sobering. "About Jesus, and Mama going to heaven. I'm sorry, Mitsu. I didn't mean it when I said I didn't believe in God."

"I know, Sweetheart." Mitsu didn't know what the minister had said to muster such a reaction, but she was delighted to see Emily somewhat returned to her normal self. Mitsu crossed the room, pulling out a chair across from Emily. She seated herself, smiling at the little girl. Though Emily's eyes were still shadowed by grief, they also shone with acceptance.

Kenshin followed Mitsu, resting a hand on her shoulder. She tensed at his touch. Bending down beside her, he smiled at Emily. "Hello, Emily."

"Hi, Kenshin."

He grinned. "Mitsu and I have something to ask you."

Mitsu opened her mouth to protest, snapping it shut at Kenshin's warning look. She knew what was coming, and she felt helpless to control the situation.

"Mitsu and I wondered if you would like to come and live with us."

Mr. Kim's startled glance rested on Kenshin. He looked at Mitsu for confirmation, but she pretended that she hadn't noticed.

Emily smiled with delight. "With Mr. and Mrs. Yakamura?"

"Yep." He looked at the minister. "I wondered if you would perform the ceremony."

"Mitsu?" the minister asked, fixing his gaze upon her.

What she would have said, Mitsu didn't know, because she was suddenly interrupted by Emily's whoop of delight. Emily jumped down from her chair, throwing her arms around Kenshin's neck. It had been over a week since Mitsu had seen such delight on the child's face. She didn't have the heart to destroy her joy after such intense grief.

Mr. Kim was watching her. He eyed Kenshin with some misgivings. "You decided then?"

Mitsu remembered the verse she had read in the Bible just the night before. A verse in the book of James had jumped out at her: *"Pure religion and undefiled before God and the Father is this, To visit the fatherless and widows in their affliction, and to keep himself unspotted from the world."*

In an earlier sermon, Mr. Kim had explained that the word "visit" in that verse meant "to take care of." His words didn't come back to her until she had read the verse again last night.

"Pure religion and undefiled." All she wanted was to give the fatherless and motherless Emily a home and the love she had been denied. She looked at Kenshin who was awaiting her reply. Her stomach felt like it had a lead weight in it.

"Yes," she answered the minister softly. "I've decided."

Chapter 7

Mitsu tugged at the skirt of her street-length white dress, pulling it into place. Since there was no mirror available, she had to hope that she looked all right.

Her mother came and sat on the cot next to where she stood. It was hard to say what feelings were reflected in her face. "Mitsu, you will make a beautiful bride," she said huskily, and Mitsu recognized the suppressed tears in her voice. Tears sprang suddenly to her own eyes. She sat down next to her mother, taking her hand and closing her fingers securely around it.

"Mama-san, am I doing the right thing?"

Her mother touched Mitsu's face lovingly with her free hand. *"Hai*, Mitsu. I think that you are."

Mitsu wasn't so sure. In her heart, she felt that what she was doing was right. *"Pure religion and undefiled before God. Whatever isn't done with faith is sin."* The words kept going round and round in her mind until she wanted to cry out for peace.

"Mitsu?"

Mitsu focused her attention back on her mother.

"Did you know that my marriage to your father was arranged?"

Mitsu's eyes widened. She hadn't known that, but it shouldn't have surprised her. That was the way things were done in Japan.

"But Mama-san, you and Papa-san love each other."

Her mother smiled. "That is true, but it was not always so. I was blessed to have married your father. He is a good man, and when we married, he treated me with courtesy and respect." Her smile widened. "He is a man who is easy to love."

Mitsu had to agree. She loved her father dearly, which was one reason she found herself in such a predicament. Her look met her mother's, and she understood the message she was being given. Kenshin would be an easy man to love too.

Her only problem lay in the fact that he wasn't a Christian, but then, her mother would never understand that. *Do not be yoked together with unbelievers.*

Mitsu massaged a spot on her forehead where a persistent ache had throbbed for days.

Her mother got up, rubbing a hand lightly over Mitsu's bent head. "It is almost time to go."

Her mother's consideration brought one more problem to Mitsu's mind. Her parents had wanted a Buddhist ceremony, but she had insisted on a Christian wedding. They had accepted her choice, but she knew that they were not happy with it.

After her mother left the apartment, Mitsu got up, roaming around the confined space. Everyone would be waiting at the church for her. She knew it would be hard on her parents, but then, this marriage idea had been hard on her. They had all had to compromise.

A knock sounded on the door, and Mitsu's heart jumped. She slowly made her way across the room, carefully opening the door. Her breath caught in her throat. Kenshin stood outside, his dark good looks accentuated by the black suit he wore. His winter coat hung open, revealing the expensive clothes beneath.

He smiled slightly. "I know it's supposed to be bad luck to see the bride before the ceremony, but may I speak with you a moment?"

Mitsu hesitated, then stood back to allow him entrance. His expensive cologne wafted to her senses when he passed her, and she sniffed appreciatively.

She closed the door, leaning back against its solid surface for support. Kenshin eyed her slowly, from her small white pumps to her dark hair twisted into a French twist. His almond eyes glinted with admiration. "You look beautiful."

Normally she would have scoffed, but it was obvious that he meant it. Mitsu's breathing suddenly became more labored under his steady regard.

"Thanks." She allowed her gaze to roam over him in the same manner. "You look pretty good yourself."

One corner of his mouth tilted slightly. "Thanks."

Silence settled over the room, and Mitsu shifted uncomfortably. "You wanted to talk to me?"

He nodded, his look never leaving her face. She motioned to the table. "We have a few minutes, I suppose. Please, have a seat."

Kenshin waited until she was seated before he took the offered chair. He took a deep breath. "I know you are concerned that I am not a Christian believer."

Surprised, Mitsu could only stare. He took another breath, looking away from her searching eyes. He focused on the blue sky outside the small window. "A long time ago, I accepted Christ as my Savior."

At Mitsu's shocked gasp, he turned his eyes back to her. He smiled with amusement and reached across the space between them. Placing a forefinger under her chin, he gently closed her mouth.

"But. . .but you said. . ."

"I know. I said that I don't believe in anything." His gaze clashed with hers. "And I'm not certain that I do anymore. This war and the things that have happened to my family—to my brother—have brought questions about God that I do not know how to answer. But I thought you should know."

Mitsu's heart began thudding. So, he was angry with God and filled with doubts. His questions made him wonder if God even existed. But God had a way of bringing His children back to Him. Suddenly, her heart felt light. Was this the Lord's way of answering her prayers? *Do not be yoked together with unbelievers.* The Lord knew before she even asked what she needed.

She suddenly remembered words that Kenshin had said weeks before: *Haven't I heard somewhere that children in the Lord should obey their parents?* She stared at him, remembering other things he had said, things from the Bible. Why hadn't she picked up on it before? In all honesty, probably because she had been so self-centered, she hadn't really noticed anything.

Kenshin sighed and a look of regret passed over his face. Mitsu wondered if much of his pain came from feeling alienated from his heavenly Father. Suddenly he smiled. The moment had passed.

He stood, holding his hand out to her. "Are you ready?"

She took the offered hand, rising to stand beside him. Taking a deep breath, she smiled. "Ready."

December blew in with an unusual cold front. The chilling temperatures continued to drop, and most of the inhabitants of Butte Camp knew enough to stay inside. Mitsu was one of them.

She handed Emily the teapot, and the child set it on the table. Emily turned perplexed eyes to her. "Mitsu, what is an orphanage?"

Mitsu had just lifted the pan of boiling water from the hot plate. She froze at the question. Slowly, she poured the boiling water into the pot, trying to ignore the sudden chill that filled her. "Why do you ask, Emily?"

Emily leaned her elbows on the table, holding her face with her cupped palms. She watched Mitsu swirling the tea in the container. "Jimmy said that that was where I was going to have to go."

Immediately riled, Mitsu had to count to ten before she could answer. Something was going to have to be done about Emily's association with her erstwhile hero. She gave Emily a cup of milk and seated herself at the table across from her, trying to gather her thoughts enough to answer the child's question without hurting her.

"An orphanage is where children go who don't have any parents."

Emily slid into her seat, her eyes wide. "You mean when their parents die?"

"Hai."

"Oh." A look of uncertainty crossed Emily's face, and her eyes clouded with fear. "When do I have to go?"

Mitsu handed her a cookie from the plate, smiling. "You don't have to go. Kenshin and I have adopted you. You're our little girl now."

Relieved, Emily took the cookie and started munching. She tilted her head slightly.

"Are there very many children who don't have parents?"

"I'm afraid so."

Emily stopped eating. "You mean they don't have anyone like you and Kenshin?"

Mitsu knew where the conversation was going. "Sometimes."

Emily settled into silence, thinking. "If they don't have anyone, who takes care of them?"

"Well, there are people, grown-up people, who take care of them."

Shaking her head sadly, Emily continued to study the problem. She watched Mitsu sipping her tea. "Mitsu?"

Mitsu waited, not certain what was coming next.

"Does Santa Claus go to orphanages?"

Taken by surprise, Mitsu clenched the teacup in her hand. *Not again,* she thought.

"I suppose," she hedged, trying to figure out a way to steer Emily away from thoughts of orphanages.

Emily obviously wasn't satisfied with that answer. "But if Santa doesn't come, then neither will Christmas."

Mitsu sighed. Before she could answer, Kenshin returned. She turned to him briefly, her expression speaking for her. His eyebrows lifted.

"What's going on here?"

He unbuttoned his work coat, hanging it on the nail behind the door. Since being assigned to Butte Camp, Kenshin had volunteered as one of the work force. He helped out wherever he was needed, but he especially liked taking care of the livestock.

He lifted Emily from her chair, seating himself in her spot and nestling the child on his lap. She smiled at him over her shoulder. Kenshin felt the warmth from that smile all the way to his heart. It hadn't taken him long to love this beautiful little girl. He hugged Emily closer. "So," he asked, "are you going to tell me what you've been talking about?"

"Mitsu was telling me about the orphanage," Emily explained.

Kenshin quickly looked across at Mitsu, wondering why she was discussing such a topic. Before he could say anything, Mitsu simply said, "Jimmy." For Kenshin, that was all the explanation needed. He smiled with sympathetic understanding.

Kenshin listened in silence as Mitsu told Emily about the birth of Christ and the reason for Christ's death. She pulled out her Bible and began to read the story in Luke of Christ's birth.

"So you see, Emily, as long as there are people who love the Lord Jesus, Christmas will always come. No matter where you are, no matter what you're doing, Christ is always with us."

Her words caused a small crack in the coldness of Kenshin's heart. He knew what she said was true. After being sent to an internment camp, then losing the farm, then losing his brother, his belief had withered. Now, the beauty of the Christmas story that Mitsu read to Emily penetrated that crack in his heart, widening the chasm until the coldness shattered into a thousand pieces.

He had been wrong to blame God. Mr. Kim had explained in his service Sunday that people either choose to serve God or else, by denying Him, serve Satan. Although Kenshin had gone to the service merely to please Mitsu and Emily, the words of God did not fall on sterile ground. He had been pondering them ever since. Kenshin could almost picture the evil smile of the one who had helped to pull him away from his relationship with God.

Emily leaned back against Kenshin's chest, and he wrapped his arms securely around her waist. He glanced at Mitsu and saw that she had noticed the rapport between the two of them. When her gaze met his, he saw a longing that triggered a response within him. He knew now that he wanted children of his own. Children by the woman seated across from him. Children by the woman who he suddenly realized he loved.

Mitsu saw the tender light that filled Kenshin's eyes, and her heart began thrumming in response. Her gaze traveled over his handsome form, recognizing the power behind his gentleness. Warmth like nothing she had ever known filled her. Always before she had been afraid of Kenshin. Maybe that's why she had pushed her strong attraction to him aside, discounting it as nothing more than imagination.

Since their marriage, however, he had shown her in a thousand ways that he cared for her. He had been gentle and undemanding, never pushing her to consummate their vows. Maybe that was why she had been able to thrust her fears aside and realize suddenly that she loved him.

She supposed she should have known it all along. The security she felt in his arms, the desire to have him solve all her problems, her willingness to abide by her father's contract: All these things added up to feelings she had done her best to ignore. She briefly considered the idea of telling him, but her fear of rejection caused her to stifle the desire.

"Mitsu?" Emily's voice interrupted her thoughts.

Mitsu dragged her gaze away from her husband, focusing instead on Emily.

"Will Santa Claus go visit the orphanage?"

Mitsu didn't know what to say, but before she could formulate an answer, Kenshin spoke. "He's probably afraid that the army will shoot him."

"Kenshin!"

Emily turned startled eyes to Kenshin's face, her own eyes rounding in consternation. Kenshin hugged her, tapping her nose with one finger.

"I was only kidding."

Relieved somewhat, Emily leaned back again. It was obvious to Mitsu that the child had taken Kenshin's words seriously. Mitsu glared at Kenshin, her lips twitching slightly at his unrepentant grin.

You ought to be ashamed, her eyes told him.

But I'm not, his laughing eyes answered.

Emily interrupted their silent exchange. "I remember when I was little my mama and daddy had a big tree with pretty lights."

Both adults turned to her in surprise. Emily and

her family had been in Butte Camp since 1942. That had been two Christmases ago, and Emily would have been only four at the time. Since Mayumi refused to agitate her Buddhist roommates, it had probably been three years since Emily had known the trappings of Christmas, but she still remembered.

Kenshin and Mitsu exchanged glances. The little girl's heartfelt concern about the holiday triggered a reaction in both of them. If there was any way possible, they would make this a Christmas to remember for Emily. How they were going to do that in a strict Buddhist household presented a problem, but they would find a way.

Chapter 8

Mitsu pulled her coat tightly about her, shivering in the cold. Kenshin had asked her to go for a walk with him after the evening meal and had suggested that they leave Emily with Mitsu's parents. He knew she'd assumed that he wanted to talk about the upcoming Christmas holiday. She was wrong.

They walked along the fence line, the desert beyond a pale reflection in the moonlight. Kenshin had heard about how when Butte Camp had first opened, everyone had been afraid to stray too near the barrier, but as time passed, restrictions had been lessened until most residents moved about freely. Now the government readily gave outside passes to internees in all the internment camps, as long as they were no longer considered a "threat." But those living in the inner sections of the compound still remained fearful and stayed close to their barracks.

For some time, Kenshin and Mitsu walked in silence until Kenshin finally pulled Mitsu to a stop, turning her to face him. The moonlight added a soft sheen to her eyes, and he had to force himself to stay still. He wanted to pull her into his arms and hold her close forever.

Instead, he allowed his hands to slide up to her shoulders and remain there.

The realization had hit him only that afternoon and had stayed with him the rest of the day and now into the evening. How would she react if he told her that he loved her? Would she believe him after such a short time? He could hardly believe it himself.

"Mitsu," he said softly. "I have to tell you something."

He could feel Mitsu's shoulders tense. He cupped her face in his palms, rubbing his thumbs over her cold cheeks. Her eyes darkened, and his heart rate accelerated. He could read the fearful uncertainty in her expression. He pulled her closer, dropping his lips until they were a hair's breadth away from hers. He decided to get right to the point, as she was so fond of doing.

"I love you," he told her, and his warm breath feathered over Mitsu's cold lips.

Mitsu's eyes widened. "Are you sure?" she whispered.

He closed the distance between their lips, wrapping her in his arms as he did so. The cold suddenly disappeared as both were caught up in the flame of their love for each other. Mitsu told him of her love without uttering a word.

When he finally allowed her to breathe, she clung to him for support. She leaned her forehead against his chest.

"I love you too," she told him breathlessly.

Kenshin tried to smother the desire her innocent kiss had inflamed in him. This was neither the time, nor the place, to think of such things. He kissed her once more, pulling back quickly and staring deeply into her eyes. "I owe you so much," he told her.

Her lips parted with surprise. "Me? I owe you!"

He smiled and shook his head. "You have given me your love and helped return me to the God I have tried so hard to deny. No, Mitsu. It is I who owe you."

Suddenly her face lit with joy. "Oh, Kenshin."

"I don't understand God's purpose," he said, shrugging his shoulders, "but I know now that whatever happens, happens according to His plan." He touched her lips with his fingers. "Everything that has happened has led me to you."

Mitsu stared at him a long moment through the mist generated by their warm breath, her feelings shimmering in her eyes.

He took her cold hand in his, twining their fingers together. "Let's go home," he said huskily. That word had never sounded so good.

Emily stood back admiring the snowman she and Mitsu had managed to build out of tumbleweeds. She smiled widely.

"He's perfect!"

Mitsu's lips tilted wryly. "Well, not quite. He's not made out of snow, but he'll do."

"I love him," Emily declared in a no-nonsense voice. Her smile suddenly disappeared, and she tilted her head in her endearing way. "Do you think the orphans have a snowman, Mitsu?"

Mitsu sighed. Emily had become obsessed with the thought of the orphans at Manzanar. No matter how hard Mitsu tried to detour the child's thoughts, they seemed to dwell on those children.

"I don't know," she finally answered, uncertain what

to do to allay the little girl's anxieties.

Emily picked up the scarf they had brought to tie around the snowman's neck. "Could we send them a picture of our snowman?"

Feeling nonplused, Mitsu shrugged. She pulled her own scarf from her coat pocket and tied it around her head, trying to ward off the cold. "I don't think so, Emily. We don't have a camera."

Undaunted, Emily studied the creation before them. The snowman looked back at her with its solid rock eyes. She put one finger in her mouth. "Could we make them one and send it?"

Mitsu choked. She opened her mouth to respond, but a voice behind her stopped her. "I think that's a great idea."

Mitsu glanced over her shoulder at Kenshin's approaching figure. As always, her heart gave a little jump at the mere sight of him. Though he looked wonderful in a suit, she much preferred him in his working clothes. He caught Mitsu's look and smiled. Placing his hands on her shoulders, he looked past her to Emily's delighted face.

"Really? We can send them one?"

"Kenshin," Mitsu warned. He squeezed her shoulders lightly.

"Maybe on a smaller scale, Emily-chan."

Mitsu's heart warmed at the endearment. She didn't know what these two would come up with, but she certainly wouldn't stand in their way.

Kenshin held out a hand to Emily. "Come on. Let's go home and see what we can figure out."

It was a few days before Christmas when Mitsu sat

down at the table next to Kenshin after Emily had gone to bed. Both of her parents had retired for the night also, and it would be only a short time before lights out.

"What are we going to do about Emily's Christmas?" Mitsu asked in a whisper, trying not to wake the others sleeping in the cots behind the hanging blankets.

Kenshin shook his head. His eyes took in her hair hanging down around her shoulders. It was so black, it shone with blue highlights. He was tempted to let his fingers run through its silky texture. "I don't know."

Mitsu smiled. "Emily seems more concerned with making a Christmas for the orphans than having one for herself."

Kenshin returned her smile, twisting his teacup in its saucer. "Isn't that what Christmas is all about? Christ came to give, not receive."

Mitsu picked up one of the little snowmen that Kenshin and Emily had made out of small pieces of lumber. Kenshin had cut out a snowman design, and Emily had painted it with supplies from the carpentry shop. Little stick arms stuck out of the small holes that Kenshin had drilled in the body.

"They're cute," she told him, grinning.

He gave a slight smile but said in all seriousness, "So are you."

Catching his look, Mitsu hastily replaced the snowman on the table. Her face colored brightly.

Kenshin bit his lower lip in frustration. Though he and Mitsu had confessed their love for each other, they still had done nothing toward consummating their marriage. He had decided to wait until they had more privacy, but he was fast losing patience waiting for that day to arrive.

She rose to her feet. "I'll see you in the morning."

When she would have passed him, he reached out a hand and caught her arm. He tugged until she fell across his lap and smiled at her flustered expression. He placed a large hand behind her neck, pulling her face down to his. His kiss was meant to be light, but it quickly took on a more serious tenor. Reluctantly, he pulled back. Tension crackled in the air.

"Goodnight," he answered softly, releasing her, and she wasted no time in retreating to her cot.

Emily roused everyone from bed at the first sign of light. Standing in her pajamas beside Kenshin's cot, she shook his shoulder. She impatiently pushed her tousled hair out of the way, curling her toes into the cold floor.

"Come on, Kenshin," she beckoned. "We have more snowmen to make."

Kenshin groaned, pulling the cover over his head. Giggling, Emily pulled it back. Kenshin growled at her, then covered his head again. At the other end of the sleeping quarters, Mitsu sat up in her cot, watching the two play.

When Emily pulled the covers back again, Kenshin growled, lunging for Emily and pulling her onto his cot. He leaned over her giggling form, tickling her sides unmercifully. Her giggles turned into peals of laughter.

Mitsu's parents sat up in their beds, shaking their heads, small smiles tilting their lips. They exchanged laughing glances with Mitsu.

Kenshin finally set Emily back on her feet. He

swatted her backside. "Hurry up and get dressed. We'll see what else we can find to do."

The child hurried to do as bid, while Mitsu and her parents took a little more time. Mitsu watched her husband dress, impressed at his strength and vitality. He caught her glance and gave her a devastating smile.

Kenshin waited for Mitsu's parents to leave and drop the blanket behind them, then pulled Mitsu to her feet, wrapping her snugly in his arms. The look he gave her would have melted an icicle.

"Come on, Sleepyhead. Times a wastin'."

Mitsu wrapped her arms around his neck, playing with the hair that extended to his collar. His look became roguish. "Keep that up and we'll never get out of here."

Laughing, Mitsu reached up and gave him a brief kiss. She tried to push out of his arms, but he wouldn't have it.

"You can do better than that," he told her, his eyes full of mischief.

Amazed at how comfortable she now felt with him, she grinned at him playfully. Knowing that she was loved had broken down all of her barriers. She felt free and alive, especially when he was near.

"You asked for it, Mister," she returned in her most sultry voice. Kenshin's eyes widened with laughter just before she pulled his head down to hers.

The kiss she gave him was more intense than any other that they had shared. He pulled her closer, only to have her push away. She shoved against him, and he released her in confusion. "Was that better?" she asked, a note of teasing coloring her words.

He reached for her again, but she skipped out of his way.

"Now, now," she purred, "we have things to do."

Kenshin stood looking in amazement. He put his hands on his hips, one eyebrow disappearing under his mussed hair. "Okay, what have you done with my wife?"

Laughing, Mitsu ducked behind the curtain, joining her parents and Emily in the main living quarters. Her mother's knowing look sent warmth to her cheeks. Kenshin was right when he said there was no privacy here.

Emily giggled behind her hand when Kenshin joined them. He grinned back, taking her hand and twirling her around. "I'm hungry, how about you?"

She nodded, and they all made their way to the mess hall, Emily's laughter lighting the morning around them.

Emily took her regular place beside Kenshin, and they playfully teased each other back and forth. Mitsu was watching them, thinking how much she loved them both, when a shadow fell over the table.

They looked up to find an elderly Japanese gentleman standing beside their table, his hat in his hand. He bowed low, then placed a carved figure of a bird on the table.

"For the orphans," he told them.

Kenshin's mouth dropped open, and he glanced at Mitsu. She shrugged, not knowing what to say. Emily had no such problem. She lifted the bird from the table, smiling brightly at the old man. "Thank you, Mr. Amaku."

Both Kenshin and Mitsu turned to her in surprise. Mr. Amaku backed away, bowing again, and departed.

"How do you know him?" Kenshin asked.

Emily lifted innocent eyes to his face. "I talk to him sometimes when I see him sitting outside playing checkers with Mr. Sei."

Mitsu sighed. The child was forever striking up conversations with strangers. "But, Emily. . ."

They were interrupted again when another gentleman approached their table. He set several origami figures on the table, the colorful paper fluttering in the breeze from the open doorway.

"For the orphans," he said, then retreated.

Kenshin and Mitsu stared at Emily in wonder. Kenshin shook his head, dazed. "How?"

Mr. Kim joined them at that moment. His face was wreathed with smiles. "I think what you're doing is wonderful. The Sunday school children want to help. They're working on cards to send to Manzanar."

Mitsu sat back on the bench. She looked at her mother, who grinned. "That's our Emily."

Mr. and Mrs. Goto stopped by their table on their way out of the mess hall. Though they normally looked at Mitsu with disapproval, this time they eyed her with respect. They smiled at Emily. "Hello, Emily."

Emily returned their greeting unabashedly.

"If you will stop by our apartment," they told the child, "we will give you something to send to the orphans."

Although Emily took their generosity as a matter of course, Mitsu did not. She was more than a little amazed that Buddhists, Shintos, and Christians were working together to help the orphans. And all because of one little girl's loving heart.

Kenshin regarded Emily with some misgiving. "What did you say to all these people, Emily?"

She shrugged, digging into her porridge. "I don't remember. I just told them what we were doing." She scooped a mouthful of the cereal, swallowing it abruptly so that she might speak. "Isn't that what Jesus would do?"

Mitsu's heart was tender. "Yes, Emily. That's exactly what Jesus would do." When Mitsu glanced at her parents, she found them squirming uncomfortably. She grew quiet, not wanting to offend them. Emily, on the other hand, seemed impervious to the tension at the table.

"Mitsu said that as long as there is *anyone* who believes in Jesus, Christmas will always come. Well, I believe."

Mitsu's parents got up from the table. "We will see you later," her father told them, not looking their way. Mitsu sadly watched them walk away. Afraid that she had hurt them once again, she bit her lip.

Kenshin took her hand across the table. "It's all right. I think they understand." He kissed her fingers, his smile warming her into a better humor. "Have faith, Honey. With your Christian witness, they can't help but believe."

"I hope so," she whispered, not entirely convinced. Still, the Bible said that God's Word would not come back empty.

They finished their meal in silence, Emily playing with the wooden bird. Then they gathered up the gifts and returned to their barracks.

For the rest of the day, people from all over the compound stopped by to give them items to send to the orphans. Their apartment grew smaller as the piles grew larger. Kenshin stood with Mitsu outside their apartment. He watched the people milling about the compound, impressed by the concern being shown for the orphan children of Manzanar. They were good people, Christian or not. Wouldn't it be something if one child's care for others helped lead the way to Christ for many of these people? Even the devout Buddhists resignedly listened to Emily's chatter about the Lord. Kenshin shook his head in amazement.

He looked down at Mitsu. "How are we ever going to get this stuff to Manzanar?" he asked.

"I think I can help with that."

They turned to find a sergeant from the administration office walking toward them. He tipped his helmet to Mitsu, then smiled at Kenshin. "Word of what you're doing reached our office. I came by to tell you that whenever you're finished, let me know, and I'll see that everything gets to Manzanar. If we take it tomorrow, they should have it in time for Christmas."

He left as quickly as he'd come. Kenshin stared after him a long time, then shaking his head again, he turned to Mitsu. "He's a funny looking Santa Claus."

Mitsu grinned. "At least he won't get shot."

Kenshin quickly pulled her into his arms, grinning down into her upturned face. "Don't bet on it."

Emily ran up to them, tugging urgently at Kenshin's pants. "Come see what we've done."

"We?"

Emily bobbed her head up and down. "The kids from my Sunday school class."

She pulled them along by their hands, her excitement contagious. Kenshin could only wonder what the child had been up to now.

Emily stopped beside the church, pointing with pride to her newest achievement. It didn't take much deductive reasoning to decide where the idea had originated. Mitsu smiled at the greasewood bush decorated with paper chains and childish ornaments. She knelt beside Emily, taking her hand.

"It's a beautiful Christmas tree, Emily. Your mama would be proud."

Emily looked at her, the excitement in her eyes tempered by sadness. "You and Mr. Kim told me to believe and Christmas would come. And it did."

Kenshin realized that for Emily, Christmas had come because she had seen someone else's need and tried to fulfill it. It was that, more than anything, that had helped her to begin to heal. He dropped to his knees beside Mitsu and Emily.

"And it always will, Emily-chan. As long as the earth shall stand, it always will."

He stood. Picking up the child and placing one arm around Mitsu, he led them away.

DARLENE MINDRUP

Darlene is a full-time homemaker and home-school teacher. A "radical feminist" turned "radical Christian," she lives in Arizona with her husband and two children. Darlene has written several novels for Barbour Publishing's **Heartsong Presents** line. She has a talent for bringing ancient settings, like the early Church in the Roman Empire and medieval, to life with clarity. Darlene believes "romance is for everyone, not just the young and beautiful."

Engagement of the Heart

by Kathleen Paul

Dedication

To Deanna Ames, Melissa Archuleta,
and Susan Simpson, my sisters in Christ,
who encourage me more than they will ever know.

Chapter 1

Betsy Alexander stepped down from the city bus in front of Michael T. Dodge Veterans Hospital. Back in the days before gas rationing, she and her parents had often passed the imposing structure on their way to visit Uncle Bert and Aunt Iola on the family farm. As a child, she had cowered down on the backseat of their DeSoto roadster, frightened by the stone walls and the big iron gate where a soldier stood as gatekeeper. It looked like a prison, not a place for wounded men to get better.

The autumn breeze blew crisp leaves down the New York sidewalk. They rattled and skittered, adding their pungent odor to the chilly air. Brown oak leaves with sharp dry edges stung her legs as they swirled around her on a merry chase. Fingers of cold air pinched at her pale skin. With gloved hands she tugged the felt cloche hat more securely over her crown of brown hair. Usually the softly waving locks tumbled to her shoulders in a becoming cascade, but in the brisk wind, the tendrils escaping from the confines of the close-fitting helmet flailed her face. Betsy clutched the heavy wool coat closer to her neck with one hand. Her other hand fingered a letter in her pocket. She pulled out the stiff green hospital letter-head and read the note once more.

> *September 9, 1944*
>
> *Dear Miss Alexander,*
>
> *I am Sgt. Kevin Coombs. Your fiancé, Jerome Frank Edgins, was in my unit. I am currently at Michael T. Dodge Hospital and have a packet of letters which Frank wrote to you. If you would come by the hospital, Ward 6A, I would like to hand them to you personally. No need to call. I'll be here at least six weeks.*
>
> *Frank was a good friend. I am sorry for your loss.*
>
> *Sincerely,*
> *Sgt. Kevin Coombs*

An MP, an older man, stepped out of the small gatehouse.

"Can I help you, Miss?"

"I. . .I want t—to visit a p—patient," she answered, walking toward him.

"Who're you visiting?" He waved a car in through the gate as he asked.

"Sgt. Kevin Coombs." She'd practiced saying the name. The syllables came out in an even flow, and she smiled at her success.

The guard raised a bushy eyebrow as he looked at a clipboard.

"Only one name listed under his for visitors." He smiled at her. "You Betsy?"

Betsy grinned at this unexpected aid to her admit-tance. She nodded, avoiding talking to the stranger.

The grizzled soldier pointed up the long, curving drive to the three-story stone structure. "You just follow the road to the main entrance. Patty is the gal at the front desk. She'll take care of you."

Again Betsy avoided words and gave her practiced nod and brilliant smile. As she was growing up, her father had often run his large hand through her bouncy brown hair, saying, "What difference does it make that you don't speak so good, baby Betz? You're smile is worth a thousand words."

Now Betsy started up the long drive, wishing that a smile alone would get her out of this mess. Her long legs marched sharply toward this meeting, responding to the nervous anticipation pulsing through her system. She stopped, took a deep breath, and began again at a slower pace. She dreaded reaching her destination. She'd never get the words out smoothly enough to present an understandable explanation. Taking huge breaths of air with each step forward, she tried to calm her nerves as she approached the stately stone porch with its two-story colonial columns and massive glass doors.

The letter had arrived on Wednesday, but she hadn't been able to get away until the weekend. Betsy baby-sat for six children while their mothers worked at various jobs to support the war effort. Her own mother worked in a local factory, running a machine that made bolts.

Three of the six children Betsy watched were her own siblings. Sixteen-year-old Rosey helped her when she didn't stay at school for study clubs or curl up with the telephone in the front foyer. Her younger sister relished any type of social encounter. Then there were her twin brothers, who exhausted each day with high adventure springing from their vivid imaginations.

Betsy was good with children, but she didn't enjoy being away from home. It had been a monumental relief to graduate from high school. Now she did the things she felt competent to do. She avoided social interaction with anyone outside her small sphere of family and friends.

She had two more brothers, one older and one younger, fighting Japanese in the Pacific theatre. Twenty-three-year-old Bob was a Marine, and nineteen-year-old Mike wrote home glowing, and heavily edited, accounts of his life as a sailor on a submarine. Betsy wished they were here now to flank her as the somber building loomed before her. With a sigh, she pushed the heavy door open.

The massive lobby oozed dank, cloying heat. Strong disinfectant and old wool combined to assault her senses. Wrinkling her nose, Betsy paused just inside to survey the waiting room. She hadn't expected a crowd, but people occupied every seat in the waiting area. Wives and mothers chatted. Children huddled next to shrunken fathers wrapped in loose, hospital-issued, faded blue robes. Some children sat awkwardly in the hard wooden chairs not designed for small squirmy bodies. Some played quietly on the floor, busily occupied with their own affairs.

The children aren't allowed upstairs, Betsy suddenly realized.

With a blast of cold air, the door behind her swung open, and three servicemen barreled past, jostling her so that she dropped her purse and the letter.

"Sorry, Miss," said one as he turned and steadied her, both of his huge hands resting on her slim shoulders.

His gap-toothed grin in a thoroughly freckled face showed more friendliness than repentance. Suddenly, his twinkling blue eyes went serious. "Hey, you're not hurt, are ya? You look awful pale."

Betsy shook her head, but before she could utter a syllable, a second soldier with a lanky body and a prominent Adam's apple picked up her handbag and began his apologies. He managed to shoulder the first soldier to the side as he handed her the purse. The third shoved in between the other two, doffed his cap, and started a polished speech.

"Hey," said Freckles, while Betsy's gaze darted between the earnest faces of her accosters. "Ain't you that zazz girl down at the USO? The one that plays on Friday nights?"

"Sure, she is!" exclaimed Adam's Apple. "Hubba Bubba! You sure make that piano swing. How come you never dance with us guys?"

"Don't mind them, Miss," said Smooth Talker. "I'm Private Wilton. Private Hayseed's straight off a Kansas farm, and Billy here is from the hills of Kentucky." He addressed the other men with pronounced patience. "She can't very well dance with you two dogface, dame-dazed goons and play the piano at the same time. What are you two going to do for brains if they split you up? It won't be convenient to keep on sharing the same gray matter if the army sends one of you to Europe and the other to the Pacific."

Freckles grinned good-naturedly and stuck his big hand out, enveloping Betsy's in his grip and pumping her arm.

"Name's Private John Hanks, Miss," he said. "I'm

from Manchester, Kansas. We let David talk like that since he's a bit inferior when it comes to lifting and carrying. He's a good friend, and we aim to make him feel better about his considerable shortcomings."

Adam's Apple grabbed Betsy's hand away from the stocky farmer and did his own version of pumping. "My name's William Chatterfield, and don't listen to either of 'em. I don't care a plugged nickel how David feels about himself, and I ain't no hillbilly. My pappy happens to be the mayor of our town, my aunt's town clerk, and Gramps has been a deputy for fifty years."

"Sounds good," said David with a grin, "until Billy-boy tells you the name of his hometown."

"Hog Holler is a thriving community," objected William.

Betsy started to giggle.

"You sing like a canary," said John, addressing Betsy with exaggerated ardor.

"You drive my poor heart wild," said William.

"On those long nights, far from home," said David in a melancholy voice, "with only the sound of soldiers snoring in the dark, I'll remember your bright smile, your lilting voice, your sweet good-bye kiss."

He planted a quick, friendly smooch on her lips.

"Oh," exclaimed Betsy with a sudden gasp. Surprised, she stood still while John and William followed suit. The waiting room burst into applause, cheers, and laughter. The three mischievous soldiers saluted and rushed down one of the side corridors, obviously knowing just where they were going and in a hurry to get there. Betsy's humiliation anchored her feet to the green linoleum.

Her hot cheeks warned her that she looked foolish.

She blinked twice and became aware her jaw had dropped open as she'd watched the retreating soldiers. She deliberately closed her mouth.

She'd never been kissed before, if she didn't count her dad's kisses and rare brotherly pecks. Now she'd been kissed three times with an audience. Her glance darted around the room. She saw nothing but friendly faces enjoying the playful interchange they had witnessed. Betsy swallowed hard and brought forth the smile that she so depended on.

A tug on Betsy's coat pulled her attention to a small figure standing beside her. The tousle-haired cherub held up the letter she'd dropped. She took it and gave him a wink. His blue eyes twinkled, charming away the last of the Betsy's embarrassment. He hopped back to his parents, and Betsy squared her shoulders, determined to find Sergeant Coombs and explain the situation.

Gripping the letter, she approached the busy front desk. Patty, with golden hair styled exactly like the movie star Betty Grable, sat in a rolling chair. One second the busy receptionist focused on the PBX and the next on the log where visitors signed in. Betsy admired how the pretty girl talked non-stop, involved in several conversations at once.

"Michael T. Dodge Veterans Hospital, hold please. Take the corridor to the left. The chaplain's office is the last door on the right. Sign in, please. How can I help you? One moment and I'll connect you. Have a seat and Nurse Becker will summon you in just a minute." Patty tossed a sunny smile around with her words.

Betsy waited patiently until she could edge herself to the counter. Patty's glance rested on her, and Betsy quickly took advantage of the moment.

"I have a l–letter," she began, holding up the note from Sergeant Coombs.

Patty nodded. "Down the right-hand corridor. See Mrs. Brighton. She's in the kitchen behind the cafeteria."

How could she know what my letter says? wondered Betsy. Before she could form a question, a sturdy woman in a calico dress shouldered her aside.

"My son was transferred to this hospital," she said, her voice quavering. "I must see him."

Betsy peered down the corridor. Perhaps Mrs. Brighton received all first-time visitors before they were admitted to the wards. She left the crowd at the front desk and started down the long hall.

The smell of cooking guided her through large swinging metal doors and into a darkened cafeteria with row after row of institutional tables. At one end an old upright piano sat on a raised dais. A warm glow of light spilled through a large opening in the wall behind the serving counter. Betsy followed the sound of clattering pots and pans and muted voices.

"Oh, glory! Help has arrived," a voice greeted her as soon as she stepped through another swinging door.

"B–but," Betsy began.

"Oh, Honey, I'm so glad you're here," a tiny woman crowned with white hair, adorned with thick eyeglasses, and swathed in a huge white apron waved her hand for Betsy to come on in. "Everyone needs to do their bit for the war effort, and it just seems like even welding at the shipyard is more glamorous than peeling potatoes these days. But these boys and their families must eat, let alone the staff."

"I'm s—supposed to see a Mrs. Br—Brighton," explained Betsy.

"That's me, Dearie." The woman's face broke into a wide grin showing perfectly neat false teeth. "You just tuck that letter in your pocket, and we'll fill out the paperwork after we get this lunch in good order. I don't normally work in the kitchen, but we're shorthanded and everyone has to do their bit. There isn't a job too small for my dignity when it comes to these young men. There's an apron hanging behind the door. You tackle the macaroni and cheese, Dearie. The recipe and ingredients are setting out on that long table next to Meg. She's doing the salad. Praise God we've got lettuce today."

"I d—don't think I—I. . ."

"Sure you can do it, Honey. Just throw yourself into the job and we'll talk later. The recipe is for fifty, multiply the ingredients by five."

Mrs. Brighton snatched an apron from behind the door and thrust it into Betsy's hands.

"There's a white cafeteria kerchief in the pocket. Put it on and tuck all stray hair in. Then wash with the carbolic soap."

The matron's delicate little figure bustled behind her until Betsy was firmly placed before an oversized galvanized sink.

Betsy tried to protest one more time. "B—but—"

"Wash up, first, Dearie. Our boys don't need any more germs."

A wide table next to a stove held boxes of macaroni, packets of powdered cheese, a gallon of milk, and sticks of real butter.

Wow, thought Betsy, *I haven't seen butter in a month. I haven't seen that much butter in six months. I guess army hospitals get extra rations.*

Mrs. Brighton guided Betsy to several pans of already boiling water and left her with a reassuring pat on the shoulder.

I can do this, thought Betsy. *Then maybe I can get someone to listen to me. I'll find Sergeant Coombs right after lunch.*

Chapter 2

Two hours whizzed by as Betsy learned exactly how a meal for 250 came together. She added a touch of garlic and onion powder to the macaroni and cheese, thinking of her mother's recipe. Mrs. Brighton approved her work then gave her another job. Betsy filled a bin of mustard and ketchup bottles and kept an eye on tray after tray of rolls as she put them into the huge oven and later pulled them out.

Just before noon a swarm of nurses' aides scurried into the kitchen and made short work of dishing up plates of food for the men who weren't ambulatory. They pushed carts designed to hold thirty trays at a time off to the wards. The rest of the food supplied the serving line. Meg, Mrs. Brighton, and Betsy began the arduous business of feeding a long line of hungry people.

"Remember to smile," said Mrs. Brighton as she passed behind the two girls dishing out vegetables.

"I feel l–like they're all st–staring at me," said Betsy to Meg as soon as the older lady was out of hearing.

Meg giggled. "They are. Oh, not the staff and the families, but the soldiers sure are. Don't worry about it. Just be glad Mrs. Tweakes isn't here. She doesn't say 'smile' like Mrs. Brighton. She practically accuses you of loose morals even if all you do is wear a little lipstick."

"Who's Mrs. Tweakes?"

"The kitchen boss," answered Meg as she piled corn into a small, thick ceramic bowl and passed it to a soldier. She smiled at him but turned a scowl to Betsy as soon as he'd moved down the line. "She's awful." Meg's pretty face crumpled into a comical expression like she'd smelled rotten eggs. "A real rusty hen, squawking and cackling and scolding and strutting around. Thankfully she's down with an awful cold. Mrs. Brighton's the personnel director for non-medical staff. She pitches in wherever she's needed, even though she really doesn't have to."

Meg looked down the thinning line. "Hey, this group of guys coming up has been through before. They can only have one more helping. Mrs. Brighton will be happy they've got an appetite."

Three men scooted their trays down the metal bars. One had a bandage that covered most of his skull, including one eye. Another had the sleeve of his robe pinned up over a missing arm. The last limped along, but Betsy could not readily identify his injury.

They began talking in rapid-fire inquiry. Their questions and comments tumbled out, running into each other and giving Betsy no time to respond.

"Hey, you're Betsy, aren't you?"

"Frank's Betsy?"

"We'd know you anywhere."

"Say, are you going to come up to the ward? Jimmy and Rosco can't come down, and they'll be disappointed if they don't get to meet you."

"Frank showed us your picture."

"Hope you don't mind."

"That was some picture. You're prettier though in person. More real."

"Of course she's more real than a picture."

"You know what I mean, less like one of them Hollywood dames."

"He read us your letters too."

"Hope you don't mind."

"Will you come sit with us after you're finished? Our table's over there. Sergeant Coombs said it would be all right."

"He said you were coming."

"We've been waiting."

"Of course we've been waiting. What else would we do?"

"We all feel like we know you."

"Because of the letters."

"Will you play for us and sing?"

Mrs. Brighton came to stand behind Meg and Betsy.

"Okay, boys," she chastised them, but with a smile. "You can't talk to the girls now. They have work to do."

"We want Betsy to come sit with us," said the limping soldier. His face molded into an expression of overwhelming gravity. "One of our squad was her fiancé."

"Okay, okay." Mrs. Brighton patted Betsy on the back. "As soon as the cleanup crew comes in. That'll be in about ten minutes. Shoo now. You're holding up the line."

Mrs. Brighton made sure the young men continued down the serving counter then gave instructions to the girls.

"As soon as those last stragglers come past, combine all the leftover vegetables into one pan. We'll start a soup for supper."

Meg cross-examined Betsy as soon as the coast was clear. Her tone held equal parts spontaneous sympathy and suppressed curiosity.

"Who's Frank? You lost a fiancé? That's tough, Betsy." She held a huge pan of corn on end while Betsy scraped the contents into the larger green bean server.

"Fr—Frank was a g—guy I wrote to. We were n—never engaged," said Betsy. She moved away to fetch the nearly empty carrot container.

"But if you wrote to him, you must have known him pretty well," insisted Meg.

"I wrote t—to twenty overseas b—boys, and I d—didn't know even one of them."

"What?" Meg's voice shrieked in surprise, and she quit scooping small chunks of roasted potatoes into the same container with the beans.

"Shh!" said Betsy. "I g—got their n—names at the USO. They w—were from all over the St—States and they were st—stationed all over the w—world."

"Twenty! I struggle to write letters to my brother. How do you write twenty?"

"I j—just write one on Sunday and c—copy it over. I do f—four on five nights of the week, and they are only one p—page or a little over. It's n—not hard." Betsy grinned at her new friend. "Easier than t—talking."

They picked up the big pot of mixed vegetables and carried it between them through the swinging doors to the kitchen.

"But you work at the USO. Those guys said you

sing. How can you do that with your stutter?"

"I only work on Friday n–nights for the d–dance. I d–don't have to t–talk to anybody. I j–just play the p–piano and sing. I don't st–stutter when I sing."

"Really? Maybe you should sing when you talk. Like opera, you know? They sing everything."

Betsy nodded. She usually sang her arguments with her siblings or when she had something important to discuss with her parents. She put the words to simple scales she had learned during private singing lessons.

"Hey! What about the picture?" Meg poked Betsy's arm in a friendly dig.

Betsy rolled her eyes. "My k–kid sister, Rosey, she's sixteen. It was her br–bright idea. We went to Dominique's Downtown Studio."

"A pin-up?" Meg's voice squeaked again.

"N–not exactly." Betsy laughed. "B–but I sure l–look good. R–Rosey's friend Sheryl d–did my hair like Judy Garland. They m–messed around with my m–makeup t–too."

"Are you working tomorrow? Oh, you wouldn't know yet. I want to see that picture. Bring it with you."

"I–I," Betsy stalled in her explanation. Too much had happened to her that morning for her to put into words. She wouldn't be coming back. This was all a string of silly misunderstandings.

"Betsy," said Mrs. Brighton from the doorway. "You can go visit with your soldiers now, but be in my office in twenty minutes, and we'll take care of the application."

"Why are you blushing like a fire truck?" asked Meg. Her shift ended, she prepared to go home as she continued to tease the new employee.

"Tr—trucks don't blush," objected Betsy as she took off her apron and kerchief and flung them in the laundry hamper, imitating Meg's final actions of the day.

"I mean your face just went red like a fire truck. You know what I mean. What's so embarrassing about talking to a bunch of guys who knew Frank?"

Betsy shook her head and waved a hand at Meg, dismissing the subject. So often she swallowed all she wanted to say. The effort to get her thoughts into words cost too much. She could never decide which made her more nervous, extreme tolerance or out-and-out impatience on people's faces. Betsy's mind turned to the soldiers waiting for her at the long cafeteria table. Five men expected her to sashay over there with confidence. She'd rather dig ditches.

Betsy watched Meg hurry out to catch her bus. She was on her own now and couldn't put off visiting with the soldiers any longer. She wove through the staff cleaning the kitchen. Placing her hand on the cold metal door, she peered through the large oval window in its center.

Father in Heaven, she prayed silently, *help me get through this. I don't know why they think I was engaged to poor Frank. He's dead and I hope he's there with You. I don't want to tell his buddies that he lied to them. But I can't lie either. What a mess. Please guide me. Amen.*

Betsy pressed firmly against the door and it swung open. Two of the men came to greet her, and as before, they began talking, giving her little opportunity to respond.

All her life Betsy had used her expressive face to cover her deficiency in speech. Now she fell back on the practiced habit and nodded, smiled, and even used her eyebrows to respond to the barrage of words coming her way. As she listened she surveyed the other three men at the table.

The man who limped had remained seated. Beside him sat a man who outwardly looked healthy. The last man caught her attention. He occupied a wheelchair and he looked emaciated. Surely this man had been gravely injured. He hadn't the vitality of the other four. Sunken cheeks, hollows under his eyes, a listless expression. Betsy wondered if he was fated not to recover after all. Perhaps what was wrong with this man could not be cured or rehabilitated.

At the table one of the men spoke to the man in the wheelchair. His gaze lifted to meet Betsy's. She smiled tentatively, but no answering response crossed his melancholy features. Betsy felt the despair in his soul hit her with a thud in her throat and chest. Her heart brimming with sympathy, she turned away and concentrated on the cheerful banter of her companions. It was pointless. She couldn't distinguish the words of babbling chatter. Even with her eyes averted, the expression of the man in the wheelchair haunted her thoughts.

Oh, Father, what do I say to someone so full of pain? I can't speak anyway, and his sorrow will stop up any flow even if I try to say something.

One soldier put a hand to her elbow and guided her to the chair held out by another gallant young man. She reluctantly sat in the space next to the patient in the wheelchair.

"I'm Harry," said the soldier with the massive turban bandage. "This is George." He indicated his friend with an empty sleeve. "I told you Jimmy and Rosco are up in the ward. Pete." He nodded at the apparently healthy man. "Nick." The man with the limp. "And this is Sergeant Coombs. He saved our skin."

"Not enough of it," said the man in the wheelchair. His husky voice showed no emotion and his face registered no change. He focused on Betsy. "Frank was our buddy, Miss Alexander. I'm sorry he isn't here with us now."

Betsy studied him, seeing the fatigue of long illness under a dark stubble of beard. Beneath his stoic façade, this man hid something. Betsy thought it must be more than physical pain. A flicker of some emotion in his dark gray eyes gave him away. A miniscule wince, a tightening of the pallid flesh of his face drew Betsy into closer observation. The strong bone structure was evident. The stubborn chin, the square jaw, the high, broad brow, and the straight nose accentuated the despondency of expression. Dark hair with a premature frosting of gray at the temples made her wonder just how old he was. He sat still but with none of the latent energy of a soldier at ease. His motionlessness reflected a lack of will. His body had been damaged, but so had his spirit.

Tears sprang to her eyes. She batted them back. These men would likely think they were tears for Frank, and she would not appear a hypocrite.

Chapter 3

Betsy hurried over the four blocks from the bus stop to her home. Mom and Dad would be there, and she had so much to tell them. If they could just work out the details, Betsy would be one of the Americans on the home front who really helped in the war effort. She opened the white picket fence gate, and Tikket hurled around the corner, a wiggling rag of fur bent on being the first and most enthusiastic to greet her.

"D–down, Tikket. Good boy." Betsy held his dirty paws away from her coat with one hand and roughed his pointy Yorkshire terrier ears with the other.

The front door opened on screeching hinges. Her little brothers barreled across the wooden porch, stampeded down the steps with clattering cowboy boots, and surrounded her.

"Betsy, Betsy! Mommy got hurt at the metal works. Daddy went to the hospital," Tommy informed her.

"She broke her foot!" said Tim.

The boys each grabbed one of Betsy's arms and dragged her to the porch. Rosey stepped out, pulling her cardigan sweater closer over the matching knitted blouse.

"Don't panic, Betz. Mom's okay."

"She's not okay. She broke her foot," said Tommy. At that volume, everyone on the block now knew about their mother's injury.

Betsy laid a calming hand on his shoulder. He immediately took a deep breath and muttered, "Sorry." As the smaller of the eight-year-old twins, Tommy voiced most opinions in a belligerent tone. The family worked together to eliminate his need to yell for attention.

"Rosey wanted me t–to know Mom wasn't seriously injured," explained Betsy. "That's what she m–meant by okay."

"A broken foot's serious," protested Tommy.

"She isn't going to die," said their sister from the door, exasperation punctuating her words. She rolled her eyes and went back into the house.

The boys ignored their temperamental sister and concentrated on amiable Betsy. For an hour and a half they rehashed a blow-by-blow description of the telephone call that had alarmed their father, the wait to find out which hospital Mommy'd been taken to, and their father's hurried departure.

"Dad was a brick," said Tim.

"He had us all hold hands in the living room and pray for Mommy's comfort," Tommy added before Tim could elaborate. "He wasn't all girly upset like Rosey."

"Rosey was mad cause she had a date tonight," said Tim.

Tommy ignored that idiotic piece of information. "Mommy's going to come home tonight or tomorrow. That's too bad."

"T–too bad?" repeated Betsy, who by this time had

the boys helping her set the table for dinner.

"If you're going to be in the hospital, you should get to stay a few days and enjoy it," explained Tommy.

"She *did* get to ride in an ambulance," put in Tim. "That'll probably make up for not getting to stay very long."

The boys then went into a description of all the neat things that happened in a hospital, riding in wheelchairs, eating all three meals in bed, nurses bringing you ice cream, fancy equipment that could see your bones, doctors in white coats with things around their necks. . . .

"Stethoscopes," provided Betsy.

There were elevators and visiting hours when all your friends would come. . . .

"Children aren't allowed upstairs," said Betsy.

"Hubba Bubba," said Tommy. "That means we could ride in the wheelchair and go down in the elevator to the lobby."

"And get our casts signed," added Tim.

"Maybe Yogi Berra would come to visit all the sick kids and sign our casts," Tommy blurted out, making a fist and thudding it into an imaginary baseball glove on his other hand.

Betsy shook her head over their wild imaginations and took the meatloaf out of the oven.

Later that evening, just before the boys went to bed, their dad came home—without their mother. He let the boys ask two questions apiece then told them they had to wait for more information in the morning.

"Your mother is just staying overnight so they can watch her, make sure she's all right. We'll bring her home probably tomorrow afternoon." He told them in his steady, deep voice.

After the boys were settled in bed, Betsy set a plate of dinner she'd kept warm for her dad on the cozy kitchen table. Maybe now she could talk to her father about her exciting day. Rosey swept into the kitchen and went to the sink. She fetched a glass of water for her father and sat down with him as Betsy returned to the last of the dishes.

"I'm right pleased to see none of your beaus are hanging around tonight, Sugar," Dad said to Rosey and gave her hand a pat. "It's nice to know you wouldn't take advantage and break the rules about callers when your folks aren't here to chaperone."

Betsy glanced over her shoulder to see her sister's reaction. Dad and Rosey often argued. The compliment didn't please Rosey. She made a moue with her rosebud lips and gave her fair curls a little shake.

"Betsy could chaperone."

"Since when did you want Betsy telling you what you can and cannot do?" he answered as he dug into mashed potatoes and gravy. "I think the rules are good the way they are."

Betsy turned back to drying the glasses in the drain and putting them into the cupboard. She tried to ignore the tension at the little table. This argument would upset her dad, and she would have to postpone asking his advice. As Betsy moved around the kitchen, her sister's little play unfolded before her.

"I'm almost seventeen, Dad," said Rosey in a falsely gentle voice of persuasion. With eyelids lowered demurely, she was the picture of sweetness. "This is my last year of high school. Next year I can get a war job. Some of my friends already work after school. Nina delivers prescriptions on her bike. Ginnie helps her dad at the *Daily Gazette*. Arnold is learning to be a mechanic at his uncle's auto repair shop." She peeked at her father and saw his cold expression. Her voice took on a hard edge. "We aren't babies, Dad. The war has matured us."

He looked down at his plate. "So what did my mature little lady do tonight?"

Rosey sat a little taller in her chair. "I organized a prayer chain for Mother."

Her father's eyebrows lifted in skeptical surprise. He glanced at Betsy, but she refused to be party to the discussion.

"And who was on this prayer chain?" he asked Rosey after a long pause.

"Friends."

"What friends?"

"Friends from church."

"And?"

"Friends from school."

Betsy watched as her father put his fork and knife down on his plate. His two large hands rested on the table. His mouth tightened in displeasure, and his eyes narrowed as he scrutinized his younger daughter.

"Rose Ellen Alexander," he said in a quiet voice. "I won't have you claiming sanctimonious holiness over your gossiping on the telephone with your friends."

Rosey's eyes widened and she huffed indignation. "I *was* calling my friends and telling them about Mom's accident."

"Give me the list then, Rose," said her father in that

awful, calm voice. "You had several hours. At ten minutes a call, you should have a mighty long list. I think I'll start calling tonight to thank these prayer warriors for their kindness in remembering your mother in petitions before the Almighty."

Rosey had no defense. She trembled with fury. Betsy's fingers tightened on the serving bowl she carried to put away in the pie safe. She wanted to escape. How could Rosey provoke their father so easily? Betsy knew from years of experience that Rosey would not feel the clenching in her stomach that already afflicted Betsy even though she wasn't directly involved in the confrontation.

"Child," said her father with a sigh, "I'm concerned about the way you think. It's time you showed some of this maturity you boast of. Betsy, put down that rag. Rosey will finish cleaning up."

"I just did my nails!" protested his youngest daughter. "Dishwater will ruin them."

Dad ground his teeth as if biting back words he might later regret. "Goodnight, Betsy," he said.

"G–goodnight, D–Dad." Betsy gladly accepted the dismissal. Why couldn't Rosey be a little smarter about living as a member of the family and willingly do enough to keep her parents from criticizing her every action? And why had her father insisted on broaching the subject tonight when everyone was upset about her mother's accident and he was tired?

As she let Tikket out the back door and stood on the porch while he made a last round of his territory, Betsy had to admit Rosey had not seemed all that upset. Being a senior in high school had been traumatic for Betsy, but why was Rosey having so much trouble? Her sister had social graces Betsy could only dream of. She was lighthearted, friendly, cute, and interested in all the right things that made a girl popular. Yet Rosey threw temper tantrums like a two year old. Her little sister seemed bent on making problems for herself.

Tikket's nails clicked on the cement walkway coming to the back door from the garage. Betsy scooped him up and gave him a hug. He rewarded her with a moist kiss.

Betsy chortled. "Bad dog," she said without malice. "You know you aren't allowed to give kisses." She snuggled the dog as she went up to the room she shared with Rosey.

Tucked in bed, sitting with the pillows against the headboard, she opened the packet of letters Sgt. Kevin Coombs had given her. As he'd handed them to her, she tried to say there was a mistake, but the rough handwriting on the top envelope clearly said Betsy Alexander. She'd taken them without a word and walked away.

Now she opened one of the letters and spread it out.

January 5, 1944

Dear Betsy,

Thank you for writing me. I don't have much family. Two uncles, an aunt, and some cousins. They live in Idaho. I live in Illinois. Or I lived there before all this happened. Now I don't reckon I have a place to name home. I'm a mechanic. A pretty good one.

I've done something you might not like, but I hope you will understand. Everybody seems to have family and friends. I don't much. I'm not much of a talker. I'm kind of ugly to boot. So when your letter came I said it was from my girl. That's a lie, I know. I'm not asking you to be my girl or anything. I just kind of feel good cause the guys think I have someone too. Hope you aren't mad. I'll understand if you don't want to write to me anymore.

God bless you, Betsy
Frank

Betsy cried softly as she read the rest of the letters. She wished he had sent them. Maybe he thought she'd quit writing if he did.

Rosey still hadn't come upstairs when Betsy turned out her light and settled under her covers. As she lay in bed, Betsy gave over her troubled thoughts to her heavenly Father.

Lord, Frank really needed me as a friend. Thank you for having his name on that list I got. Please comfort the little bit of family he had. I hope they know he was a nice man.

I think Sergeant Coombs is lonely and hurting too. Send someone to comfort him.

I've got to talk to Dad. I probably won't get to work at the hospital now that Mom will be home and needing help. I guess I ran ahead of You and didn't pray about whether You wanted me to take that job. It was a nice dream. Help me give it up if that's what You want.

And Father, please help Rosey to think more of others. She really has a good heart. You know that. Help her to listen to Your guidance. Help Dad to have patience. Help Mom get better quickly. And Sergeant Coombs, Lord, . . .well, just help him find peace. Amen.

Chapter 4

The next morning, the Alexander household burst into activity right after the alarm clock announced eight o'clock. They hurried through breakfast to make a quick run by the hospital before church. Only Dad and Betsy went up to see Mom and brought down news that the doctor hadn't said when the patient could come home.

"We'll stop by after church," said Dad and ushered them back into the blue Packard. The return trip to the hospital failed to bring more definite news. Spirits were low by the time the family, minus the all important mom, sat around the table eating fried chicken from Uncle Bert's farm and green beans and corn from their victory garden.

"Why don't they let kids go up to see their own mom?" asked Tommy. He'd asked the same question using different phrasing ever since they'd left the hospital.

"Because little kids," answered Rosey impatiently, "don't know when to be quiet."

A glare passed between brother and sister.

"Don't spoil your digestion." Dad pointed his fork first at Tommy then at Rose. Turning to Betsy, he said,

"Tell us about your visit to Sergeant Coombs yesterday, Betz."

Because there was no chance she'd be able to take the job Mrs. Brighton had offered, Betsy's enthusiasm had dwindled. In spite of that, she knew her brothers needed a diversion and she knew they would enjoy the story. So she started recounting her adventure, leaving in all the funny bits about the three soldiers who kissed her and about struggling in the kitchen with fifty pounds of macaroni to drain.

"Tell us about the wounded soldiers," demanded Rosey, leaning over the table with eyes full of curiosity.

"They were nice. They t–talked a lot." Betsy blushed remembering the attention they'd showered on her.

"Well, that's good," said Rosey, "if it means you didn't have to try to carry on a conversation."

Betsy nodded and their father cast a warning glance at Rosey. She ignored him.

"So why did they think you were engaged to this Frank guy?"

"Frank said w–we were." Betsy wanted to defend the dead soldier. "He was k–kind of shy, and they said he was t–tall and sk–skinny. He d–didn't talk m–much except when he t–talked about me. I think he j–just wanted to fit in so he pretended he had a g–girl back home."

"Well, you told them the truth, didn't you?" asked Rosey.

Betsy didn't answer.

Rosey rolled her eyes. "I knew I should have gone with you. You were there for six hours, and you didn't once find a chance to set them straight?

"It didn't seem important to tell them their friend had l–lied." Betsy looked at her father instead of Rosey. "I thought I would t–tell Sergeant Coombs and let him decide what to t–tell the others. But I never g–got a chance."

"Six hours and you never got a chance?" Incredulity raised the pitch of Rose's voice.

"You never listen," said Tommy. "She was making 250 pounds of macaroni and cheese."

"Servings," corrected Tim.

"And I played the p–piano for them and sang a c–couple of songs," said Betsy.

"Whatcha sing, Betz?" asked Tommy. "Did you sing 'Shoo Shoo Baby'? I like 'Shoo Shoo Baby.' "

Betsy nodded.

" 'Deep in the Heart of Texas,' " guessed Tim.

Betsy nodded again.

" 'Jingle Jangle Jingle,' " said her father with a grin.

Betsy grinned back and nodded.

" 'Don't Sit Under the Apple Tree with Anyone Else but Me,' " crooned Tommy.

"Oh, for Pete's sake," said Rosey with teenage indignation.

"Can't say I remember that tune," said their father. He began to sing a made up tune, trying to use "for Pete's sake" as the lyrics.

Tommy and Tim dissolved into giggles.

Betsy saw her sister's eyes narrow and watched as storm clouds shadowed her pretty face. Betsy didn't want to give Rosey the chance to pour cold water on their Sunday supper.

"I had a j–job interview t–too," she hastily inserted.

Dad raised his eyebrows and waited for her to continue.

"Mrs. Brighton had sent l–letters to girls who had applied to come interview. That's what everyone thought my l–letter was about. I finally g–got to explain when I went to her office."

"She offered you a job?" Rosey's horrified voice drew attention to her side of the table.

"What would be so bad about that?" Dad asked.

"Betsy has work here. And with Mom's broken foot, she'll have lots to do right here." Rose's lower lip extended in a pout.

"Rose, you are mature enough to take over some of Betsy's responsibilities. This could be your contribution to the war effort, freeing your sister to work in the hospital."

Betsy concentrated on her plate of half-eaten food. Her hand clenched in a tight ball as if she could hold the tension and crush it in her palm.

"I don't want to be stuck at home with children while Betz gets to go be with soldiers everyday," complained Rose. "What good would she be? She can't talk to them and cheer them up. It's not fair. You only let me go to the USO once a week, and then I *have* to go with *Betsy*."

"You're children too," yelled Tommy. "And Betz is nicer than you. The soldiers will want to talk to her. She listens good."

"Tommy, this isn't your fight," said his father. "Rose, go to your room. I'll be up to discuss this in a minute."

Without a word, Rosey flounced out of the room. Dad turned to Betsy, covering her tight fist with his own huge hand. "What did you tell Mrs. Brighton about the job, Betz?"

"I said I'd t–talk t–to my d–dad."

He nodded. "I'll talk to your mother. It may be a good thing for Rose to take over your job. Spending more time with your mom would be good for her too. With so many mothers working and fathers working extra jobs to make up for the men at war, our young people are suffering. Paper said just a few days ago that juvenile delinquency is increasing. God expects us to meet the needs of our families. Rosey is definitely in need." He turned solemn eyes on his boys. "I want you to find nice things to say to your sister. Tell Rosey when she does something you like."

"That's gonna be hard," said Tim.

"Keep your eyes open like a spy, Timmy-Todd. I trust you to spot one good thing she does a day."

"Is Sergeant Coombs married?" asked Rosey hours later when the lights were out and Betsy had almost drifted off to sleep.

"Hmm? I d–don't know," responded Betsy.

"Is he handsome?"

"He looks sick," said Betsy. "But I g–guess he might have been g–good-looking before he was wounded. Harry said he t–took six bullets and shrapnel, but he crawled through the t–terrain and guided them out of the ambush."

"Where?"

"Sicily."

"I'd like to go to Sicily."

"Rosey, Sicily is in the m–middle of a war zone."

"Not now, in a year or two, when the war's over."

Outside the wind rattled the dry leaves on the huge golden maple. The furnace kicked in and a musty smell wafted from the floor registers.

"Betz?" Rosey's voice sounded small and insecure.

"Hmm?"

"Do you think the war will ever be over?"

"Yes."

"We read about a hundred-year war in history."

Betsy was surprised. Rosey didn't often bother with subjects she didn't like. English held her attention when they studied literature, but she didn't clutter her mind with many academic subjects. Dad was right. Rosey was in need. Confident, carefree Rosey feared the future.

"God has seen lots of w—wars, Rosey. Long ones and short ones. He won't desert us, and there will be joy in the morning. This is the d—dark. Morning will come."

Chapter 5

On Tuesday, Betsy reported for her first day of work at Michael T. Dodge Veterans Hospital. Mrs. Tweakes squawked just as Meg had said she would. The stout old lady's feathers were easily ruffled, and Betsy appreciated Meg's whispered words of advice. The kitchen boss fussed behind her two cooks and hurried them along, getting in the way as she gave instructions for the day.

Mrs. Tweakes objected to the men loitering in the cafeteria when they'd finished eating. After several weeks, the glares she cast at both Betsy and the soldier patients would have burnt blisters on the back of a camel. But the men persisted, and as soon as Betsy had a break, they escorted her to the piano, begging her to play for them.

One afternoon just after the men had dispersed back to their wards, the chaplain intercepted Mrs. Tweakes as she barreled across the empty room, obviously intent on having her say. The gentle pastor convinced Mrs. Tweakes that Betsy's music lifted the wounded men's morale. Thwarted in her purpose, she begrudgingly agreed the men deserved some light entertainment. With one last indignant look at Betsy at the piano, Mrs.

Tweakes bustled back to her kitchen.

Chaplain Browne sauntered over to Betsy.

"Would you be willing to play for our chapel service every Sunday?" he asked.

"I think so," she answered. "I'll have to figure out a w—way to get here."

The idea appealed to Betsy. She liked Chaplain Browne. His gray hair and thick glasses told why he wasn't serving overseas. His wisdom could have been used there. The men at the hospital obviously respected him.

On Tuesday and Thursday mornings, the chaplain led a mid-morning Bible study in the cafeteria. Sometimes Betsy followed the interesting discussion while she worked. She'd noticed Sergeant Coombs attended the sessions, but she'd never heard him speak.

She admitted to herself that she watched the battered sergeant whenever she had the chance. For some reason his despair touched her heart, and his face came to her mind at the oddest moments. She took that to mean she should pray for him and did so with an astonishing frequency. The other men looked stronger. They talked about being released and going home. Not Sergeant Coombs.

"I have to tell you, young lady," said Chaplain Browne, "you've done a lot to encourage the men."

"I—I haven't d—done a thing," objected Betsy.

"Oh, but you have. The men who heard Frank read your letters have been retelling the stories you wrote. Those type of letters on the frontline remind soldiers why they're risking their lives. And now the same stories act as balm on their wounded hearts. They've come back injured, some of them maimed for life. Your hopeful perspective on everyday happenings helps them to focus on the positive."

Flustered by his compliments, Betsy felt her face warming in a telltale blush.

"I'd like to meet Tommy and Tim," said Chaplain Browne.

"My br–brothers?"

He nodded. "Did they really set fire to the house, trying to send smoke signals through the drainpipe off the eaves?"

Betsy nodded. Her brothers always managed to fall short of actual disaster. "It was a l–little fire," she said. "We p–put it out with the g–garden hose."

"And they both climbed into a garbage can, pretending to hide in a mine from 'Injuns,' only to get jammed in there too tight to get out." The chaplain chuckled as he related the tale he'd heard.

Betsy nodded.

"And you greased them with chicken fat you'd been collecting for salvage."

She nodded again, smiling in response to the merry twinkle in the chaplain's eyes.

"My favorite. . . ," a gravelly voice interrupted from behind them.

Betsy and Chaplain Browne turned to see Sergeant Coombs. He had wheeled his chair back into the cafeteria. Betsy felt an odd flutter of pleasure at the sight of him. The sensation gave her apprehension as well as joy. She needed to concentrate on being a friend to this wounded soldier and forbid any silly romantic feelings.

"My favorite was the story of Tikket cornering the

neighbor's cat," he said as he rolled to a stop. "The cat went up a tree. Tikket jumped onto his dog house, then onto the shed roof, onto the house, and onto a limb of the old maple tree outside her bedroom window. Betsy heard the dog barking and the cat howling. When she looked out the window, Tikket was clinging to a branch at eye level, fifteen feet above the ground."

Both men laughed. Betsy marveled at the change in Kevin Coombs's expression. She'd never seen him show any emotion. As she smiled at him, his face settled into its habitual guarded expression.

"I came back to ask you if you'd come up to the ward and sing, Miss Alexander." Sergeant Coombs looked away from her. His eyes scanned the windows overlooking the vast lawn as if something outside of great interest held his attention. Betsy followed his gaze but saw nothing unusual. The sergeant continued. "Rosco found a guitar and he can play. He and Jimmy are eager to hear you sing."

Betsy didn't hesitate to volunteer. "I'll be r—right up, Sergeant."

He looked at her for a second as if he would say something else. Instead, he nodded and moved on. Betsy watched him turn his chair and move rapidly out the door.

"That's a fine young man," said the chaplain.

"He s—seems very sad."

"He'll come around. He's a man of faith. God will heal his heart." The chaplain sighed. "His men told me he used to read Scripture to them at night. Even the nonreligious men said it calmed their nerves. He'd read a bit then talk about it. His father's a preacher."

"Is he g–going to get well?"

"His body will mend when his heart is unburdened."

"Will he be able to get out of the wheelchair?"

"The doctors say he doesn't apply himself to the physical therapy. He needs encouragement. Maybe you can give him a little of that, Betsy. And. . ."

"And?"

"And he's trapped in memories, memories he doesn't like."

"Wh–what happened?"

Chaplain Browne stood silently for a moment, then laid a hand on her shoulder. "Maybe you're the one he'll tell, my dear."

Kevin stroked his hands across the top of the wheels, propelling his chair down the hall. He wanted to get away. Talking to Frank's fiancée tightened his stomach into a hard ball. He felt the sweat on his brow and stopped to wipe the sleeve of his robe across his face.

He blamed weakness from his injuries for the sudden cold sweat but didn't discount the uncomfortable feelings that overwhelmed him every time Betsy Alexander came into the room. Yet he couldn't tear himself away. He stayed to listen to her sing, to watch her fingers play over the ivory keys with seemingly little effort, and to enjoy the gift of her smile.

Her letters had been important. To tell the truth, he figured most of the men were just a little bit in love with Betsy Alexander, the girl back home. No other mother, sister, wife, or girlfriend wrote with such vitality. Betsy told of incidents that could have happened in any American home—trouble her siblings got into, mishaps in everyday living, excitement over small normal happenings. She focused their attention on just what they were protecting from the Axis. At the time, Kevin had thanked God for her letters, faithfully arriving every week. On those occasions when some of her letters were held up in transit, the men's waiting would finally be rewarded when a fistful of letters arrived. The young woman had a gift for putting heart into the discouraged, battle-worn men.

Frank always stopped reading just before reaching the end of his sweetheart's letter. He'd hem and haw and say the rest was personal. Every man in the barracks longed for those last few private words to be directed at him.

Kevin heaved a big sigh and once more pushed his chair down the hall. He'd rolled only a few yards when his left arm cramped below the shrapnel-damaged muscles. The searing sensation coursed up through his elbow and set the wound throbbing. With an uncontrolled jerk he sent the chair crashing into the wall. The jolt stabbed the other injuries. For a moment the hallway darkened, his stomach clenched in nausea, and he fought the moan welling up in his throat. Kevin propped his right elbow on the arm of his chair and let his head rest in his hand. Swallowing, he concentrated on breathing slowly, waiting for the throbbing to subside. Immersed in the pain, he scarcely recognized his surroundings until he became aware of the cool touch of a soft hand on his arm. It stayed there, a connection to the world outside his agony.

He felt someone's arm come around his back, holding him. When he could lift his head, he first saw the chaplain bending over in front of him, his face full of concern. Turning slightly he found Betsy stooped beside his chair. She cradled him as if he were a hurt child. He felt comforted instead of embarrassed and fleetingly marveled at the sensation.

"Is it b–better now?" she asked softly. "May I p–push you to the ward?"

Kevin closed his eyes and nodded. The small movement sent an explosion of pain down his neck and into his shoulder. He heard the mumble of a deep voice, but his muddled mind focused on the throbbing in his temples. He didn't know what the chaplain had said. Betsy stood, withdrawing the comfort of her touch.

She didn't speak as she maneuvered the chair down the corridor and into the elevator. Kevin gratefully relaxed. Nurse Brackett met them as the door opened. Her hands on her hips and a disapproving frown told him he was in for a scold.

Kevin managed a weak smile. "How did you know?"

"Chaplain Browne rang up to the nurses' station." The nurse took over her patient, wheeling him rapidly through the crowded ward. "If you're Betsy," she called over her shoulder, "Rosco is waiting over there." She let go of the chair long enough to wave haphazardly toward the south side of the room.

Kevin let Nurse Brackett help him into his bed, listened to her soft-spoken badgering, and gratefully took the pain medication and muscle relaxant. Reasonably comfortable at last, he closed his eyes and listened to the banter of the men around him. Laughter floated above the normal chatter, and Kevin realized it came from Betsy and her circle of admirers. They'd decided what to sing, and Rosco strummed a chord. First the two sang "Chattanooga Choo Choo" and "Jeepers Creepers," but then just Betsy sang "Blueberry Hill."

The song lured Kevin out of his deliberate attempt to remain aloof. He opened his eyes and watched Betsy's face as he listened to the gentle words. A lump rose in his throat, tears sprang to his eyes. The too familiar sensation irked him.

God, my heavenly Father, why can't I get past this? This depression is going to kill me. I can't, I just can't, accept this defeat in my spirit.

I know You give peace. A week ago I found Elijah's words in the Bible. "I have had enough. Lord, take my life." Suicidal thoughts are a sin. I know that. I can't control my thoughts. Take every word in my mind captive, Jesus. Help me. You worked miracles in Elijah and through him, even after his failure. I can rest in that. You are the same today. You can do the same for me.

I can't go home for Christmas as I am today. My family doesn't need my lack of faith. The best thing I can do for them is stay away.

Listen to me! I vacillate like that ship tossed on the ocean. What good am I in Your service? What good am I at all?

Even as he prayed his eyes were taking in the beauty of Betsy as she sang. She turned and smiled at him.

Look at her, Lord. She's so innocent and pure. How can she smile at me? Doesn't she know Frank's life was my responsibility, and I failed?

No, that's wrong, isn't it? Those guilt feelings are from the Father of Lies. I followed orders. I got as many of my men out of that ambush as I could. You helped me have the strength and wisdom to save the few I could. Why don't I feel like a hero, God? Why do I want to die?

Chapter 6

T his is prob–b–bably n–not such a g–good idea,"
Betsy whispered to her large satchel purse as
she slung the long handle over her shoulder and
stepped off the bus in front of the VA hospital. The bag
bumped against her side.

"B–be still," she commanded sternly under her
breath.

"Good morning, Betsy," said the guard at the gate.

"Hello, Sergeant T–Toliver."

"I thought today was your day off."

"It is," she answered, holding the leather pouch
firmly with her elbow.

"You just visiting the men on the ward?"

She nodded.

"Wish I could come up to hear you sing."

She smiled.

"Everyone says you sing like an angel."

"You could c–come to chapel on Sunday, Sergeant."

The guard ducked his head and pulled on the rim
of his white helmet. "Well, now, I don't know about
that. I haven't been to church since I was a kid."

"I'd like t–to see you there."

"I'll think about it." He touched the brim of his hat again in a brief salute.

Betsy walked past him, glad to be beyond the first checkpoint. She sent up a little prayer that Sergeant Toliver would come to chapel and then marched up the drive, determined to get this over with as quickly as possible.

On Saturday mornings the hospital teemed with visitors. The spell of sunshine and warmer air this late in October had brought people out to walk on the grounds. Betsy nodded at several people she knew, but she didn't dare stop to converse. If she hurried she could get in and out in forty-five minutes, time enough to meet the next bus.

Very little physical therapy took place on the weekend, and the nurses relaxed their vigilance. That's why the men on Ward 6A had suggested this would be a good time.

"This is c—crazy," Betsy muttered, then patted her satchel. "J—just a few more minutes, Tikket, and you c—can get out."

She'd been manipulated into agreeing to this escapade. After several weeks of working in the kitchen and spending every spare minute visiting the wounded soldiers, Betsy felt she had acquired thirty more brothers. They all flattered her but with an exaggerated sincerity that felt comfortably like brotherly teasing.

Private Nick Berinotti had bemoaned his fate. He was to be released to go home on Monday. He'd never see Betsy's charming smile again. Never hear her sing. Never meet the twins. Never see Tikket do the tricks he'd heard about for months. Somehow the men coaxed

Betsy into agreeing to bring the dog to the hospital. She thought Nick could come out to the lawn. The men thought she could bring Tikket in.

"They don't even allow children up here," she'd protested.

"Please," said a sad-eyed soldier who'd lost a leg. "They won't let me come out."

What was Betsy supposed to do?

Be careful, that's what, thought Betsy as she opened the heavy door to the hospital. *If I get caught, I'll lose my job.*

A few wounded soldiers and their families sat in the lobby. Betsy made a beeline for the elevators. She stepped in with two orderlies and a nurse. As soon as the doors closed, Tikket growled a soft protest against his continued imprisonment.

The three other passengers turned inquisitive eyes on Betsy. She felt her face warm and knew her complexion had turned tomato red. She placed a hand on her stomach and smiled.

"I d–didn't eat m–much br–breakfast."

The orderlies grinned, but the nurse arched an eyebrow and turned cool eyes back to the elevator doors. The nurse got off at the second floor. When the doors opened on the third floor, Betsy nodded at the two men as they got off with her and breathed a sigh of relief when they turned down the opposite corridor. Passing the nurses' station, Betsy smiled with what she knew had become a painted-on grin. The nurses greeted her and she went on. Having passed the last checkpoint where someone might have asked about her unusual bag, she scurried down the short hall and turned left.

She stepped through the swinging glass doors into Ward 6A. Three men stepped forward.

"Betsy's here."

"You made it."

"Is Tikket in there?"

One took her arm. The others hovered behind her. Betsy allowed them to hustle her to a corner of the large room far from the prying eyes of nurses.

She placed the satchel on a vacant bed and unclasped the latch with a snap. Tikket pushed his tiny head out before she had a chance to widen the opening. Peering around him with apparent interest, the little dog's ears perked up, and he yapped one bright bark of greeting.

"Shh!" said Betsy and scooped him out. The dog squirmed in eagerness as the men passed him around the circle of admirers. Each got their faces licked; each laughed with good humor. Betsy's heart hummed with joy. This silly prank cheered the men, and she was glad she'd talked herself out of her qualms.

She showed off Tikket's tricks. He could sit, speak, lay down, roll over, and play dead. But he could also whisper, sneeze on cue, and play hide and seek.

"How come he's named 'Ticket'?" asked one of the men. "Did you buy a raffle ticket and win him?"

Before Betsy could answer, Jimmy—one of the men from Frank's squad—spoke up.

"Nah, it's because of the noise his nails make on the floor. Tikketikketikketikket." Jimmy turned to look at Betsy. "Tell it, Betsy. Tell about the night Tikket scared your mom."

Betsy looked around at the crowd of men lounging

on the beds, in wheelchairs, and on crutches. She panicked. Nearly a hundred eyes looked at her, expecting her to speak. Until that moment she had not realized that most of the soldiers in the ward had gathered close. A familiar lump rose in her throat, paralyzing her vocal chords. She wrapped her arms across her stomach and clasped a hand on each elbow, squeezing to release the tension. But despite her best efforts, she could not open her mouth and even stutter an answer.

"Tikket," said Sergeant Coombs as he wheeled himself into the center of the ring, "was just a puppy." Betsy smiled her gratitude and scooted over so he could situate his chair beside her. She looked down at him for a moment and saw his concern.

"Thank you," she whispered.

He nodded once and continued. "They'd had him only a day. He looked like a fuzzy rat without the long hairless tail. The twins put him in the laundry room but didn't close the door properly."

Betsy listened in amazement. Kevin Coombs repeated the story almost verbatim as she had written it in the letters. Since she always wrote the first letter on Sunday afternoon, then copied it over and over during the week, the phrases often were indelibly etched in her brain.

"Tikket slipped back into the kitchen and must have hidden. Someone closed the laundry room door and everyone went to bed. Soon after lights out, a strange noise could be heard in the house. Tikketikketikketikket.

" 'What's that?' asked Mom, giving Dad a good poke in the ribs.

" 'What?'

"Tikketikketikketikketikket." Kev imitated the sound. Betsy saw the men grinning in response to his theatrical telling. He used different voices for Mom and Dad.

" 'That,' said Mom, squealing.

" 'Nothing,' said Dad. 'Your imagination.'

" 'It's a rat!'

" 'We don't have rats.'

" 'That was before the war. We didn't have rats before the war, but now we could have rats.'

" 'What does a war have to do with whether or not we have rats?'

" 'They're just like everybody else,' explained Mom in a whisper. 'Rationing, you know.'

" 'What?' " Kevin's explosive intonation of the question had all the men roaring. When they quieted, he continued in the outraged husband voice. " 'What does rationing have to do with rats?'

" 'Don't get all bothered with me, Fred Alexander. There is a scarcity of commodities. Everyone knows that. And wherever that rat used to get his commodities, he can't get them there now. So he's come into our house looking for our commodities.'

"Tikketikketikketikket.

"Mom gave Dad another good poke.

" 'Fred, get up and get him. That rat's in the upstairs hall.'

" 'There isn't a rat, Lillian.'

" 'Just go see.'

"Fred threw back the covers and swung his feet to the floor.

" 'Put on your slippers.'

310

" 'Why?'

" 'So he won't bite your toes.'

" 'Humph! There isn't a rat.'

" 'Put on your slippers anyway.'

"Dad put on his slippers and went out into the hall.

" 'Nothing here,' Dad said.

" 'He must have gone downstairs. Oh, Fred, the puppy! The rats will hurt the puppy.'

"Dad went down the stairs, and Mom sat in her bed in the dark with the covers drawn up to her chin.

"Tikketikketikketikket.

" 'Fred!'

"Tikketikketikketikket.

"The sound came down the hall, through the door, and right up to the bed. A tiny creature began leaping at the covers, trying to scramble up the sheets.

"Mom's hysterical screams brought Tim and Tommy, Rosey and Betsy, and Dad, who turned on the light.

"The boys cornered the 'rat' under the bureau. And the puppy was named Tikket for the sound he made running around the house trying to find his people. He now sleeps upstairs with Betsy."

The men laughed and clapped. The noise bothered Tikket and he ran to Betsy, bouncing against her legs, asking to be picked up. She scooped him into her arms.

"Suppose we could hear his nails on this linoleum?" asked Rosco.

"Sure," said Jimmy. "Everyone be quiet."

A hush descended upon the room. Betsy put the dog down on the floor. No one moved, waiting to hear the silly noise that had scared Betsy's mom half out of her wits. The dog stood still.

"Come on, Pooch," urged Rosco from his bed, leaning far over the side with a hand extended toward the floor. Tikket responded and hurried across the open space.

Tikketikketikketikket.

"What in the world are you doing?" asked a shrill voice from the door.

The nurse. Not just any nurse, but Nurse Binger, Bringer-of-Bad-News Binger. The nurse with the longest needles, the coldest hands, the hardest heart, and meanest streak on the continent of North America.

Chapter 7

Kevin watched as the men shifted, seemingly headed back to their beds, but amazingly most of them chose to go through the route directly in Nurse Binger's path. He grinned, knowing they were delaying the nurse on Betsy's behalf.

"Quick, hide Tikket," he told the pale girl beside him.

Betsy called softly. "Hide and seek, Tikket. You hide."

Tikket scooted under a nearby bed and sat next to the wall.

"Betsy," said Kevin in urgent undertones, "sit on my bed and open my Bible."

She hopped up on the unmade bed and grabbed the book.

"Lamentations chapter 3, verses 22 through 26." Kevin wheeled closer to her.

She opened to the right page.

"This is the passage I've been memorizing," he explained. "I put it to music to make it easier." Kevin glanced over his shoulder and saw Nurse Binger emerging from the crowd. He put a hand on Betsy's shaking one and gave it a little squeeze.

"You listen and make sure I don't skip any words."

He sang softly in a pleasant baritone.

"It is of the LORD's mercies that we are not consumed, because his compassions fail not, fail not, fail not. They are new every morning, new every morning: great is Thy faithfulness. The LORD is my portion, saith my soul, saith my soul; therefore will I hope in him, in him. The LORD is good unto them that wait for him, for him, to the soul that seeketh him, seeketh him. It is good that a man should both hope and quietly wait for the salvation of the LORD, hope and wait for the LORD, hope and wait."

He delighted in her smile, and when she asked him to sing it again, he did so gladly. She joined him in the simple tune.

"Lovely," commented Nurse Binger when they finished. "But surely your singing wasn't the center of attention just a minute ago."

Kevin leaned back in his chair and eyed the matron in her starched uniform. Too many of his thoughts had centered on himself since the ambush. He hadn't paid much attention to the various nurses other than to be annoyed when they insisted he interact with them in some way. Vaguely he identified this nurse as being particularly belligerent. He couldn't let her bully Betsy.

"I can't say what the men were up to, Nurse, but Betsy may sing this passage in chapel tomorrow."

"Humph!" answered Nurse Binger and began to move up and down the aisles of beds. Her eyes scanned each man and his little niche in the ward, obviously looking for something out of place.

Tikket started to crawl away from the wall.

Kevin saw the movement out of the corner of his eye.

"Betsy." He nodded to the bed beside them.

"No, Tikket, stay," she whispered.

"We'd better get him out of here," said Kevin. "You sneak him into the bag, and I'll give the men their orders."

He quickly wheeled away and spoke to several of the patients close by.

He returned to find Betsy sitting on his bed with her large satchel in her lap.

"Ready?" he asked.

She nodded. She looked nervous, biting her lower lip with small straight teeth. Her intense gaze darted around the room scouting for trouble.

"Relax," said Kevin. "Try not to look so guilty."

Betsy rewarded Kevin with a glance his way and a tiny smile.

"The men are going to create a diversion, and we'll make good our escape," he assured her.

She nodded briefly and kept her eyes on the nurse across the room.

Betsy's like a tiny bird, a canary, thought Kevin. *Shy. Skitterish. Delicate. Not feathered in a gaudy way, but soft and homey looking. Whatever did Frank do to deserve such a rare bird?*

Two men complained loudly from the side of the room farthest away from the door.

"Nurse Binger, Nick's taking the radio with him. He's packed it in his bag. That's company property, not his."

Several men joined in the loud debate as to whether the radio they commonly used was government issue or Nick Berinotti's private property.

"Our cue," said Kevin.

Betsy stood up.

"I'll carry the bag. You push," Kevin ordered.

Betsy looked at him, confused.

"I'm escorting you out to make sure you don't run into any problems." He reached up, took the bag with Tikket in it, and placed it on his lap. "Come on, Betsy, move on out."

Betsy shook herself out of her stupor and grabbed the handles on the back of his wheelchair, whirled him around, and pushed rapidly toward the exit. A patient stood ready to open the doors.

"Thanks, Betsy," he said as they went through.

She nodded and smiled, not trusting her voice. Her heart didn't stop racing until they were outside and breezing down the long tarmac trail toward the duck pond.

"You can slow down, Betsy," said Sergeant Coombs.

"Oh, I'm sorry." She immediately shortened her stride and eased up her pace.

Kevin Coombs pointed to the left. "There are some benches. Would you like to stop?"

"I've already missed my b–bus. I forgot to watch the t–time when the men were playing with T–Tikket."

"Doesn't that mean you have time to waste before the next one?"

"Yes, yes, it d–does."

Betsy guided the chair over to the benches which circled the trunk of a tree. The number of people roaming the grounds had dwindled since her arrival.

"Are you cold?" she asked, looking up at the thickening clouds.

"No, but it does look like our Indian summer is

coming to a close."

"We'll probably have snow n–next week. We usually d–do by Halloween."

She sat down next to the parked wheelchair, feeling awkward. Conversation centering around the weather always seemed so artificial. She wanted to thank him for rescuing her. Twice, actually. Once when she couldn't tell Tikket's story and later when the nurse came in.

They both started speaking at once, then burst into laughter.

"You first," they chorused and laughed again.

"Ladies first," said Sergeant Coombs.

"I d–didn't know what t–to do. Thanks for g–getting me out of there."

"You're welcome."

He smiled at her, and she reached for the bag in his lap to avoid looking into his eyes. He'd mellowed some in the past month. She noticed he didn't always wear that frown that had marred his good looks. Maybe he was healing.

"Do you think we c–could let T–Tikket out? I don't think he l–likes it in there."

She surveyed the surrounding territory. Only a few brave families had stayed out in the wind. Blustery and chilly, it had chased more timid souls inside.

Sergeant Coombs nodded.

Betsy opened the bag and affectionately cuddled the tiny dog before setting him down in the dry leaves.

"They need to rake," she said. "Tikket c–could get lost."

"They probably haven't taken into account short dogs."

"I'm glad I brought him t–to see Nick. I'm not very

brave. I had to t–talk to myself sternly to g–get on the bus this morning."

"You know the things Frank told us about you gave me a different picture. Brave, outgoing, life-of-the-party, fun. You're quieter than I expected."

Betsy didn't know what to say. This was a perfect opening to tell the sergeant that she had never met Frank. She worked over the right words to use.

"You're taller too."

"T–taller?"

"Yes," said Sergeant Coombs. "Of course, Frank was tall so when he said you were petite, he might have meant in comparison to his height."

"Um."

"He never mentioned your stutter either."

"He. . .he never d–did?"

"Nope, not once. I guess he thought it was kind of cute. I think it's kind of cute."

Betsy couldn't think of anything except he thought her stutter was cute. Was he making fun of her? She peeked at his earnest face. No, he wasn't.

"He really loved you, Betsy. You were his ideal girl and the rest of us envied what he had. I really am sorry he didn't come home to you."

"Sergeant C–Coombs," Betsy started, hoping to finally get the mistake taken care of.

"Call me Kev."

"Kev, there is something I n–need to t–tell you about Frank and me."

He nodded and waited, his gaze on her face.

"Puppy!" The toddler's exuberant call interrupted them.

Tikket bounced through the leaves toward an obvious admirer.

"Oh dear," said Betsy and dashed after him. Tikket didn't often play with small children, and she wanted to be sure he didn't snap when his tail or ears got pulled. She talked to the young mother and child for some time. Her bus pulled up at the gate and left again. She knew her visit had just been extended another forty-five minutes.

When the mother and child went back to the main building, Betsy returned to sit on the bench next to the solemn soldier. What topic of conversation would be best?

"Who will be the next to go home?" she asked.

"Pete, George, and Harry. They should go home for Thanksgiving."

"And you?" She turned sideways to study him as he spoke.

"They say Christmas, but. . ."

His face remained closed. The topic didn't interest him. She tried again.

"Where do you live?"

"Bakerton."

"There's a nice Bible college in Bakerton." His expression had changed for a moment, too quickly for her to read its significance.

"It's closed now." He moved his hands over his knees, rubbing up and down.

Betsy decided the school must interest him in some way.

"Just for the duration, right?" she probed.

"Yes."

"Did you go there?"

"Yes."

"Do you have family up there?"

"Yes."

"Who?"

"My father, mother, and grandfather, two sisters, a sister-in-law, and a nephew."

Betsy scowled, trying to remember if she'd seen someone beside his bed or walking with him in the corridors, someone who wasn't a patient or hospital staff.

"Nobody comes to visit you."

"I told them not to." His lowered tone, the hardness of his jaw told her he didn't like her questions.

"Why?"

"They have enough to keep them busy."

"They love you. It would relieve their minds to see you."

"No, it would make them wonder what's wrong."

Betsy took a deep breath. As she slowly released it, she said a quick prayer. Whether it was a good idea or not, she asked her next question. "What is wrong?"

"I haven't forgiven Him yet."

"Him?"

"God."

"For what?"

"For allowing me to live."

She examined his tense form, his face turned carefully away from eye contact, his hands now clenched in his lap.

"I d—don't understand," she whispered.

"My two brothers are dead and my brother-in-law. Jake was a powerful speaker. He would have been the kind of preacher my dad is. Matt was a brain, a real scholar. My grandfather is the president of that little Bible college you mentioned. Matt would have followed in his footsteps, and he has a little boy who doesn't have a father now. My brother-in-law could fix anything. He and my sister were going to be missionaries. Me. . ."

His face twisted in disgust. "I never could figure out where I fit in. I was one of the first to enlist. It was obvious I had the least responsibility at home, no clear future. Yet I came back. They didn't. The last battle. . . the ambush—that should have been the end. I was supposed to get my men out, and I lost five. Why couldn't those five have lived, and why didn't He take me instead? Butch had kids, Beano had a family restaurant to inherit, Joe wanted to farm, Kelly wanted to write the great American novel, and Frank had you."

The tirade came to an abrupt stop. Betsy held her breath, waiting for him to continue.

He didn't.

"I'd better go in now, so you won't miss your bus again."

Chapter 8

Betsy could not get Kev Coombs off her mind. As soon as she got into the house, she ran down the hall and peeked in her parents' bedroom door. Her mom lounged on the bed with her foot up on a pillow. Her dad sat in an upholstered chair with his feet up on the matching ottoman and his nose in the sports section of the Saturday paper.

Her mother promptly put down her book. "What is it, Betz? You look worried."

"Did you and Tikket get caught?" asked her dad. He folded his paper and put it aside. His reading glasses slipped down on his nose, and he examined her over the top.

"Oh, Tikket," said Betsy. She unslung her satchel from her shoulder and gently placed it on the bed. Tikket scrambled out as soon as she opened it. Wired for excitement he raced from one person to the next, barely delivering his greetings before wiggling down and running to someone else.

"Put him out back," said Dad, "before he wears us all out."

Betsy scooped the squirmy bundle up and deposited

him outside, where he circled the yard at high speed. She returned to the bedroom.

Her mother patted the bed, and Betsy sank down beside her.

"Tell us, Betsy. What has you all in a dither?"

"Sergeant Coombs," she answered. She saw her mother and father exchange a knowing look. "No," she protested. "Not l–like that. I'm not ro–romantically d–dithered." She wasn't about to admit to the acrobatics her heart did whenever she looked at the man, so she laughed good-naturedly at her parents' look of disappointment and plunged into her concerns about the wounded soldier's mental state. "How d–do you help someone who is utterly d–depressed?"

"Well, your uncle Bert has had some problems with depression," said her dad in his slow, mellow voice.

Already Betsy began to relax. Her parents would have good advice.

"Yes," chimed in her mom. "Seems to me Iola said they memorized Philippians 4:8 to combat the despair. And then put it into practice, of course. Let's see, 'Finally, brethren, whatsoever things are true, whatsoever things are honest, whatsoever things are just, whatsoever things are pure, whatsoever things are lovely, whatsoever things are of good report; if there be any virtue, and if there be any praise, think on these things.' My, I can still say it."

"But how can I use that to help Sergeant Coombs?" asked Betsy.

"The negative thinking, the worry, the loss of hope," said Dad, "become a habit. He needs to break the cycle. He consciously has to address his problems instead of trying to escape. You say he doesn't tackle the physical therapy, doesn't want to go home. He's withdrawing."

"Can you think of something I c–can do? I mean, I know the d–doctors and the people at the hospital all are trying, but they have so m–many patients. I don't want to just pray for him. I want to do something."

Her parents sat quietly, considering the problem.

"He needs to laugh," said Mom. "You know, 'A merry heart doeth good like a medicine.' "

"He laughed at Tikket," said Betsy. "He laughs at the stories about the boys."

"Do you think he's better than when you first met him in September?" asked Dad.

Betsy contemplated the weeks in between. "Yes. He's gained back a little weight, and his complexion isn't so sallow. His eyes look alive now. He seems more interested in things, but he still doesn't contribute to conversations or the Bible study."

"What about that song he wrote to go with the Bible verse?" asked her mom.

"It's quite good."

"Didn't he suggest you sing it in chapel?"

"Not exactly."

"Why don't you talk to the chaplain tomorrow? If between the two of you, you could persuade Sergeant Coombs to sing for the men, that would be a step forward. He'd be giving something of value, and that always makes one feel better."

Her father nodded. "That was Bert and Iola's strategy. Bert forced himself to be involved with others. Sergeant Coombs needs to turn his thoughts outward for a change instead of dwelling on his failings, his mistakes."

"I don't understand why he thinks he is so useless." Betsy picked up one of her mother's lace-edged throw pillows and crushed it in her arms, hugging it into a wadded ball. "You should hear the men rave about him. They really care, and I think it depresses them to see their hero this way."

Betsy's mother patted her arm. "We'll pray, Betz, *and* we'll think of practical ways to cheer your sergeant up."

"I'll go start dinner, Mom." Halfway to the kitchen she remembered her mother's words, *your sergeant.*

A smile settled on her lips. "My sergeant." She heaved a sigh. If only it were true. She could write letters to a slew of men, she could be sister to a whole ward of wounded soldiers, she could pull bouncy tunes out of a secondhand piano while couples danced to the swing beat, but to be the sweetheart of one man—it had never happened yet, and she had no idea how to make it so.

At dinner that night, Dad prayed for Sergeant Coombs's full recovery. Of course, the twins wanted to know all about him.

"We'd be glad to go cheer him up," offered Tommy. "I could take my baseball cards. He'd like to see them!"

"Maybe he'd like to go to the Saturday matinee," said Tim around a mouthful of corn. "I see lots of soldiers from the hospital there with their wives and kids. Danny Drucker says they get a day pass."

Mom passed the applesauce around. "If he can get out for the day, maybe you can bring him for dinner, Betz."

"Does he have friends?" asked Rosey. "Ones that aren't too bad?"

"What d—do you mean by 'not too b—bad'?" asked Betsy.

"You know, maimed, sick. You said he was emaciated."

Betsy felt an unusual rage rising within her. The muscles in her face hardened. Her lungs expanded as she drew in a long breath, ready to expel it with a hot diatribe against her sister's pitiless, self-centered outlook. She closed her eyes and saw the men on the ward. Most were cheerful in spite of their suffering. All were brave beyond her expectations. Instead of the hateful words that had perched on her tongue, Betsy sighed.

"You need to know them, Rosey, you j—just need to know them. Then you c—can see how b—beautiful their souls are." She paused, steadying her voice. "They are beautiful."

"Guys are handsome, Betz," corrected Tim, "not beautiful."

Betsy thought of Sergeant Kramer, whose face was scarred from burns. "I stand corrected, Tim. Their souls are handsome."

Tommy giggled. "You're sitting, Betz."

Dad covered Betsy's hand and gave it a squeeze. "Hard to have a serious thought with monkeys at the table, isn't it?" His sympathetic eyes twinkled.

"We know what you mean," said Mom. Her attention turned to Tommy. "Tikket doesn't like lettuce either, so quit sneaking your salad under the table."

Tommy made a face but forked the next bite into his own mouth.

Later that evening Rosey bounced into their bedroom after a phone call from her current leading male admirer. "Are you reading those letters again?" she asked as she opened the closet door and threw her shoes under her hanging clothes. "Why? The guy is dead."

"I think there is something in here that w—will give me a clue as to how to help Sergeant C—Coombs. Frank talks a lot about the other m—men in his squad and especially Kev."

"Kev?"

"He said I could call him that."

"Are you in love with him?"

Betsy considered. "Yes, I think I am," she said after a moment. "I don't know if it is the forever k—kind of love like Mom and Dad's. I can't imagine he w—would ever love me."

Rosey plopped down on the edge of her twin bed.

"Oh, Betsy, how *could* you?"

Betsy didn't answer. She didn't know what her sister meant. Rosey watched her with eyes honestly dismayed. Searching for the right words, Betsy made an attempt to explain. "He's nice. He's hurt badly, and he k—kind of stays to himself, but when he d—does do something, it's usually for someone else. I know a lot about him b—because the men t—talk and there's these l—etters from Frank."

Rosey picked up an old stuffed teddy and cuddled it. "You are so good, much better than I am. You deserve the best, and you never go after it. Betsy, you just can't throw yourself away on this soldier. He may not even live. If he does, he may never get out of that wheelchair.

"You may not believe it, but I really love you. You're a great big sister. You taught me to dance. It's things like that that drive me crazy. You're a great dancer, but you never dance."

"Bob and Mike taught me to dance."

"Brothers!" Rosey exploded. She jumped to her feet, threw the ragged teddy down, and paced the room. "Dancing with brothers doesn't count. Dad doesn't let us do slow dancing, only jitterbug, so I'm not talking using dancing for romance. Betsy, don't you get it? You don't have to be in love with a loser. You've got potential. You could be having a lot of fun. You just don't try!"

Rosey's voice held a note of hysteria as she continued. "What's wrong with having a good time? What's wrong with dancing and going to the soda fountain to have a few laughs with your friends? This war is going to kill everybody. Half the people I know have someone dead in their families because of those crazy people on the other side of the world. Why, Betsy? Why is this happening?"

Rosey stopped in front of the mirror and looked at her tear-streaked face. She turned away as if the image frightened her. Her arms wrapped around her middle.

Betsy threw back the covers and jumped out of bed. She grabbed her sister's frigid form and hugged her tight. Rosey collapsed against her and sobbed.

"It's all right to be scared, Rosey. God will probably never t–tell us why, but He'll always hold us tight, just like I'm holding you now. Jesus had all sorts of human feelings when He was here as a man. He d–did that on purpose so we would know He understands how scared we c–can be. No matter what happens, we'll b–be all right. Even if the worst possible thing we can think of happens, we'll still be all right. Cause we're special, Rosey. We're His."

Chapter 9

B etsy stepped out of the elevator onto the third floor of the Michael T. Dodge Hospital and abruptly halted.

"You're standing!"

Kev Coombs, on crutches, hobbled fifteen feet away. Beside him Nurse Binger paced with her arms crossed, not even giving him the support of a hand on his elbow. On the other side, a gray-haired, white-jacketed doctor followed closely with a clipboard in hand.

Betsy hurried forward and stopped just in front of Kev. She studied his face. A fine beading of sweat showed on his upper lip and forehead. Tight lines revealed the strain of this physical effort, but in his eyes the look of accomplishment sparkled. He smiled down at her.

"Is this your first t—time up?" she asked.

"This is the first time they've let me walk in the hall."

Betsy felt tears prick the back of her eyes. The last thing she wanted to do was cry and make a spectacle of herself. She laid a hand on his right arm and turned to the doctor.

"This is g—good, isn't it?" The question sounded corny, but her hopes had soared for the wounded sergeant, and she couldn't form a more profound question.

The doctor nodded. "Should be home by Christmas."

Betsy turned back to Kev. The look on his face shocked the joy out of her.

"I have to sit down," he said.

"Fine," said Nurse Binger. "Your chair's right over there." She pointed toward the end of the corridor.

Betsy immediately started for the wheelchair, but the doctor hooked her elbow and gave a slight shake of his head. Kev turned and slowly made his way down the hall with Nurse Binger ambling along beside him, not offering a word of comfort or encouragement.

"Why doesn't she help him?" whispered Betsy.

"He doesn't need help," said the doctor. "He needs a goal. And going home for Christmas isn't it." He released her elbow and marched down the hall headed for Ward 6A. Betsy easily caught up with Kev and Nurse Binger. Irritated by the sober nurse's lack of encouragement, she began to talk to him as he labored with the crutches and his recalcitrant legs.

"You're d—doing well. Just a few more steps and we'll b—be there."

He stopped and gave her a tired smile. Between pants he managed to say, "Betsy, you are sunshine. You are spring rain. You are the first snowflake and the last bird's song before sunset."

Nurse Binger growled. "Sergeant, you are procrastinating. I have other things to do. Please proceed to your chair."

Kev crooked an eyebrow at Betsy, winked, and

struggled forward. Once he was seated, the nurse made notations on a chart, then turned to Betsy.

"Young lady, this man just said you were glaring, wet, destined to melt away, and twittery. I suggest you find someone less poetic and more determined to get his health back."

Betsy's mouth fell open and she uttered an indignant "Oh!" as the ramrod stiff back encased in a white uniform disappeared toward the nurses' station. Betsy looked down to see Kev's face dropped into the palm of his right hand. His shoulders shook. Biting her lip, she sat down in the metal chair next to the wall and reached across the arm of his wheelchair to take his left hand in hers. She watched in horror as a tear slid down Kev's cheek.

"That woman should be rep–rep–reprimanded. She should be fired."

Kev lifted his gaze to hers, and she saw the grin on his face. He snorted, then chuckled, then laughed out loud. He winced with pain as he laughed, but still he could not stop. He wiped the tears streaming from his face on the sleeve of his robe. He tried to speak and broke out in fresh laughter. Betsy, who saw nothing funny in the situation, let go of his hand, crossed her arms over her chest, and stared straight across the hall at a poster that said, of all things, "Loose Lips Sink Ships."

Minutes passed before Kev composed himself.

Betsy arched an eyebrow at him. "If I speak t–to you are you g–going to d–dissolve into those ludicrous g–giggles again?"

Kev snickered, clamped his mouth into a controlled

grin, and shook his head.

In her heart, Betsy enjoyed the red-faced sergeant's efforts to control his mirth, but she didn't understand what had set him off and that enabled her to keep a straight face. "Are you going t–to t–tell me?" she asked.

"What?" Kev's voice bubbled over with the re-strained laugh.

Betsy clamped her lips together and turned her eyes back to the poster. She avoided eye contact because she feared she too would burst into laughter and she didn't even know what was so funny.

"Tell me," she said between clenched teeth.

Kev took a deep breath. "Well, it occurred to me that our Nurse Bringer-of-Bad-News Binger actually does have a sense of humor."

Betsy looked into his twinkling eyes. Blue invaded the usually gray irises. She wondered if the color changed with his mood or the lighting in the hall or because she wore a cornflower blue shirtwaist. "I don't get it."

"She took my ramblings on your very lovely attrib-utes and put them in the worst possible light. She demonstrated cynicism so thoroughly that it must be a put-on. I think the sinister Nurse Binger hides a more pleasant personality than she wants us to discover."

Betsy nodded.

"Do you want me to push you back into the ward? I bet you're tired."

He agreed, and together they went past the nurses' station, down the hall, turned left, and went through the heavy glass doors.

Betsy had worked out just exactly how she would

gain Kev's cooperation in getting a day pass to come spend time with her family, but first she had to give a few of the men in his ward their parts in the little maneuver.

Dad picked up Betsy, Rosco, and Kev after chapel on Sunday. He drove the big Packard. Betsy made the introductions. They put the men in the backseat and the wheelchairs in the roomy trunk.

"I see it worked," said her dad as they used a string to secure the trunk lid, which couldn't quite close.

"Shh!" warned Betsy casting a look at the men comfortably settled in the car.

"They can't hear us," her dad reassured her.

"Rosco said he wouldn't g—go to some stranger's house for dinner," she explained in a whisper. "He'd feel ill-at-ease. But if the sergeant went with him, he might not feel so awkward."

"Your mother will be pleased to have the boys for dinner. The twins are beside themselves with excitement. And Rose has done her hair three different ways since she got up this morning. Had it real pretty for church and tore it all down as soon as we got home to fix it different."

Betsy laughed. "Dad, you're a peach. Thanks for everything."

"What have I done out of the ordinary?"

"You did make a ramp so they could get up the front porch steps."

"And your brothers have been galloping plastic horses up and down it since the first board was in place. Seems like we've been needing such a thing and didn't even know it."

Betsy gave him a hug and hurried to get in the car.

The next week Jimmy wouldn't go without the support of his sergeant. Rosco said he was too tired, which was the excuse Jimmy had used the week before.

Three days later Betsy took her twin brothers to the hospital. Kev came down to the lobby on his crutches and sat talking to them. He listened to their stories of cowboys and Indians. At home the two played out elaborate tales spawned from their own imagination. They entertained half of the lobby as they enacted the rescue of the good Indian "Tall as a Tree" from the ornery rustlers in Dry Gulch. Kev taught them to play Go Fish, but he renamed it Herding Cattle. The cowpoke with the most steers won the game.

Frank's girl, thought Kev and tried to be annoyed that she again perched on the end of his bed and chattered away about silly little things. He couldn't raise the ire he needed to stay cold and indifferent to this unusual beauty.

With both hands, he caught the beach ball she threw and tossed it back. The doc had said his coordination would improve with the exercise. Betsy always seemed to know what the prescribed exercises were and engaged him in them.

Engaged. She'd been engaged to Frank. Frank had been loved by this girl, accepted by her wonderful family, and had looked forward to a life together with her. Kev missed the ball and watched as Betsy slipped off the foot of his bed to retrieve it. She hopped up again, smiled, and tossed it to him. He frowned at her; she ignored him and went on with her tale of the neighbors' efforts to mulch the winter garden with old newspapers.

One of the soldiers in a bed close by gave her some advice to pass on to the Millers, the old couple who shared the produce from their victory garden. She flashed him one of her heart-stopping smiles. Did she know how many of these men were hopelessly in love with her?

The first time she'd come she'd been shy to the point of speechlessness, probably because of the stutter. He hardly noticed the repeated consonants anymore. He did notice the way his own heart skipped a beat at the first sight of her, the way his blood zinged at the sound of her voice, the swelling of emotion when she smiled his way.

Frank's girl. She'd lost her love and didn't deserve any more pain. He'd stay away from her. As much as he wanted to catch her attention, earn her love, he knew he wasn't good enough for her. In the end, he'd walk away, and she'd be left behind again.

She tossed a comment over her shoulder to Jake, who struggled by on his crutches. Jake was a nice fellow. Or Jimmy, or Rosco, or that crazy New Yorker the next bed over. All of them were decent guys. Any of them would be a better choice. Any of them would make Betsy a good husband. Anyone but him.

Kev missed the ball again.

Chapter 10

Heavy gray clouds threatened snow. For many, Thanksgiving would be as cold and relentless as the steel gray sky. However, most of the men at Michael T. Dodge Veterans Hospital had escaped a dreary holiday. In the Alexander home, the family warmly welcomed six men from the hospital. While Mom had been waiting for her foot to heal, she had enlisted women of three churches to get most of the patients out of the hospital and into homes for Thanksgiving Day.

Three of those wounded soldiers played Hearts with Rosey. Two played Herding Cattle with Tim and Tommy. Sergeant Coombs had the unfortunate experience of being cornered in the living room, where Betsy's dad asked the young man about his childhood, his family, and his dreams for the future.

Betsy peeked through the dining-room door for the tenth time in the last hour.

"Relax," said her mom as she placed serving spoons on the rich brown tablecloth. The dark linen on the long oak table set off her best china and silverware. "Your dad won't bite him."

"Mom, he k–keeps asking questions." She shook her head in despair. "So many questions."

The older woman put an arm around Betsy's shoulders and gave her an affectionate squeeze. "Just testing the waters, Dear."

Betsy looked at her with bewildered eyes.

Her mom winked. "I believe my father grilled your father in much the same way just before we became engaged."

"B–but it's not n–needed. Kev Coombs has no ro–romantic interest in m–me."

"I wouldn't be so sure about that, Betz." Her mother looked at her with a contemplative eye and sighed. "All right, you can rescue him. Announce dinner and start moving the men to the table."

Sometime during the festive midday meal, a winter storm quietly descended on the town. Snow rapidly covered the ground. When Tommy peered out the window late in the afternoon, he exclaimed, "Look at that! Big wet snowflakes, perfect for snowmen."

"But not perfect for driving," said his father.

Since Dad had to make two trips to take the soldiers back to the hospital, they started the first journey earlier than previously planned. Four men, showing obvious signs of fatigue, bundled into the Packard first. That left Kev and Rosco to visit with the family while Dad made the forty-minute round trip.

The twins, Mom, and Rosco battled away at Chinese checkers in the dining room.

Kev sat on the family-room davenport, one leg propped up on a pillow on the coffee table, content in the fading light of the day. Betsy played a soothing

Debussy melody on the spinet. A small lamp illuminated her sheet music and gave her hair an angelic glow. The fireplace crackled, giving out a flickering light.

Bored, Rosey flipped through a copy of *Ladies Home Journal.* Her chair backed up to a picture window, and she read by the dim natural light. With a sigh, she tossed the magazine on the table. Her head swiveled from the silent sergeant to her sister and back again. Impatience flashed across her face, and she moved from her chair to sit on the couch beside Kev.

"We'll probably have a skating party now that the really cold weather has come."

Kev reluctantly shifted his attention from Betsy to her sister. "You'll like that."

Rosey smiled with enthusiasm. "I like having fun. Not like Betz. Betz likes doing worthy things." She rolled her eyes, showing what she thought. "I get along with people. I enjoy thinking up games, instigating mischief, making the gang laugh. Poor Betsy doesn't like to talk. . .you know. . .it makes her uncomfortable. She never dated."

"What about Frank?"

"Frank?"

"Her fiancé?"

"Oh, him. You mean she still hasn't told you? That's just like her." Rosey ran her fingers through the curls at her shoulder and tossed an exasperated look at Betsy. "Honestly, sometimes I think I'm the older daughter, and she's the kid sister. She was never engaged to Frank. She just wrote him letters. He wasn't even anything special to her. She writes to. . .I think now it's sixteen enlisted men. She got their names at the USO."

The music stopped. Kev looked up to see Betsy staring at him. He could see her waiting for his reaction. Absolutely still, she looked like a startled doe, large eyes shadowed by apprehension, watching him, ready to flee if he gave a sudden, aggressive movement. He smiled at her, trying to convey reassurance.

Kev shifted his gaze back to the pretty teenager.

"You love your sister," he said in a quiet tone. "You even wish you could be like her in some ways."

Rosey gasped and drew back a little. Kev saw the retreat and continued.

"You fill your time with activities without any real peace in your soul. It doesn't have to be that way."

Rosey's expression fell into a frown. "You don't know anything. How could you? You don't know me. You don't know anything about me."

"I watched you, Rose. I listened to you. Some people cry when they're worried or scared. You don't want to cry, so you laugh. You laugh too much. You play too hard. You never relax. Relaxing is hard, isn't it, Rosey?" His voice lowered as compassion cushioned the words. "Because that's when you can't stop the thoughts that bother you."

"It doesn't have to be that way?" she said, echoing his words.

"No," he whispered. "You rush into life. I shut down, blocking out the world. But I've learned I don't have to do that. You know what helped?"

Rosey sat with large eyes, concentrating on the sympathetic man beside her. "What?" The word escaped on a breath of air.

"Words, or maybe I should say the Word. Words like 'Casting down imaginations, and every high thing that exalteth itself against the knowledge of God.' That means taking what my mind conjures up as great big threats and believing God is bigger and stronger. I replace the anxiety with the hope that I have in Christ."

"It works?"

"It works."

The front door opened and Dad stomped in, shaking snow from his coat and knocking it off his boots.

"D–Dad," said Betsy. "You've b–been gone over an hour."

"Yes, and I have permission to keep Kev and Rosco here." He took off his hat and turned a face reddened by cold to his family. "We've got the makings of a blizzard. I stopped on the way home to put chains on the tires. And then to help a family whose car slid into the ditch on Mason Avenue." He reached in his pocket and pulled out a paper bag. "Here's medicine for Rosco and Kev from the hospital. Rosey, my dear, see if you can rustle up a cup of coffee. I'm frozen."

Rosey went to the kitchen with her father following.

Betsy turned to find Kev looking at her. Their gazes met and held.

"I'm sorry," she said.

"For what?"

"For d–deceiving you."

"About Frank?"

She nodded.

"You didn't want us to know he was lying."

Nodding again, she came over and sat down beside him. "How d–do you d–do that? How d–did you know why I d–didn't t–tell?"

"I guessed." He reached out and took her hand, holding it tenderly between his two. "It's a motivation that fits your personality. It's just something you'd do."

"I tried t–to tell you. I thought I'd t–tell you and you could decide what to tell the others. But do you realize how very little t–time we've spent t–together when no one else was around?"

Kev chuckled and squeezed her hand. "Very little time."

She leaned back against the cushions of the sofa and slipped her other hand into his, content to sit in the gathering darkness and hold hands.

"Kev?"

"Um?"

"What you said to Rosey about getting better. . ."

"Yes?"

"Will you go home for Christmas and see your folks?"

His hands tightened on hers. "They're awfully busy, Betz. You don't know."

"Tell me."

"It'll be bad at Christmas."

"Tell me."

"My dad's a powerful minister. He writes books and does conference speaking. My mom writes articles about the godly woman. Granddad's the president of the Bible college. At seventy-three, he's still a dynamo. My brothers and brother-in-law were the same kind of go-get-'em Christians. I don't fit the mold."

"You d–don't have to fit their mold; you fit the mold God designed for you."

He didn't respond, and in the darkened room, Betsy couldn't read his expression.

"Kev, you had the right words for Rosey. If she had you to talk to, she could work through these fears boiling inside her."

She felt his shoulder rise and fall in a silent shrug.

"You help people one by one, Kev. God uses your family to share His love *en masse*. But individuals need God to touch them one by one. He uses you for that."

Kev remained silent.

"You don't believe me." She sighed, then she sat up abruptly. "The letters. Frank's letters." She stood. "Stay right here."

Kev watched her dash out of the room. Through the doorway, he saw her charge up the stairs. In a moment he heard her rapid footfalls as she plunged down. She flew into the room and turned on the end-table lamp. Plopping down on the couch, she sat sideways, facing him.

"Listen," she ordered as she sifted through the pages in her hand. She found one, skimmed it, then began to read. " 'Coombs reads to us from the Bible each night. Some of the guys pretend they're not listening, but I think they are. Beano, the one who has an Italian restaurant to go home to, he gets real still. He's listening, I'm sure.

" 'Coombs just reads a little bit, maybe a verse or two. Then he talks. He believes that stuff and it makes me want to believe too. I don't think it's just being out here so far from home and the sound of guns firing and all. It has something to do with how his voice sounds when he talks. He sounds confident, like he'd stake his life on what he's saying.' "

She shuffled through more pages and began to read again. " 'Tonight I heard Joe crying, not loud, you know, just kind of sniffling. Maybe he wasn't crying at all and just had a cold or something, but Coombs went and sat beside him. Didn't touch him or anything, just started talking about some guy in the Bible who was in a horrible place, a pig sty, I think. Joe's folks own a farm. They've got hogs. Anyway, it was a horrible place to be, kind of like our camp. We aren't too comfortable here, Betsy.

" 'Back to the Bible story—Coombs said when it was time to go home, the son knew it and went home to his dad and got a big welcome. I'm getting this kind of mixed up, but the point was there was a better place to be and God is our Father and He would want us to come home. Coombs said when we belonged to God it's like our hearts go ahead of us to that home, and someday our bodies will catch up. Meanwhile we can tap into that feeling of being at home, any time, any place. If we believe in God's Son, even in this camp, in this war, we can have peace. Does that make sense, Betsy? To carry heaven in your heart—that would be good.' "

She flipped through two pages.

" 'Coombs talked about being adopted tonight. You know I don't have much family. It's kind of nice to think I could have God as my very own Father.' "

Another passage: " 'Kelly was writing in that book he keeps. You know what he said to me? He said, "I just wrote down that today's my birthday." I said, "Happy Birthday," and he grinned. He said it was the birthday Coombs talked about, not the cake and ice cream kind.

You know what, Betsy? I'm a Christian now too. I believe in Jesus. And you know what? I bet half the men in our squad, maybe more, believe too. Sergeant Coombs just talks about God, Betsy, and it all sounds true. It is true. I know that.' "

Betsy held the papers tightly in a fist and shook them at him to emphasize her point. "Do you see, Kev? Your family wasn't there in the camp with those men. You were. Your father's b—books, your mother's articles, your granddad's classes d—didn't help those soldiers. You helped them. You did because you were where God put you. You understand people, Kev, and you t—talk to them just the way they need to be talked to. Your mind isn't busy with great big projects. You have t—time for people, one by one."

The dark room mellowed as she waited for his response. Her own tension ebbed away. She thanked God for helping her with the words and prayed Kev's heart would receive what she'd tried to say.

"Betsy, may I read those letters?"

She put them in his hand and, seeing that he needed time alone, went to the kitchen. She kept her hands busy helping her mother, but her mind focused on Kevin Coombs. Her thoughts formed prayers, each one pleading that God would help Kev make the final surrender, leaving aside the expectations formed by his family and accepting God's plan in his life. She moved about her parents' kitchen, but her heart stood before the throne of God.

Chapter 11

"Tim, go tell Sergeant Coombs the sandwiches are ready," Mom called from the kitchen later that evening. He turned away from the game and hopped out of his chair, running as soon as his feet hit the floor.

In a moment he held the door wide as Kev maneuvered through with his crutches. Betsy held her breath as she studied his face. The hard lines of pain and weariness had softened. Even his hollow, sunken cheeks and eyes looked less gaunt. He paused inside the door and surveyed the room. When his glance met Betsy's, it stayed. Laugh lines deepened at his temples and spread to lift the corners of his mouth. Betsy's heart loosened and sent a fluttering rhythm pulsing through her veins. She loved this man. Even if he never returned that love, she'd be happy knowing he'd triumphed over his depression. But she'd be happier if she could share his future.

Betsy turned away, finding it absolutely necessary to butter the bread and place it in the oven to toast. In just a few minutes, she felt an equally compelling need to talk to Kev alone. Her brothers claimed the chairs on either side of the sergeant. She had to sit opposite him. Once they cleared the table after supper, her father brought out a board game. The last thing Betsy wanted to do was buy and sell little wooden houses. Facing the inevitable, she soon relaxed and joined in the spirit of the game. But she kept stealing glances at Kev. It didn't help that each time their gazes met, an unspoken communication ran between them. She knew he wanted a word with her as well. The anticipation of what those words might be kept tugging her attention away from the game. She went broke before anyone else, even Tommy, a notoriously wild speculator.

She missed a chance to speak to Kev again at bedtime. Mom relegated the twins to the older boys' upstairs bedroom. She designated Betsy supervisor of getting them settled while she and Dad made their guests comfortable in Tommy and Tim's downstairs quarters.

Amazingly, though sleep eluded her, Betsy woke up early and jumped out of bed. How soon could she expect Sgt. Kevin Coombs to be up and ready for breakfast?

"I heard you open the back door for Tikket."

Kev's voice startled Betsy and she almost dropped the coffeepot in the deserted kitchen. She whirled around to greet him but froze. He stood propped on crutches in the doorway. His disheveled hair drooped over his forehead. A stubble of beard shadowed his chin. She'd never seen a more attractive man. He put forth a hand, and she walked across the room to take it. Betsy waited, holding her breath, hoping what she saw in his eyes truly meant he loved her.

"I have something to say to you."

His gravelly voice sent lovely chills down her spine. She found she had nothing to say at all. With her chin tilted up, she looked into his eyes.

"I knew how I felt for a long time," said the man of her heart, "but I didn't think I had the right to say it out loud. First I didn't dare hope that my heart was really returning to life. Then I wondered if God could really be offering me a love I didn't deserve. Then I realized I couldn't pursue my dream in this shattered body. That's when I started working at the physical therapy. Betsy, I'll never run another race, but would you be willing to walk down the path God ordains with me?"

She nodded.

A frown creased Kev's face. "You're sure?"

She nodded again.

"Say it," he demanded.

"I w–will."

"Oh, Betsy," he groaned as he let his crutches clatter to the floor and pulled her into his arms. His lips gently caressed her temple then captured her mouth. "Will you come home with me at Christmas and meet my family?"

"I st–stutter."

"You do?"

She giggled. "I do."

"Ah, but you said that very well, without a stutter at all. And that's what I want you to say before God and His witnesses."

She hugged him, enjoying the feeling of his arms around her.

"Betz?" he whispered in her ear.

"Um?"

"I'm sorry, Sweetheart, but I have to sit down unless you can prop me up. My legs are about to give."

"Oh." Betsy released her hold and immediately grabbed him again when he swayed. "Do you want to sit in the family room or here at the kitchen table?"

"I won't make it to the family room. Where are my crutches?"

"On the floor."

"Well that's a fine how-do-you-do. How are we going to get them without my falling over?"

"I'll get 'em."

"Here, let me." Two small voices spoke simultaneously.

Tommy and Tim wormed past Kev's and Betsy's legs and quickly thrust the crutches at them.

"Can we go with you at Christmas?" asked Tommy.

"Don't you think you'd rather stay here and go after?" said Tim. "It won't be much of a Christmas with Bob and Mike and you gone."

Betsy assisted Kev to the kitchen table and breathed a sigh of relief as he sunk into the wooden chair. She then turned on her little brothers.

"How long have you been here?"

"Long enough." Tim grinned.

"If you're finished with the mushy stuff, can we have breakfast now?" asked Tommy.

Betsy turned to look at Kev. He shrugged. "I'm starved too."

"What would you like?" She gazed at his face, comparing his handsome features to the haggard look she'd seen the first time they met. She knew God had given her what she most wanted.

"Hugs and kisses," said Kev, promptly.

"Yuck," said Tommy. "I'll have anything but oatmeal. I've had enough mush for one morning."

"Me too," said Tim. "Can't we just get on with life now that you two have figured out you're in love?"

Kev reached over and gently clapped Tommy on the shoulder. "Sure we can, Bud." His gaze drifted back to his love. "And I for one am looking forward to it."

KATHLEEN PAUL

Kate lives in Colorado Springs with her eighty-six-year-old mom and a college-age son. Her married daughter also lives in town and is expecting the first grandbaby! "Everyone in our family reads voraciously. I already have two bookcases filled with children's books to read to that precious grandbaby."

In the house, two small dogs, Gertie and Gimli, provide entertainment with their outlandish antics. The dog in this story is modeled after her own.

Kate's hobbies include oral storytelling, mentoring new writers, and knitting.

A recent **Heartsong Presents** novel, *To See His Way*, won second place in the national Romance Writers of America/Faith Hope and Love Historical Short Fiction contest.

A Letter to Our Readers

Dear Readers:

In order that we might better contribute to your reading enjoyment, we would appreciate you taking a few minutes to respond to the following questions. When completed, please return to the following: Fiction Editor, Barbour Publishing, Inc., P.O. Box 719, Uhrichsville, OH 44683.

1. Did you enjoy reading *Christmas Letters?*
    - ❏ Very much. I would like to see more books like this.
    - ❏ Moderately. I would have enjoyed it more if _____

    _____

    _____

2. What influenced your decision to purchase this book?
    (Check those that apply.)
    - ❏ Cover ❏ Back cover copy ❏ Title ❏ Price
    - ❏ Friends ❏ Publicity ❏ Other

3. Which story was your favorite?
    - ❏ *Forces of Love* ❏ *Christmas Always Comes*
    - ❏ *The Missing Peace* ❏ *Engagement of the Heart*

4. Please check your age range:
    - ❏ Under 18 ❏ 18–24 ❏ 25–34
    - ❏ 35–45 ❏ 46–55 ❏ Over 55

5. How many hours per week do you read? _____

Name _____

Occupation _____

Address _____

City _____ State _____ ZIP _____

E-mail _____

JHEARTSONG ♥ PRESENTS

Love Stories Are Rated G!

That's for godly, gratifying, and of course, great! If you love a thrilling love story, but don't appreciate the sordidness of some popular paperback romances, **Heartsong Presents** is for you. In fact, **Heartsong Presents** is the only inspirational romance book club, the only one featuring love stories where Christian faith is the primary ingredient in a marriage relationship.

Sign up today to receive your first set of four never-before-published Christian romances. Send no money now; you will receive a bill with the first shipment. You may cancel at any time without obligation, and if you aren't completely satisfied with any selection, you may return the books for an immediate refund!

Imagine. . .four new romances every four weeks—two historical, two contemporary—with men and women like you who long to meet the one God has chosen as the love of their lives. . .all for the low price of $9.97 postpaid.

To join, simply complete the coupon below and mail to the address provided. **Heartsong Presents** romances are rated G for another reason: They'll arrive Godspeed!

YES! Sign me up for Hearts♥ng!

NEW MEMBERSHIPS WILL BE SHIPPED IMMEDIATELY!
Send no money now. We'll bill you only $9.97 postpaid with your first shipment of four books. Or for faster action, call toll free 1-800-847-8270.

NAME _____

ADDRESS _____

CITY _____ STATE_____ ZIP_____

MAIL TO: HEARTSONG PRESENTS, PO Box 721, Uhrichsville, Ohio 44683